PROMISCUOUS
Lies

Listen real close, sweetheart

Spread those pages, then get your toys because tonight, the only person you will be thinking about is me.

Sincerely,
Your book husband.

WARNING

This book contains sexually explicit scenes and adult language and may be considered offensive to some readers. This book is intended for adults ONLY. Please store your books wisely, where they cannot be accessed by under-aged readers.

BLURB

I use my body to make men fall to their knees. I just wasn't expecting a man as powerful as my boss to fall for the act.

Dutton Taylor is a man who is not used to hearing no. Good thing denying dangerous men just so happens to be my specialty.

The past broke me and I refuse to be tempted by promiscuous lies. I'll do whatever it takes to protect my son and the new life I've built for us.

We should keep our distance. But my body doesn't get the memo... and neither does he.

ONE
POSIE

I didn't plan to work here; it wasn't exactly on my career path. I didn't wake up one day and say, *today is the day I will become a stripper.*

But here I am, two months in, working as a fucking stripper. If my parents were alive, I'm sure they would be really fucking proud.

Not.

But that's what happens when you have bills and a body you can use to pay those bills.

A fucking stripper.

Yep, that's what I grumble in my head every night when I have to pay the babysitter to watch my son so I can shake my ass for men who are more than likely cheating on their wives.

Fuckfaces.

"Posie, you're late," Paula says. I roll my eyes because I'm always late. It's the one constant about me. She should be used to it by now, but I make up for it when I bring in the money. I only work here twice a week, sometimes only once. And I make enough on those nights to pay my bills and put food on the table. At the moment, that's what I'm happy with; it's all I need. Once my son starts school, it will be a different scenario, but right now, I want to give him all of me like my own mother did for me when I was a kid. So I work one to two nights here instead of getting a full-time job because it pays the same.

"I'm here," I reply, throwing my things on the counter and pulling out my makeup bag. "You know I can get ready quickly." I slip off my dress, revealing hot-pink lingerie.

Paula is more adamant about my tardiness tonight as she stands behind me while I touch up my hair and makeup. "I told you I needed you to be on time tonight. The boss doesn't usually come in, and you still haven't met him." She throws her hands up in the air. "You know he likes to meet everyone."

So I've been told.

And I still don't care.

I don't work as much as the other girls do, and ass-kissing isn't exactly my thing.

"Is he still here?" I ask, in between applying my soft-pink lipstick. I don't care if he is, but I'm pretending to be at least a little bit interested.

"He'll be leaving soon," she says, side-eyeing me.

"Okay, next time, then."

She sighs and walks away, shaking her head. Paula and I have an interesting relationship. She gave me a job when I desperately needed it, and I work my ass off to bring in good money and tips. She won't admit it, but I know she likes me.

"You really piss her off," Samantha, one of the other dancers, says next to me. I can't help but smile, not even attempting to deny it.

"Posie, you better be ready because you're up in ten," Paula calls out. It irritates her that I'm always ready and presentable for my sets despite being late.

I throw a barely-there cover-up over my lingerie and smirk as Samantha waits for her turn to dance. "Have fun," she calls out as I wave her off and open the door to wander the main floor. The lights are dimmed to focus everyone's attention on the current girl dancing on the stage. Seats circle the stage, with private booths scattered throughout the main room. In the center is a bar, and one of the other girls stands there, waiting to take her customers' drinks out.

I admire the woman on stage, but I know all eyes

will be drawn to Samantha when she comes out. She earns the most tips. I'm second to her, and she fucking works her ass off for it. She's an amazing dancer who is studying it as a profession, but like all of us here, she struggles to pay her bills, let alone pay for dance lessons. Working here fixes that.

I skirt along the edges of the room, eyeing the night's patrons. I smile as men's gazes roam what is usually off-limits, although, for the right price, they can touch. I rarely let that happen. Men are easy. They want what they can't have. And they're willing to pay for it.

When I overheard two women discussing what strippers could potentially earn, I looked into clubs in Manhattan. Two weeks later, I met Paula by chance at the hospital. My son was running a fever, and her husband was sick that night as well. Although I usually keep to myself, we were in the same room, and she mentioned her workplace. Pearl is an exclusive, invite-only gentlemen's club, which means the clientele has plenty of money to spare.

Most importantly, this one has the best reputation for keeping the girls safe. And they do. I get walked to my car every night. And if I feel unsafe, I even have the option of having security drive me home. So if I have to dance my ass off for money, I want to do it somewhere extra safe.

As I walk past the side of the stage where a group of men are watching the main dancer, I caress the men's shoulders. Some look my way, and I offer them a small wave.

"Anything I can get you, fellas?" I ask, standing to the side. One in particular stares at me with lust in his eyes while the others rattle off drink orders. I smile and head to the bar, passing their orders to the bartender.

"Looking good, Posie," Mike, the bartender, says. He's well-groomed, with light brown hair tucked behind his ears. He has a long earring dangling from one ear, making him look edgy in a pretty-boy way. I wave him off with a flattered laugh. He always says that to me, and at first, it made me uncomfortable, but now I know he's not hitting on me; he's just playing. Now we enjoy bitching about the men together and admiring his failed dating app attempts. But, hey, at least he's trying.

"Thanks, Pookie." I wink at him as I lean over the counter. "Been busy this week?"

He nods as he starts making the drinks. "Boss has been in all week, so everyone's been on edge. One of the girls stumbled down two steps when she saw him across the room because she was so nervous," he tells me with a sly smile. But then he looks back out over my shoulder toward the floor. "He's here right now; just a heads-up." I make no move to turn around. I don't care about the boss. I come to earn money and go home. As long as I have a job and am not doing anything wrong, I don't see the problem.

"Good to know." I place the drinks on the tray and walk them over. Leaning down, I place one in front of the man who hasn't taken his eyes off the dancer, and the other two, I make sure to show my cleavage when I bend down to hand them their drinks.

And like usual, their eyes track to my tits.

"Is that all, boys?"

A cheer erupts, and they look to the stage as Samantha struts out.

Two of the men hand over a nice tip, only one of them taking their eyes off Samantha. I pocket the cash with a smile and go back to the bar with the empty tray.

"How's the kid?" Mike asks.

"Good. Didn't want to sleep tonight, though," I say, rubbing my temples. That's why I was so late tonight.

Mike laughs and shakes his head before cutting himself off quickly as a customer approaches the bar.

I eye the man because I haven't seen him before, and he certainly looks like he has more than enough money to tip handsomely. He's dressed in a suit, with light brown hair, blue ocean eyes, and a watch that probably costs more than everything I own combined.

Another cheer erupts, and I turn to watch Samantha basically backflip in her heels on stage and can't help but smile. Gosh, she's good. I mean, I can move my hips and climb a pole, but what some of these women can do is mind-blowing.

Not a chance in hell that I am trying to do that stuff unless I want to break my neck.

It's then that I feel suffocated. When I look over my shoulder, I understand why. The man in the nice suit is standing in my space. No, he's consuming all of it as if entitled to do so. It's so unnerving that I step back while faking a smile.

"Hello," he says, and his voice is sweet as honey but with a lethal edge that raises the hair on my arms. It's a confusing mix, considering how pretty he is. He doesn't look any older than me—in his mid-twenties—but there's a cold calculation in his gaze that ages his presence.

"Hi, handsome. What can I get you?" I push my breasts out, and he notices. Not once has he smiled, and even as I stand here smiling at him, he doesn't reciprocate it. Instead, he looks... disgusted. "Nothing, then?" I ask, raising a brow flirtatiously. He remains silent, simply studying me.

"Is this your first time at a gentlemen's club, sugar? Don't worry; it doesn't cost you anything to talk to me." A lie, of course. I make any man who occupies my time pay for it. I go to step past him and tap his shoulder, but his hand snatches my wrist before I can touch him.

"I don't think we've met," he says. I try to pull my wrist out of his grip, but his hold won't budge. It's only when he finally releases me a few moments later that I'm able to regain my composure.

"We don't need names, sugar. Do you want a dance?" I ask, batting my thick eyelashes.

"Is this how you are with all the clients?" he questions. I flick my long blonde hair over my shoulder and smile at him, even when I would much rather tell him to go fuck himself.

"How would you like me to be?" I ask with a sultry smile. I glance past him to find Mike staring at me, eyes wide, mouthing "no" to me. Confused, I look back at the stranger. Sure, he's dressed in a nice suit, wearing an expensive watch. Hell, even his shiny shoes scream wealth, but he's just a pretty boy, and all boys go weak at the knees for a little bit of attention.

"I'd like you to be more..." He trails off as he puckers his lips, trying to think of the right word.

"Mr. Taylor." Paula hurries over and stands next to him, her gaze flashing worriedly between us. "I see you've met Posie Quinn, one of our best. I know you requested Samantha, but she hurt her ankle on stage just now. I can guarantee Posie will be just as amazing." I'm so confused at first, then his gaze rakes down my body before he nods, as if barely approving, and walks off. When he does, I turn to Paula.

"Okay, he seems like a total ass. Did Samantha seriously hurt her ankle?" Must've been the flip.

Paula gasps, and before she can speak, the man interrupts me from behind. "Yes, a total fucking ass who is about to pay you a lot of money."

Shit. I really should have checked he was gone before I said that out loud. Turning, I find him already walking off. Paula pulls me by the arm and drags me backstage.

"Do you know who you just insulted, Posie? Please check yourself before entering that room, because it's full of powerful men. Clients you haven't entertained before."

My eyebrows dip. "Who is that, the fucking president or something?"

"No. Worse. He's your boss."

TWO
DUTTON

Entering the private room, I find my clients seated and waiting with drinks in their hands. There's a buzz of energy in the air as they wait with anticipation. When I want to win a business deal, I always bring my clients here because I know this will close it; men are always more inclined to say yes when beautiful women are around.

The door opens, and in she walks. The one with the sickly-sweet smile but sharp tongue. With every seductive word she said, her eyes were screaming for me to go fuck myself, and I don't tolerate anyone who doesn't either have immediate respect, lust, or fear in their eyes after meeting me. As far as first impressions go, Posie's wasn't great. The main thing I got from her was that she has a bad fucking attitude.

I'm aware she's one of the new girls, but every time I've come in since she was hired, she's been off, and as far as I'm aware, she's been working here for months. I don't tend to fraternize with the girls, but I do like to meet them to make sure they're up to my standards, such as not taking drugs or being affiliated with anything that might look bad for my business. Paula has hired a few girls in the past who had drug issues, and we helped them with rehabilitation programs.

Posie's golden gaze meets mine as she comes farther into the room. Her long blonde hair is down in waves, and the pink lingerie she's wearing is cheap. All the dancers and waitresses here are offered access to my father's lingerie store for work purposes at a very generous discount. The store is exclusive and carries the best items in the city. Clearly, she hasn't made use of that offer, and her half-assed approach irritates me.

Her gaze quickly moves on from me as she saunters into the room with that fake smile plastered to her lips. She takes a moment to scan the room, then approaches the nearest man, running her hands along his chest as she looks down at him and asks him what he would like to drink. It's not her job to only offer drinks, but it warms up the clients.

"Dance," he commands, not even bothering with a drink. She giggles, and I know it's fake because I know sharp-tongued women like her. But she's good at what she does, stepping back and turning around to show him her ass. She pushes it out and bends over to touch her ankles, looking back over her shoulder at him.

This promiscuous little vixen would rather be gouging this man's eyes out right now.

"Do you like what you see?" Her voice is sultry. The man nods approvingly, and I sit, grinding my jaw as I watch her. I'm not sure why it agitates me so much. Perhaps because she wasn't the original girl I requested for tonight, and I don't like plans changing at the last minute.

She pushes his hand away when he reaches out to touch her, and then she moves on to the next man. She touches everyone, smiling as they stare at her body and not her face. I can't blame them; it's bewitching how her waist pinches in and gives her the perfect hourglass figure. Her ass is high and firm, her legs toned, and her breasts are more than a handful.

She dances around the room and finally reaches me, not making the mistake of touching me, though. Instead, she looks down her nose at me when she leans over and puts her tits in my face as if intentionally antagonizing me. My gaze remains trained on her mischievous golden eyes. "Not interested?" she asks.

Leaning in, careful not to touch her but close

enough to hear her shallow breathing, I smirk, pleased to know she's not entirely indifferent to my charm, no matter how much she might like to pretend to be.

"Do your job," I instruct, pulling back as she stretches to her full height. Her gaze narrows ever so slightly, and then she turns and widens that fake smile.

She dances for each man, intentional in the way she handles them. She touches and teases them but is careful not to let them touch her, moving on at the first twitch of their hands toward her. Her hips gyrate, practically hypnotizing the group. I can see why Paula hasn't fired her yet; she's good.

Posie giggles as she sways her hips, and when one of the men offers her a few hundred-dollar bills to take off her bra, she does. She makes it a game, a tease. By the time she removes it, three more men have slipped her another hundred each.

It's an art what these women do, and I only employ the best. Whether it's in their skill of tricks on a pole, flirtatious glances, or simply knowing how to keep to a beat with the movements of their body, they all have one thing in common: conducting a room's attention. It's just as powerful as any man in a boardroom. And at its finest, it's beautiful.

When my main client becomes more demanding

and encourages her to sit on his lap with his cock clearly pressing against his pants, I interrupt.

"That's enough. Send Maria in," I tell Posie calmly.

The client looks like he's about to argue with me, but I offer him a tight smile I know doesn't reach my eyes. He swallows but applauds like the other men and eagerly awaits the next woman.

Posie doesn't let the emotion show, but I can tell she's pissed at being replaced. She probably thinks she's underperformed. If anything, it's the opposite, but I'm not in the business of complimenting people. She seductively waves to everyone, but before leaving, she saunters over to me, those hips swaying from side to side, and stops abruptly in front of me. Then she holds out her hand. I glance at it, then meet her eyes. She's only in a G-string and a pair of stiletto heels.

"Yes?" I ask her, raising a brow.

"My tip," she says expectantly.

This little brat needs to be taught a lesson. My jaw tics at her boldness. No one demands *anything* from me. With the exception of my younger sister, Billie, perhaps, she's the only one.

"Leave and send Maria in if you want to keep your job," I advise. Her golden eyes widen, and she pulls her hand back. I feel triumphant as she grinds her teeth, but only briefly before her mask slips back into place and she turns to leave. I watch her ass as she does.

The men laugh over some shit and keep talking business as we wait for the next dancer. Ten minutes go by and Maria hasn't showed yet. I excuse myself from the room to figure out what the fuck is happening. When I reach the back room, I notice Posie, fully dressed now, heading for the door. Paula follows her, throwing up her hands in defeat. I follow both and watch Posie climb into a rundown car and take off.

"What happened?" I ask, and Paula startles, hand on heart as she faces me.

"Mr. Taylor, I didn't see you there," she says, licking her lips. Her cheeks are stained pink, and she is most likely embarrassed by what I just witnessed.

"Where did she go?" I ask, nodding in the direction Posie went.

"Oh, sorry. Did you need her? I'll organize another girl straight away."

My irritation rises at my previous order not being fulfilled and Paula purposefully evading my question. I don't often have to ask for things twice. "Paula, where did she go?"

Paula sighs before she answers, "Home."

"Her shift has barely started," I remind her.

"I know, sir. She seemed to have an emergency pop

up," she replies, and I've worked with Paula for long enough to know when she's trying to cover for someone. Paula's a woman in her fifties and she treats most of the women here like her daughters. It's a privilege they don't even realize they have, and that's precisely why I hired her to manage the dancers. I know the women are being looked after emotionally as well as physically. This line of work isn't easy for everyone.

"What did she say?" I demand. She bites her lip and looks away. "Paula, I expect an honest answer."

She offers me a nervous smile and exhales heavily. "It was something along the lines of..." she mumbles under her breath, and I don't quite hear what she says.

"Repeat that clearly."

"She said, 'That stupid-ass fucking boss thinks I dance for free. Who would ever do this job for free? He can go fuck himself and the horse he rode in on. I'm out.'" Had I not already been slapped with the aggressive nature of Posie's sharp tongue, I'd find it entertaining how Paula mimics her attitude.

"Thanks for that, Paula. Please send Maria into the room." I turn around and head to the office.

"Wait, Mr. Taylor. Please. She's a good girl and a hard worker, I promise you," Paula calls out after me, but I don't respond.

Someone is about to be taught a lesson.

THREE
POSIE

The moment I pull up to my house, Amy steps outside and says, "He fell asleep as soon as you left. You're home early." She pulls on her jacket. It's been chillier lately as the season is changing.

"Early knockoff. Thanks again for watching over him, Amy." Someone parks across the road as I watch her get into her car.

I spare a glance at the grass, which is in need of serious cutting. I might have time to do it this weekend. I wave to Amy as she drives away and briefly admire my modest two-bedroom house. It's a small rental, but it works, and I can afford it.

As I'm opening the front door, someone calls my name. I turn at the sound of the voice and find my boss,

Mr. Taylor, leaning against his car. *How the fuck does he know where I live?*

He doesn't move to come closer, and for that, I'm thankful. Because my first thought was *where is my weapon?* I have a bat just inside the door, but that's it. Usually, that's enough to dissuade someone from entering my home uninvited.

"Why are you here? You do know how fucked-up this is, right? To follow your employee home?" I say, carefully inching my hand inside to find the bat. When I grip it, I feel relief straight away. Holding it but not showing him, I wait for him to answer. Fuck this, I'm not at work. I don't have to pretend shit for this asshole.

"You left before the end of your shift," he says matter-of-factly. It's two in the morning, the neighborhood seems so quiet, and his voice carries effortlessly.

"Yeah, I have that privilege." He doesn't seem to like that response because he pushes off the car and stalks toward me. My grip tightens on the handle of the bat.

"So I take it you don't want your money, then?"

"You could have called," I tell him as he gets closer.

I don't know this man. Yes, he's my boss, but tonight was the first time I met him, and he seemed anything but friendly. He also has a dangerous aura around him I don't trust. I've stepped away from men like him for a reason. And him being a total ass is another checkmark against him. And I let Paula know that.

He reaches into his pocket, and I lift the bat in response, gripping it with both hands. He pauses at the end of the path. Even in the dim glow of my porch light, I can see the slight tug of his lips before they pinch into a thin line again. He continues coming toward me, unfazed by my weapon. As I raise the bat higher, making a note that I have no hesitation in using it against his striking features, he pulls out an envelope and offers it to me. My gaze dips to the envelope curiously.

"What is that?" I nod toward it.

"Take it."

"No."

"Take it," he repeats.

"What is it?" I ask again.

He sighs. "You don't make things easy, do you?"

"And do you follow all your employees to their homes?"

"No, just the special ones, it seems." He drops the envelope on the ground between us, and money spills out of it. "If you pull that shit again, you won't have a job," he warns before turning and walking back to his expensive-looking car. He doesn't look my way as he shuts the door and then drives off. Momentarily, I wonder what it might look like after it takes a couple of hits from my bat.

When he's gone, I lower the bat, reach for the envelope, and peek inside. It's not just *some* money. It's a lot. Baffled, I head inside and shut the door behind me, making sure it's locked.

Is that really how much the girls make when called to perform for his favored clients? Shit, maybe I should've waited around if the pay is this good. Though I was confident, he was going to fire me.

I go to Bentley's room and lean against the doorframe, studying him as he sleeps peacefully. I hate being away from him, even when I'm working to pay our bills. It's just the two of us, and sometimes I wonder if I'm doing all I can to offer him the best future.

I yawn as I walk to the kitchen and begin counting the money on the counter.

Once I reach $1,000, I start to smile. Some nights, I can earn that much, and others, I'm lucky if I get four hundred. On those good nights, I put the money away to make up for the nights I don't.

I get giddy when I reach $2,000. I could go shopping tomorrow. Take Bentley to get some new shoes.

He's growing so fast; the ones I got a few months ago are already getting too small.

$3,000. *Holy shit!* I have never earned that in a single night, let alone for just a few hours. While I hate my boss, I'm really fucking happy right now. Even if I was going to hit him in the head with a bat, I consider maybe he's not all that bad. Well, at least my savings thinks so.

"WHY IS IT PINK?" Bentley asks the following day as we sit in the shoe store. He's too clever for an almost five-year-old.

I'm grateful I get to spoil him a little today.

"We can look at the blue ones," I say, pointing to different shoes.

"I like purple," he tells me with a smile, and I can't help but return it. I love him so much it hurts. I wish he'd stay this age because the years have already flown by so quickly.

It's challenging at times as a single mother, but I wouldn't have it any other way because it's even more rewarding.

Sometimes, it makes me sad to think what my life would be like without him. Most likely a disaster. I'd probably be dead. When I ended up pregnant with Bentley at eighteen, I had no one to ask for guidance. It turned out I just needed someone to love and protect enough for me to get my shit together.

I was shocked when his father wanted nothing to do with him. I thought I loved that man. It turns out that I loved the *idea* of him, not actually him. My parents died in a boating accident when I was sixteen, and I was young and impressionable when I met Bentley's dad. I fell for his fake promises and loved a man who only loved himself and the power to control others. I did all of that narcissist's bidding until the minute I saw that stick turn blue, confirming my pregnancy. That's when I saw him for who he truly was.

An asshole.

And so I ran and left him off the birth certificate.

I'm not a religious person, but I pray every night he never finds us.

Bentley doesn't know anything about him and hasn't yet asked. I know one day, this will change. At some point, he'll want to know all about his father. But for now, I want to protect him as much as possible so he doesn't feel like he's missing love anywhere.

How do you explain to a kid that their father is a narcissistic killer?

You don't.

"You can have the purple ones," I tell him. He starts school soon, and I'm dreading it. But I don't want to keep him from being the social butterfly he is.

"For my birthday?"

"No, just because I love you. You'll get other things for your birthday," I say, hugging him. I'm so grateful he got my blonde hair. But he has his father's brown eyes.

"Is Amy going to come to my birthday?" he asks. While he doesn't spend heaps of time with Amy, he knows her. She is really the only person who comes to my house, and even though I'm protecting him, I wonder if I'm also coddling him. We don't have many friends, and we have no family here. It's part of why I want him to interact with other children his age. He's only ever been used to adult conversation, and I don't want to squash his childlike curiosity.

"We can always ask. What do you want for dinner this week on your birthday?"

It's a tradition that we go out every year for our birthdays. Since we don't eat out often, we pick any restaurant we want.

"I want pasta."

"Pasta it is," I agree, my heart melting when his little hand grips mine.

We pay for his shoes and then head for the car.

He's watching a couple across the road on a park bench with a newborn, and I can't help but wonder at times if I'm failing him. But I know we're better off not having his father in our lives. When I look at Bentley, I still see Bobbi. But as he gets older, I see more of me in him. And it's selfish, but I hope it remains that way.

FOUR
DUTTON

"She didn't come in?" I ask Paula. She shakes her head and looks anywhere but at me.

I'd shown mercy because Paula had promised me Posie is one of the best, and I can see that from the revenue she brings in on the few nights she does work. The roster states she's supposed to be in tonight, but there's been no sign of her yet.

Even after I gave her such a generous tip.

"No, she didn't," Paula replies, looking at her feet as she stands in my office.

"Then I'm going to fire her."

Her head snaps up. "Please, sir, she's really good."

"She also doesn't show up for her shifts, leaving the other girls doing more," I remind her. "Why do you have such a soft spot for her?"

Paula looks down again as she answers. It's not like her to go this far for someone. "I like her," is all she says. *She likes her?* You shouldn't give employees a free pass just because you like them. Especially if you want your business to succeed. "And..." She seems hesitant but then meets my eyes and blurts, "Look, she came from a rough part of Boston. She didn't tell me much, but she made sure before stepping into this line of work that we weren't associated with any biker gangs, and I think she's trying to create a better life for herself. I'm sure there's a good reason she's not in today, and I want to help her. She just needs a hand."

A biker gang from Boston?

I wonder if it's the same one my cousin, Eli Monti, was having issues with a few months ago and is now in negotiations with.

Interesting.

I don't believe in coincidences, nor do I leave things up to chance.

"You're dismissed, Paula."

She seems uncertain whether what she just told me helped Posie's case. Ordinarily, I wouldn't care for sob stories, but I'm curious about Posie's potential connection with the Boston Delinquents.

I call Eli, hoping for once he isn't balls-deep in his wife and is actually conducting business. It's only one in the morning, so he should still be working on whatever lucrative deals he's brokering as the new head of the Italian mafia. His father officially handed him the reins a few months ago.

If Posie is connected to that gang, I don't want that association to draw ill-fitted patrons to my club. Still, that information might benefit Eli since we're always cautious about uninvited guests snooping around.

When I'm almost sure he won't answer, he finally picks up. "Taking your time answering calls, aren't you?"

I hear a man scream in the background. And then a scream from what sounds like a second person. "Well, considering I'm busy, you're lucky I answered at all." In other words, he's torturing someone. Most likely two by the sounds of it.

"Give me your location. I have some information for you," I say, removing my jacket and leaving it hanging over my chair. The less clothing I have to get bloody, the better.

"Oh? And what do I need to give you in return for this *information?*" Eli asks, and I can imagine his raised eyebrow. I smirk because my cousin knows me well.

I have plenty of vendettas in this world. I'm regarded as the proper and perfect son publicly. For anyone who looks deeply enough into my family ties they'd realize my mother is an Italian mafia heiress, and my father runs all matters of sexual fantasy, going to great lengths to keep his empire in the top position.

And then there's my baby sister, Billie. She's only a year younger than me, but I'm extremely protective of her because I know what men are like. So I remove them from her life, and it's turned into a hobby of sorts —clearing out the trash.

"Trea Lissor recently asked my sister to a ball," I say, business-like.

"The audacity," Eli replies dryly. "I'll have Hawke and Ford locate him and bring him in so you can give him a stern talking to."

"Appreciated," I say with a sadistic smile. "Oh, and make sure there's a sharp knife waiting for me."

I ARRIVE at an abandoned warehouse favored by Eli and his two seconds. Ford and Hawke are tenacious little fuckers. The twins were adopted at fifteen by Anya Ivanov and her husband, River, who civilized the brutes. I don't know much about them, but they've been hanging around us for the last decade, and one thing is certain. No matter what, they have my cousin's back. And that's good enough for me.

They're also very efficient in what they do. Hawke, the one with shorter black hair, is pleased with his handiwork as he ties up a sniffling man who's still wearing his long PJs and has a bag over his head. Ford, the quieter one, is busy on his phone, ignoring the pleas echoing around the empty space.

The fact that there isn't a second man tied to a chair leads me to believe the other man my cousin was torturing when I called may no longer be with us, and the body is being dumped God knows where and how.

"You'll never believe it," Hawke says, almost laughing. "This guy actually left his backdoor unlocked. What an idiot."

Ford's gaze slides from his phone to me. "His fucker of a dog bit me."

"So, did you get rid of the dog?" Eli asks.

"Why would I?" Ford replies, affronted. "I would've done the same thing."

We all stare at him in silence.

I'm never quite sure about Ford's dry humor, nor do I want to ask him to elaborate if he would've bitten someone if they were to break into his home.

Eli grins as he polishes his knife fondly. He's had that one since his wife threw it into his leg. Love at first sight, apparently, even though she was a hitwoman who was hired to toy with and then kill him.

"I don't care if you kill this guy, but he is the son of a politician, so this information better be worth it."

I know my cousin would've gotten this man for me even if I didn't have information to share with him. I do, however, pull an envelope out. When he opens it, his eyebrows shoot up to his hairline. Inside are explicit photos I'd paid someone to download from the computer belonging to the asshole tied to the chair. Very incriminating and graphic images that, once they're aired, which they will be, will guarantee he won't make it through his first year in prison. I also gathered this to justify the way that I'm about to destroy his fucking life, irrelevant to the information I'm about to provide Eli about Posie and her potential connection to the biker gang in Boston.

Before I proceed to enjoy myself torturing the man, I pull Eli to the side. "You said recently you uncovered a spy from Boston Delinquents, didn't you?" I ask him.

"Yeah. We got rid of him. But I've just been in negotiations with their new president, Waylon Striker. Why?"

I contemplate this. It wouldn't be impossible for their new president to attempt to infiltrate my company. Eli's businesses and mine are closely linked, considering we're blood-related and our fathers have worked closely together for almost forty years. And although Eli might be in negotiation with Waylon Striker, it doesn't mean he's not gathering his own intel. Negotiations aren't a done deal or treaty.

"I might have someone associated with them in one of my clubs. It's a stretch, and I'm not sure, but I'll look into it."

He frowns. "One of your men?"

"No, a dancer."

His brow furrows. "Make sure she's not an assassin or something."

"That might be your kink, but it's not mine," I say, thinking of the scars that mar the tattoos down his back. Something his wife gave him while he fucked her that he's very proud to show off.

I'm certainly not kink-shaming. Everyone has their own thing. I, however, prefer carving into other people as punishment, not pleasure.

I take the knife out of Hawke's hand and sigh with relief as he removes the bag from Trea Lissor's head. Whenever I'm in this space, about to give in to my darkest of demons and carve messages for fun, I feel most at ease. It's the only way I'm able to release the stress of my busy life. The only way to satire my inner darkness that's always clawing to reach the surface.

"Look, man, I don't want any trouble. My dad can

pay fo—" Trea's words die on his lips as he recognizes me.

"Do you know who I am?" I ask rhetorically.

He swallows hard. "Dutton Taylor."

"And I'm sure I've made it very clear that my baby sister is not to be touched. So either you're new, ignorant, or stupid. Which one is it?" I say as I slice the tip of the blade down his shirt. His legs are shaking, and he's hyperventilating.

"I'll l-leave her alone. I'm s-sorry. I'll n-never g-go near her again," he stutters.

I smile, his fear music to my ears. I get my hands dirty often in my line of work, having a cousin run the mafia makes it so much easier and acceptable. I've never bothered to question whether I'm a good or bad person. If it makes me a profit and protects my family, that's all I care about.

"But what about all the other women, Trea?" I ask with a smile that clearly terrifies him. "What about all the videos and photos I found on your computer? Are you sorry about them?"

"I-I—" He starts to scream wildly and painfully as I carve the first letter into his chest. I ignore all his pleading and crying. Thick trails of blood begin to run down his chest and stomach. I've barely finished before he passes out, which makes it far less fun.

I don't consider myself the next Picasso, but I do appreciate my handiwork.

'Sex Offender' is carved into his chest. I consider cutting his dick off but know that someone in prison will do it for me.

"When do you want the photos and videos leaked?" Ford asks, looking over my shoulder curiously.

I shrug. "Let him cower in his home for a week. When he thinks he can face society again, blast it."

Eli smirks, and I frown, noticing the blood splatter on the cuffs of my shirt. I was so preoccupied with my craftsmanship that I forgot to roll up my sleeves. I undo the shirt and then hand it to Hawke. "And burn this."

"They don't work for you," Eli reminds me under his breath.

"No, but we're all friends here, aren't we?" I smile handsomely. "Now, who feels like a drink? My treat."

I'm grateful Bentley's fever went down in time to celebrate his fifth birthday. When we returned from shopping, I noticed he felt warm, and it progressively got worse. It wasn't until he finally fell asleep and his temperature started lowering that I could message Paula, but half of my shift was already over. I'm hoping I don't lose my job for it, but no matter what, Bentley comes first.

I spot Paula straight away as I enter the club. Tom, the security guard who usually walks me out at night, offers me a nod as I pass him and go straight to the back.

"Mr. Taylor wants to see you before you take the stage," Paula says with an apologetic expression. I figured it was coming. I technically did a no-show for my last shift. But why is that asshole around so much lately? How had I been so lucky to avoid him for two months, and now he seems to be here all the time?

"Sure," I say with a bright smile. I show everyone what they want to see. The smiling blonde, the happy-go-lucky girl. All the things I am anything but. When Paula leaves, I move closer to Samantha. I look at her ankle and notice it's not bandaged, so she mustn't have done too much damage last weekend. "Care to swap?" I ask her as I wiggle my brows.

"My song's up next." She rolls her eyes as I unpack my bag. She's always considered me a troublemaker, but I know she secretly loves it. And I help her out when men get too handsy without paying. Where she might be the best dancer, she still has a lot to learn in the way of intentionally influencing men by being sickly sweet and sometimes being a little rougher when need be.

I quickly touch up my makeup. "I can dance to that. You have plenty of songs, right?"

She nods and glances in the direction that Paula just left. Farther down the hall is the office where I'm assuming Mr. Stalker Boss is. "You won't get in trouble?" she questions.

"I'll probably get fired, but I would at least like to

make some money before I do," I say, taking off my loose dress, my work lingerie already on underneath.

She lets out a bark of nervous laughter but agrees. I change into the schoolgirl outfit and slide on my black heels before I lean down and kiss her cheek. I wait only a few moments before the music starts playing, then I open the curtains. Men catcall, but I don't give them the privilege of eye contact. I sway my hips as I go straight for the pole. I grab it and hook a knee around it, twirling in circles as I eye those closest to the stage, spotting which of them I think are the biggest tippers.

I come to a stop, gripping the pole with both hands, with a smile, as I throw my long blonde hair over my shoulders. I drop down into a crouch and look over my shoulder, winking at the man who looks like the biggest fish here. I lift my skirt, smack my ass, and grab a handful of flesh. Men begin cheering and throwing money on the stage. I smile as I lay down on the stage. My hands caress down my body until they reach the waistband of the skirt, and then I shimmy it down my hips until it's off. I turn around to get on my hands and knees. As I reach for the pole again, someone lifts me and drags me off the stage.

"What the fuck! Put me down!" The men boo as I'm carried off over a shoulder, even as I kick and punch. I don't recognize who it is until we are behind the curtains, and he speaks.

"You. On now," he roughly commands, and that's when I notice Samantha.

"Get my tips!" I yell out after her. She slips through the curtains, and the moment they close, I'm a fiery, chaotic bitch.

My boss lowers me to the ground, and the moment my heels touch the floor, I shove him away. This infuriating man stares at me, and I fucking glare back. Most men would ogle my body, the G-string and barely-there schoolgirl top. Not this man. He takes me in as if he's entitled to my every movement, never averting his gaze from my eyes. He's fucking intense and purposefully trying to intimidate me.

Good fucking luck.

Dutton is dressed in a black suit. His lips are pressed in a hard line as if expecting me to actually be scared. I don't ever feel intimidated by men. I've been around all types of powerful men in my life. And although none of them have ever put me on edge like Dutton does, I fucking refuse to bow at his intensity just because he expects it.

So, I might be a brat.

I don't give a fuck.

When I don't say anything, a tic runs through his

jaw, and he grudgingly breaks the silence. "I requested you to come see me when you got here, and you ignored that and went on stage."

I place my hand on my hip.

"I was coming to see you after work to display why I'm a valuable asset." I beam at him, and the vein in his temple throbs once, then twice before he shakes his head.

I know he wants to call me a smartass. I can see it written all over his face.

"Is this fun for you? You do need this job, correct?" he asks, crossing his arms as if trying to look at me in a different light.

"I do need a job, but I don't do well being micromanaged by a man who doesn't know how to shake his ass or show his tits," I throw back at him.

The corner of his mouth twitches, and I'm not sure if he's trying not to laugh or if he's so furious that his face is starting to spasm in weird places.

"I should fire you. I have fired women for far less."

"Fire me then if that's what you want to do. But at least get my tips off that fucking stage. I earned that money." I point in the direction of the stage. His gaze remains on me.

"Are you always this much of a brat?"

The question surprises me but also fills me with a weird amount of pride. "So it seems."

Wait. Am I getting away with this?

"Stay off the fucking stage for the night," he orders, and it's like a bucket of cold water thrown over me.

"I need my tips," I yell out as he turns and walks away. "I don't work here for free!"

He's gone, and I throw my hands up in disbelief. Maybe I wanted to get fired or for that asshole to return to whatever trust fund hobbies he was up to before he decided to make weekly visits to his club.

Huffing, I walk back into the dressing room, remove the shirt, and then head out to the bar area in my lingerie.

I'm a woman who lives off technicalities. He said I should stay off the stage, but that doesn't mean I can't make money from working the floor and performing personal dances.

I spot him standing at the bar with Mike, but their conversation comes to an immediate halt when his gaze lands on me. I offer him a small wave before I focus on my job and start walking the room. I feel him tracking me, even when I do my best to ignore him. I sit on the lap of a guy who offers me a hundred-dollar bill, and I stroke his tie as I ask what he'd like to drink.

"You're really beautiful," he says, and my nostrils flare at the offensive smell of alcohol on his breath and the wedding ring glinting in the lights from the stage. Disgusting, really. His wife is probably at home, clueless about what's happening here. And men wonder why women have trust issues. It's because men act on impulses and always want what they can't have. I've been burned by this personally when I discovered Bentley's father was cheating on me throughout our relationship. I hate myself because, even at the time, I had my suspicions. It wasn't until I became pregnant I gathered enough courage to leave.

But I'm here to make money to give my son everything he deserves.

So, unfortunately, I have to ignore my moral compass.

"Well, thank you, handsome." My hand pauses on his chest. "How about a dance?" He nods eagerly, and I stand, offering him my hand.

"She's booked," Dutton says and pulls me to him by my waist.

Fucking hell.

Really?

Is this man hellbent on making me lose all my clients tonight? For what purpose? To teach me who's in charge?

Fuck that. I'll just find another job and tell him to shove this one up his prim and proper trust-fund-baby ass.

I don't say that in front of the customer, but my fists curl as I wait to explode when he escorts me to the back. Except he doesn't guide me to the back; instead, we step into a private room.

He shuts the door behind us, then turns to look at me.

I cross my arms over my chest. "Do you plan to fuck with me my entire shift?"

"Fuck with you?"

"Yes. I'm here to work and earn money. And you keep on fucking that up," I say, frustrated.

He scoffs. "You seem to mistake me for a member instead of your boss."

"I don't care who you are. I only care about who's paying."

"I pay you to work here," he reminds me.

His harsh blue eyes never leave mine, as if he's studying me like I'm some sort of oddity. Then he reaches into his pocket and drops a wad of hundred-dollar bills on the table. My eyebrows furrow as he takes a seat and leans back, his arms stretching along the back of the couch as he nods to the money.

"But if that's not enough for you, then dance," he commands.

I don't completely understand what his game is, but that's a fuck ton of money that would usually take me multiple private dances to make. We don't earn that much for a private dance unless the client is an excellent tipper. Even then, it's very rare. There's easily a thousand bucks on that table.

I lick my suddenly dry lips, then say, "Okay." I approach him slowly. When I do private dances, it's about matching the customer's energy and anticipating their needs. Luring them to believe they're getting more than a dance. But with Dutton, there's an uneasy energy around him. He's so fucking cold and calculated I can't figure out what he's thinking, let alone what he might want. And I don't know if I want any fucking insight into this asshole's mind, either.

If my boss wants me to dance for him, I will make him fall hard.

He wants my paid services, then this asshole's about to get the most incredible show of his life.

I place my hands on his knees and separate them, keeping eye contact with him the whole time. He doesn't blink or pull away as he watches me. It's intimidating, but I don't bend to the will of powerful men. I rest a knee on either side of him, pushing my tits against his body as if riding him.

"Why do you keep stopping me from working?" I ask.

"Did I ask for a conversation?" he replies.

I lean in close to his lips, careful not to touch them. It's the first time his gaze dips lower, and I curve a satisfied smile. This man doesn't seem like the type to let people touch him, which gives me confidence that I can rattle him. I place my hands between us and caress his inner thigh as I roam my other hand up and over his stomach to his chest.

"I want to know. You are my boss, after all."

"Yes, and you would do well to remember that." His gaze flicks back to mine knowingly.

It's disturbing how I can't seem to break through that fucking icy wall of his. I don't dance for other men like this, *ever*. But I want to ruin his night the way he's ruined mine.

But maybe I'll have some fun in the meantime.

"Do you get all your women to dance for you?" I ask huskily as I lower my hips and start grinding them, purposefully brushing myself against his cock. I smile with satisfaction as I notice his eyes dilate.

"Only the annoying ones," he replies, and I can tell

it's taking all his discipline to keep his hands on the back of the couch.

I smirk as I stand and turn, bending over in front of him and looking over my shoulder at him. There's still no music playing in the room, but there seems to be a tune and rhythm only we can feel.

I sit back down on his lap, my ass directly on top of his cock. It fills me with satisfaction that he's hard, so he's not entirely immune to my charm.

"Some would say you're the annoying one since you keep stopping me from working." I move in his lap, and he keeps his eyes trained on me. "I'm a very *hard* worker, you know."

"You're working now, aren't you?" His voice is gravelly.

"Seems very unprofessional that you're getting me to dance for you." I pout over my shoulder, and when I look back at him, his eyes remain an icy blue, but an inferno rages within them.

I bounce once on his lap, with a grin, and then twice, fully bringing his cock to attention. Okay, maybe I'm enjoying this way too much because I notice a sudden heat trickle into my lower abdomen. A sexual curiosity that has been dormant since Bentley's father.

He smirks, as if he knows, and I hate that he *sees*

me. His arms lift from the back of the couch, but when he goes to touch me, a knock comes at the door.

"Come in," he commands as he lazily places his arms back where they were. I continue to move in his lap.

The door opens, and two men walk in. I haven't seen them before. They look like criminals, and it's obvious they're twins. Both seem surprised to see me as they take seats near him.

Suddenly, the room crackles with dangerous energy, and I'm certain the men who just walked in are not law-abiding citizens. The bulkier one speaks first. "You paying for entertainment tonight?"

"Pay for us as well," the one with the shoulder-length hair says, not looking up from his phone.

"You can both afford it yourselves," Dutton says. "And, no, she will not be dancing for either of you."

His hands finally land on my waist, halting my movements. When I look over my shoulder at him, he orders, "Take your money and leave."

"Greedy." The bulkier one chuckles.

"You don't want me to finish dancing?" I ask, standing and laying my hand on his chest with a pout. I can tell he's agitated when I put on the childish act that everyone else usually devours.

His hand covers mine, and he leans in. "Take your money and fucking leave. You're done for today."

Fucking asshole.

You don't have to tell me twice.

Smiling, I grab the cash and saunter out, knowing his gaze is glued to my ass.

An ass he'll never have the chance to grab again.

What the fuck is wrong with that man?

SIX
DUTTON

"Why did you send her away? We could have had some fun," Hawke says, admiring Posie as she exits the room. My hands tighten on the back of the couch, but I bite my tongue. It's not the first time they've been here, but it is the first time I've been mad at them for wanting to give one of my women attention.

I stare at the door momentarily, half expecting her to return because that seems like something she would do.

"It's unlike you to pay for your own services. Feeling lonely?" Hawke bites back a smile, and I suddenly want to get very stabby. Or at least have a drink so I can tolerate him a little more. As usual, Ford remains quiet compared to his obnoxious twin.

I hit the button beside my seat, which calls for

someone to service us. Samantha enters, her eyes lighting up the moment she sees Hawke. It's no secret the muscled beefcake is popular amongst the women, and although I'd usually let them play, I want to get straight down to business.

"The usual, Samantha, with three glasses." She looks disheartened, and Hawke is about to argue when I raise my hand to him. She leaves without a word.

"Wow, you really are all work and no play. That's funny coming from someone who goes around running clubs that provide pleasure," Hawke says, disheartened.

"Might I add that it's not a necessity for you to fuck every woman in this city?" I say, undoing the top two buttons of my shirt and readjusting my cock. Posie dared to touch and taunt me in ways that no other woman has. Even the women I do fuck don't get the privilege of being so... intimate... so playful. She acts like it's her personal mission to unnerve me.

"No, but it's a preference," he replies with a smart-ass smile.

Samantha saunters back in with a bottle of my finest whiskey. She pours it into three glasses with ice and then slides one over to each of us, her gaze focused on Hawke. I swallow the harsh drink, trying to cool my temper.

I've considered a few different reasons or angles Posie might be here. It could very well be what Paula said—that she's trying to build a better life for herself, but I leave nothing to chance. I've watched her these past few weeks. Well, when she shows up for work, of course. I could easily have someone trail her, but that feels like a waste of resources. Or I could pay Will Walker, a family friend, and the best tracker around, to dig up dirt on her.

I tap my finger contemplatively. So why haven't I done that yet? Money's not an issue. I could have all the answers right now in front of me, but for some reason, there's the allure of the mystery surrounding her, which could be just as damning. There's also a pleasure in extracting information from someone, whether it be through torture, pleasure, or various other entertaining means. Whether she likes it or not, she is my current obsession because I don't like anyone I haven't yet figured out.

When Samantha leaves and closes the door, I bring the glass to my lips. "I saw that Trea Lissor was taken into custody today. The press is eating him alive," I say with a smirk.

Hawke chuckles. "Would you believe he never left his house after we returned him? The guy was terrified."

"His father approached Rya Monti to get his son out of this situation," Ford says before he downs half the glass in one mouthful. Interesting. Rya is the best criminal lawyer in New York, and my aunt. She has, in many ways, influenced Eli's and my way of thinking, especially his, considering she's his mother.

"Did she take the case?" I ask because I can imagine the hefty amount of money his father is willing to offer, but if she did take him on as a client, I might have to have a private discussion with her. If she even considers it, I'll kill him myself before he can make bail.

"Nah. Eli explained the situation, and she's trying to take fewer cases as she and Crue settle into this semi-retirement shit," Hawke replies.

I roll my eyes at my aunt and uncle. I love them both dearly, but retirement doesn't suit the busy mafia family. "Speaking of... Where is Eli?"

"Probably trying to get his wife pregnant. That's all those two do these days." Hawke rolls his eyes.

"I've walked in on them twice, and Eli had the audacity to bark orders at me as if I were the intruder when they're fucking in public," Ford says under his breath.

"You know peeping is a real kink, brother. I don't judge you if that's your thing. Just don't do it with me.

You'll feel inadequate." Hawke grins widely. He's already pouring his second drink and then goes to top off mine and Ford's glasses.

The door bursts open, and Billie barges in. I internally groan as she points her finger in my direction. Behind her is Hope, and I'm even more uncomfortable having Alek Ivanov's daughter in one of my clubs. The notorious killer and black-market auctioneer is no doubt as protective of her as I am of my sister. But at least the twins are here, so they'll get the lecture before me because they're family.

"What the fuck did you do?" Billie demands with hands on her hips. "Trea asks me to go to the ball and then ghosts me, and one week later, he's being imprisoned?!"

I try to hide my smirk. "Hello, Dutton's little sister. It's good to see you're studying hard in your final year of college," Hawke says.

"Don't give me that shit!" she snaps as she strides over to Hawke and swipes the bottle from his hand, then takes a long swig. I sigh. She's obviously in a mood. She drops onto the couch between the twins, and I know she's done it intentionally because it pisses me off when she positions herself so closely to any male.

"Hey, mini tornado!" Hawke says, going to throw

an arm over her shoulder. He pulls his arm back when I give him a deadly glare. He chuckles, knowing it will irritate me.

"Far worse than a *little* tornado," Ford corrects.

Billie glares at him as Hope quietly takes a seat across from me. I've never been able to understand the star pupil much. Her sculptures are already renowned worldwide, and she is as much in the spotlight as her famed mother, Lena Love, who is a singer. And yet, there's a quiet edge to her that reminds me very much of her father, Alek. And that makes her silently dangerous.

Unfortunately, she and my sister have been friends since they were kids. Hope is two years younger, though, with my sister's immature mood swings, you would never know it.

"Oh, Ford, don't tell me you've started growing a personality," Billie bites back.

"Unless you brought him sweets, he isn't going to bite back," Hawke jokes, immediately redirecting her wrath to me.

"So what did you do to Trea, hmm?"

If only she knew. I don't think I'd be her favorite if she knew I carve messages into the chests of people who try to become friendly with her. But it's the role of a big brother. My father taught me to look after my family, which I take very seriously. He's aware of my antics and doesn't see anything wrong with them.

"I'm talking to you, Dutton! I'll tell Mom!" she yells.

I see the corner of Ford's lip curve up, and Hawke begins to laugh.

I place my drink down. "We're past the point of 'telling Mom.' And do you think it's so bad that I had a hand to play in exposing his dirty little secrets? Do you agree with what he was doing?"

Her shoulders sag, and the fight begins to leave her eyes. "No. He should be put behind bars for what he's done, but that's not the point, Dutton, and you know it. I'm a woman, not a child. You need to let me date like a normal person! Let me make my own mistakes and fall in love!"

Love is a criminal notion. Everyone seeks it, pines for it, then wallows when they lose it. All of which alters their fucking brain cells because they don't think critically.

"You're too young to love. Focus on your studies and—"

"I'm not a kid anymore, Dutton!" she says, exasperated. "Your overprotective nature will literally drive any woman to insanity."

Ford is looking at his phone as he casually hands his glass to Hope, who takes a sip.

I sigh. Is my sister intentionally trying to humiliate herself in front of this group?

"I keep women safe. It's what I do." It's what my father taught me to do. "So, no, I won't apologize for deterring the wrong type of men from getting close to you."

"What, are you a matchmaker now?" Billie hisses. "And who will be good enough for me, Dutton?"

I stare at her, taking a sip from my whiskey. It's the same look I give her whenever I'm done with a conversation.

She throws her hands in the air and screams, "Well, thank fuck you're leaving the country for two weeks! Who knows how many cocks I might get in my holes while you're gone!"

My grip tightens on the glass as she swipes the bottle from the table and flicks her honey-colored hair over her shoulder. "Come on, Hope. Fuck these guys. Let's go pick up Ivy and have our own fun."

"Wait, don't take the bottle!" Hawke yells at her back. Hope hands Ford the glass, and he watches them silently as they leave. Billie slams the door shut.

"You're going to break that," Ford says, and that's when I realize how tightly I'm holding the glass.

My teeth grind. I'll be gone for two weeks, opening another gentlemen's club in Italy. I'm flying over there to keep the grandparents at bay. Something Eli hasn't done for two years now, which I always hear about. Which is exactly why I'm the favorite grandchild. Surprising, considering I still don't know if my grandfather, even in his old age, likes my dad. But over the last two years, I've been going every six months, at the very least, as I expand our businesses.

"How much will it cost for me to have one of you trail my sister for two weeks?" I ask the twins.

Hawke chuckles. "You know we work for Eli, not you. And I have a feeling Eli might agree with her on this one. You have to give her some breathing room."

I glare at him, and he holds his hands up in defense.

Nothing great ever comes from love, and I wish my sister wasn't so sucked into the notion of it. I have loving parents in a successful marriage. I see its advantages, but I also know the level of dependency it creates, and I could never imagine myself being so invested in another's wants and desires above my own.

It either makes me a profit or protects my family.

That's all I need.

SEVEN
POSIE

Dutton hasn't been at the club for the last two weeks, which I'm thankful for. But to say I haven't been looking for him would be a lie. Because I'm certain he's going to try and ruin my fucking night.

When I think of the boss of a gentlemen's club, I think of an old, rich man who is a sleaze. But Dutton is definitely not that. Assuredly, he's an undeniable asshole, but I've realized he barely interacts with any of the other dancers. The dancers, however, gossip behind his back as to how they all wish they were fucking him. If only they understood what they were asking for. Yes, the man's beautiful, in the same way an ice sculpture is. He looks like he's been built by God's divine hand, but his personality could freeze over the Sahara Desert.

That's most likely why I can't bite my tongue around him. I'm positive that this man is used to everyone obeying him and throwing themselves at him, and I just can't do it. I promised myself I'd never do that for a man again. I wonder if that's why he's so hard on me because he's not used to someone telling him no.

Tonight, the club is closed to guests but open for the staff to celebrate three years of being open. Dutton supposedly puts on a celebration every year and hires caterers. In those three years, he's allegedly also opened another eight gentlemen's clubs internationally. And I heard that's why he's been gone the past two weeks; he's in Italy to open another one. That's what one of the girls said, but they gossip about everything, so who knows if that's fact or if he's off conducting other lucrative business. Or maybe he's on a pleasure trip because, for sure, that man is up to no good in his spare time.

I only agreed to join the party for a few hours tonight because, apparently, he's never attended the celebration, and there are prizes to be won. One of the girls bragged about winning a twenty-carat diamond bracelet last year, so it's fair to say I'm intrigued. Again, rumors are a wild thing here.

I considered taking the night off, but when Amy was readily available, I thought, *why not?* Apart from work, I don't really do anything without my son, and that's not exactly social. I just hope it's worth it, so I don't consider paying the babysitter tonight a waste of money.

So here I am, walking into the club—without lingerie on for a change—and finding mostly everyone already here. I know I'm late, and it's not that I intentionally do it to piss people off, but I prefer to have dinner with my son before I leave.

I place my bag on the table in the back, then reapply my lip balm—the cold has been wreaking havoc on my lips—and I ease into the sound of everyone enjoying themselves out on the main floor.

"Late as usual," someone says from behind me, and Dutton walks in.

My breath hitches because I forgot how intense his ocean-blue gaze and dangerous aura are. Two weeks without this man is not long enough to wipe away the fact that despite being beautiful, he's an asshole.

I focus back on the mirror and pucker my lips. "Seems I'm right on time if the boss is only arriving now." He briefly looks me up and down before coming to a stop behind me with his hands in his pants pockets. I'm sure it must be different for him to actually see me in clothes for once, and yet, somehow, I feel even more judged than when I have my body on display.

I'm dressed in jeans tight around my waist and ass, which flare at my ankles, a shirt that says something about riding a cowboy, and my hair is up in a bun.

Samantha bursts through the door, wearing a short pink dress. "Yay, you're here!" She runs up to me and almost tackles me in a hug.

"How much have you had to drink?" I ask her. It's only then that she realizes Dutton is in the room, and her demeanor changes, if only slightly, because the alcohol won't let her act any other way. He's taken two considerable steps back, however.

She wisely chooses to ignore him and place her full drink into my hand. "You have to catch up, come on." She grabs my hand and pulls me toward the main floor.

I sniff the drink and am blinded by the toxicity of the vodka. "Jesus, Samantha, did you put a dash of orange juice in this just for kicks?"

"That's what happens when the brats get into the liquor cabinet like dirty little raccoons," Mike says as I'm dragged past him. "Want me to get you something drinkable?" he quietly whispers to me, and I nod silently.

A few of the other girls with whom I don't work many shifts are dressed more presentably than we usually do. I'm sure this is a warm-up for a wild night out.

Paula steps in front of Samantha, cutting her off, and I'm so fucking grateful I could kiss her. *"Help me,"* I mouth.

Paula keeps her expression composed as she asks Samantha to give us a moment.

"Okay, but you better have finished that drink by the time I return! I'll pour us another one!" Samantha says giddily. I don't even know if she'll make it out tonight.

She skips to the bar despite premade drinks being readily available by a hired bartender.

Mike walks over to Paula and me, and she says, "I didn't think you would come."

"Free food? How can I pass that up?" I say with a smile as I place the toxic concoction of Samantha's drink on the high-top table beside me.

"Well, I was shocked you left your house," Mike says, pulling me in for a side hug and placing a flute of bubbly liquid into my hand. "Here, have this, these taste great."

"Thank you. I didn't think I'd come, but here I am," I say triumphantly as I notice Dutton speaking with one of the security guards; however, he's staring at me. I take a sip of the drink and focus back on Mike as he complains.

"You never come out when I ask; it hurts my feelings," he says, brushing my shoulder with his playfully.

I laugh. "You know I don't go out. Ever. It's too expensive, and I'd rather be in my PJs at home."

He rolls his eyes. "You sound like a woman in her fifties, not a twenty-four-year-old."

"Hey!" Paula interjects. "There's nothing wrong with being in your fifties."

Mike lays his hands over his heart dramatically. "But, madam, you don't look a day over thirty. I never knew."

"Smartass." She smirks, and takes a mouthful of her drink. I follow her lead and sip from my own. It tastes festive and decadent but too sweet for my liking. However, the buzz it offers me isn't all that bad.

Paula excuses herself from our conversation to start the games.

Mike cozies in as we watch Samantha drunkenly grind on the pole with two of the other girls. We're laughing as one of them stumbles. They're having the best time, and it's moments like this that remind me I'm only in my mid-twenties. I imagine this is what a lot of women around my age are doing—going out and having fun. I can't remember the last time I had fun. Well, at least like this.

"How come you don't go out now and then? You're

hot as shit," Mike says as he places his empty flute behind me. I swallow the rest of mine and set my glass next to his.

I shrug. "My money can go elsewhere. I don't want to jeopardize my financial security. It just doesn't seem worth it."

Mike leans against the counter. "You never really told me much about your family. Do you not have any here?"

I don't remove my gaze from the girls. I don't like sharing much about myself. I overshared on the night I met Paula in the hospital, but it was to my benefit, I suppose, since she offered me a job. But that doesn't mean anyone else needs to know more about me; keeping everyone at a distance is better.

"Nope, just me and Bentley," I tell him.

"Bentley?" a voice cuts in, and Mike and I both jump. Dutton is standing behind us, holding two glasses of champagne. He offers me one and then holds the other out to Mike, who takes it with a nervous smile. "You don't wear a ring, so I didn't think you were married."

"I'm not," I reply flatly as I raise the glass to my lips and turn my back to him to watch the girls again. He stands beside me, unfazed by my obvious want to shut the conversation down. I don't like people prying into my personal life.

"So, who is Bentley?" he pushes.

"How about you tell me about the last woman you fucked, and then I can decide if I want to share that information with you."

Mike chokes, half his mouthful dribbling back into the glass. "Don't mind me," he wheezes.

"I don't usually share that information, but since you asked so nicely..." Dutton turns to Mike. "Care to give us a minute?"

Mike nods hastily, as if appreciative of being excused, then walks off, still coughing. I internally sigh. I'd much rather spend my evening with Mike than with Frosty the Snowman over here. Yet, I'd be lying if I said there isn't a small part of me that's curious. What kind of woman is my cold-hearted boss into?

I cross my arms over my chest, trying to shake off the cold intensity of this man when his undivided attention is on me. It's unnerving.

"Why do you look like you want to run?" he asks.

"I Googled you," I tell him, gripping my glass. He raises a brow. All sorts of wild speculation came up in my search. Him being involved with the mafia. Associates he's had that have simply vanished—the type of wealthy family with parents who've been able to provide him with absolutely everything.

I know his type.

Dangerous.

Cunning.

Often with a God complex.

And that matches the description of this asshole, without a doubt.

"You did?" he purrs, and for some reason he sounds satisfied.

"Yes."

"And what did you find?" His voice is like honey, coaxing in a way that probably makes many people fall for his charm. I'm not that type, though.

"That you come from money. And you opened this place yourself to escape your father's businesses. There's speculation you're attached to the Italian mafia as well. Killed anyone lately?" I ask rhetorically.

He smirks. "Are you asking for my body count? And who can trust those gossip blogs? Nasty little things, they are."

"Okay, so tell me the truth." I don't expect this man to give me a lick of truth because why should he?

"The truth, huh? Okay. Your first question was who I last fucked. Last month, I met a girl named Tamina. We attended the same function, and I took her out the back door of the event, fucked her in the alley, and went about my night. Since then, no one. I've been too busy."

"A man too busy for sex? That's a first," I mumble into my glass as I take another sip.

"I'm constantly surrounded by sex," he says matter-of-factly.

"Yes. I suppose you are." I take another sip, unsettled by how he stares at me even when I watch the others. "Do you fuck your employees?" I ask, and finally look up at him.

"No, I do not."

A relieved sigh escapes me, and I glance away, hoping he didn't notice. But he did.

"That appeases you. Tell me, Posie, did you think I wanted to fuck you?"

"I never said that."

"You didn't say no either. And I'm certain 'no' is your favorite word."

"I just thought how sad it'd be if the turnover rate of the dancers were high because you can't keep your dick in your pants."

He chuckles then, and I'm so surprised that I stare at him in bewilderment. "Oh my God. He understands humor, after all. Frosty the Snowman can actually laugh."

"You don't seem to be able to refrain from speaking your unfiltered thoughts to your boss, do you?" I look away, uncomfortable with the mesmerized state I was in simply because he chuckled. Jesus, maybe these drinks are more potent than I think.

"Now, since we're getting to know each other, why don't you tell me when was the last time you had sex."

I consider lying. I don't like that he's asking personal questions, but I have to take it if I can throw it his way.

"About six years ago." I don't usually share that with anyone. It's the truth, but I also want to rattle him with the information. I'm curious about his reaction, and it disappoints me, to say the least. I expected him to express a bit of surprise, but I got nothing.

"You hate men?" he asks curiously.

"Who said I don't like men?"

"True. So you hate women?"

I go to take another sip and realize I drank it all. He waves over a waitress, who provides me with another glass and takes the empty one. Damn, is this asshole trying to get me drunk?

But then I glance over at Samantha, who is wearing a bucket on her head, and decide I'm nowhere near drunk.

"I don't hate women either. I have a lot going on,

and my last relationship didn't really leave me with high hopes."

"Was it with a man or woman?" I can't help but smirk at his question. He's very inquisitive.

"With a man." I pause, considering the women in front of me. "Though women are beautiful, so I may be in the wrong lane."

"You aren't," is all he says before the security guard near the door waves him down. He excuses himself and walks off. I feel relieved the moment he's gone, and I don't entirely understand why he puts me on edge.

EIGHT
POSIE

The evening is more fun than I anticipated. I join in on a game because Mike is insistent, and I'm surprised when I win a fucking laptop. If I knew the games were giving out these types of prizes, I would have joined in sooner. I thought it was a joke they played on newbies when they mentioned someone winning a twenty-carat diamond bracelet last year, but the prizes are all extravagant in their own way.

I could do so much with a laptop. I haven't seen it as an essential, but now that I have one, I'm itching to go back to my designs online, which I was doing before Bentley. I hadn't picked it up since he was born because I sold my last laptop for extra cash.

The minute I found out I was pregnant, I started

saving. I saved and saved so I could move away. And I eventually got there. I sold everything and started fresh. And it worked until I started running out of money. I began working at a local cafe and was there for a few years before I realized it wasn't paying enough. Then I found out about the club, and even though I'd never stripped before, Paula hired me. My first paycheck was only a few hundred, but that money was a saving grace. I quit the cafe and just kept this job. And I haven't looked back since.

But now... I could dabble in my designs again, which makes me ridiculously happy. Or maybe it's the slight buzz from the drinks making me feel this way. When I think it's about time I leave, Mike pulls me to the side with a mischievous grin.

I want to slip out before the others start heading for other clubs that I have no interest in attending.

"Do you want this?" Mike asks. He opens his bag, and I see a brand-new cell phone inside. I look up at him, confused.

"You won that?" He nods with a triumphant twinkle in his eye. He opens another small bag, which has another phone in it. "You won two? How is that possible?"

"Lucky, I guess." He shrugs. "I don't need two, and

seeing your cracked screen makes my eye twitch. But if you don't want it, it's all good. I can just sell it."

"No way. I want it. Can I pay you for it?"

"No. Why would I charge you? I won it, so take it. Consider this my down payment to receive all the gossip of whatever happens between you and the boss."

I laugh because he's genuinely a devilish gossiper. "Nothing is happening between us."

He looks me up and down. "Girl, you're delulu if you think he's once taken the time to speak with the dancers, let alone bring them a drink."

I wave him off as I accept the bag. Then I throw my arms around him because I'm already on my third glass of the champagne mixture. He's startled but hugs me back since I'm not usually the affectionate type.

"I know it's a pity phone, but I love it." I clap my hands. "Best work party ever."

"Yep. So, are you going out with the girls tonight?" he asks.

"I think she's had enough to drink, don't you?" Dutton says, appearing behind us again, and we both startle. *Is this guy a fucking wraith?*

"You need to stop sneaking up on people like that. It's fucking creepy." I sigh. And then I glare at him. "Are you trying to control me? Because the last man who did that never saw me again."

"Noted. Though, that won't work here while I pay your bills," he says in his superior, asshole-ish tone.

Mike bites his bottom lip, trying to hide his *I told you so* expression. I glare at him as if to say, *There is definitely nothing between me and the boss.*

I lean toward Dutton. "Technically, your clients pay my bills. Not you."

"How are you getting home?" he asks, nodding to the glass of champagne.

"I'll call a cab," I tell him, looking down at my phone.

"I'll drive you. Grab your things, and let's go."

Mike coughs next to me, and I don't miss the mischievous twinkle in his eyes again.

"And Mike?" I ask Dutton. Dutton glances at him as if only noticing him for the first time.

"Get your shit too."

Mike straightens his back and nods, picking up his bag. I can't help but giggle at his smug-ass smile.

I grab my handbag from the back and thank Paula for the evening. She's the only one we say goodbye to because we want to slip out quietly. Well, Mike and I, that is. Dutton is already waiting outside beside his car, hand casually tucked in his pocket as he talks to someone on the phone.

This car is different from the one he drove to my

house. It's a G-Wagon and looks just as expensive as the last. Does this asshole have multiple cars at his disposal? Most likely.

Mike leans in and quietly whispers, "He's never personally driven any of the girls home."

"Well then, it might be your lucky night." I nudge his shoulder.

He laughs as he throws his hands in the air and yells, "Shotgun for the back!"

Dutton finishes his call and opens the doors for both of us. Mike doesn't even try to hide his smile, and it's contagious as I try to hide my own as I slip into the front.

"I feel so bougie," Mike whispers as Dutton walks around the car. "There's so much space back here, you two could fuck in here, for sure."

"You have a one-track mind." I laugh.

"Yeah, I'm a man. And, also, girrrl, you've seen him... That man is a snack."

"And an asshole," I quip.

"A *rich* asshole," he sing-songs before Dutton opens the door and slides into the driver's seat.

"Do I want to know what you two are giggling about?" Dutton asks as he starts the engine.

I drop my head back against the seat and smile. "I

was just saying this car is fancy, and I wonder if you'd hate me if I spilled something in it."

He doesn't reply, which I take to mean he regrets asking me. He shoots a glance down at the bags at my feet.

There's barely any traffic at this time of night, and we start our drive to Mike's house after he tells Dutton the address. Mike giggles in the back as he shows me a profile of an attractive man, then whispers, "It's actually his address I'm going to, but who cares."

I smirk, envious of his freedom to bounce through men. Prioritizing myself and my needs has been long forgotten since having Bentley. And the thought of bringing anyone around Bentley horrifies me. Then again, maybe having a fuckbuddy with no strings attached isn't a bad idea. It's been a while since I've seriously thought about it.

I know Dutton intentionally asked Mike his address so he could drop him off first. He already knows my address, but Mike doesn't need to know that. It will only give him more fuel for his speculation that something is going on between me and our boss.

I side-eye Dutton as Mike makes small talk with him about cars and motorcycles. Neither of which I have any interest in.

I take the time to study Dutton's face. It's truly

cruel how beautiful he is. Even his shirts, which are likely made to fit so tightly, effortlessly show off the lean muscle underneath. And those eyes? Even in the dark, with only flashes of the streetlights, they look like a brewing storm. The shadow of growth around his jaw looks like it'll leave some serious beard burn, and those fucking lips look like they could do some damage.

He glances my way, and I immediately avert my gaze, realizing I was staring for too long.

I mean, I can't imagine he'd be that bad of a lay. I think back on when I danced for him, and the size of the dick I felt pressing against his fly felt more than adequate. A heat begins to pound between my legs, and I try my hardest to ignore it. There's something about this man that puts me on edge. Most likely because he's, without a doubt, dangerous, and that's never gotten me into good situations. I should be running the other way, and yet, I'd be lying if I didn't admit he's attractive.

When we park in front of the address Mike gave, he stops singing whatever was on the radio and jumps out of the car. Coming to my door, he pulls it open, leans in, and kisses my cheek before he starts singing another song as he skips his way to the apartment building for a rendezvous I'm most likely going to hear all about on our next shift together.

Without Mike, a palpable silence and tension fill the car.

It might be the slight buzz of alcohol or the encouragement from Mike, or maybe the frustrating pounding between my legs that has me deadpanning, "So, I know you said you don't fuck your employees, but what about giving and receiving head?"

NINE
DUTTON

Did she say what I think she did? I immediately pull over and turn to face her. She smiles at me, and I don't think she meant it because she likes to toy with me. However, I take it very seriously especially since this little vixen has been haunting my dreams, unsolicited, for the last two weeks.

"You want me to fuck you with my mouth, Posie?"

She shrugs casually. "Was just a question."

Not only do I want to uncover her association with the Boston Delinquents, but I've also never met a person who so easily says no to me, but she also equally intrigues me. And every time she challenges me, I want to see how far I can push her. How much is she able to take before she crumbles?

"Get in the back," I order as I get out of the car. I

pull open the back door, and she's staring at me in disbelief. I'm not wasting any fucking time on this invitation as I impatiently wait outside the car, parked beside a bush.

"There are cars driving past; we're on a busy street," she blurts, shocked.

I parked behind a bush that half hides the car, and I silently dare her to eat her own words. If she pushes me, I'll push right back and play whatever little daring game she thinks she's toying at.

"And you will be lying on the back seat where no one can see you, so climb back here and drop your jeans. Don't worry; the windows are tinted, and the car is bulletproof."

Her mouth drops open as if she's about to ask me about it being bulletproof, but instead, she settles for, "Are you usually this demanding?"

She's still not moving, and I lick my lips, restraining myself from dragging her over the seat. This woman tests my patience like it's her favorite fucking game.

"Do you plan to move, or am I going to move you myself?" I ask because fuck if I'm not tasting her after she instigated it. My patience can only last so long until she realizes there are consequences to her taunting me.

"You don't fuck employees," she reluctantly states,

and I can see her inner struggle. She most likely didn't think I'd take her up on the offer. She thought she'd get another jab at me. She thought fucking wrong.

"I'm fucking you with my mouth, not my cock," I clarify. Semantics. "Do you often go back on your word?" I challenge because I know this woman, under no circumstances, will let me have the upper hand in this mental wargame she likes to play.

She swallows, still staring at me, then quietly says, "Okay," before undoing her seat belt and climbing between the two front seats. The moment she lands in the back, she looks at me, and I dare say it might be the first and only time I see a degree of nervousness in her expression. "This is a bad idea."

"Sounds like a win-win to me. You need a release, and I get a taste of you."

I graze my callused hand over her inner thigh all the way down to her ankle, where I yank her possessively towards me as I stand outside the door. She sucks in a sharp breath when she comes to a halt, half hanging out of the car while I'm looming over her like a monster waiting to pounce in the dark. She looks over my shoulder at the bush behind me.

"No one will see you. Now, lie down." I nudge her back, and she slowly lowers to the soft leather.

In what I assume is disbelief, she laughs to herself

as she lifts her hips and shimmies off her jeans. "This is so bizarre. I don't even like you."

"You like me enough to want my mouth on your cunt," I point out.

"That's true," she agrees as she pushes her jeans to her ankles. I help remove them as I drop to my knees, undisturbed by the wet grass. Then I start exploring, my hands grazing over her long, smooth legs. I smile, staring at that ridiculous shirt that says, "Save a horse, ride a cowboy."

I keep my gaze on her golden eyes, not wanting her to look away, as I run my hands up her inner thighs. Her body's tense and I notice the small telltale signs of her apprehension.

My life revolves around sex, noticing people's subtle shifts in mood, and discovering and exploiting their pleasure is what I specialize in. I reach the curve of her hip and black panties and then pause.

"Are you sure?" I ask. She doesn't look away as she swallows and nods her head. I still don't break eye contact as I lean down and kiss her through her panties. I swirl my tongue against the material, licking between her folds and circling her swollen bud. She looks transfixed. I lick deeper, and a small moan escapes her lips, and her hips tilt up to meet my wet stroke.

I smirk, quite enjoying how responsive her body is. I push her panties to the side and slide a finger between her folds. The moment I slip my finger inside her, her head tips back.

"Don't look away," I demand. Her head snaps back to attention. Once I have her gaze locked on me again, I begin to play with her, pumping into her with long, leisurely strokes.

Another small moan escapes her, and I can't help but dip my gaze to her lips. Lips I've been watching all night. When she spoke, when she took a drink from her champagne flute, and when she laughed. I imagined what they might look like around my cock.

Fuck.

My cock is painfully pressing against my pants. Her hips tilt up to meet my second finger as she slowly begins to ride my hand.

"Posie," I growl, noticing her attention starting to waver as she looks from my face to where my fingers are fucking her. I want her to know exactly who's making her come undone.

"Hmmm?" she replies in a haze, her gaze shifting back up.

"Do you want me to fuck you with my mouth?" I ask, placing a kiss on her folds. Her hips immediately raise—needy little thing.

It's been a long time since I've so desperately wanted a woman to shatter into pieces because of me. In spite of me. And I fucking love knowing that as much as she wants it, she can't stand me, and this fact alone makes it all the more rewarding.

"Yes," she breathes.

"Good girl." I suck her clit into my mouth, and her legs immediately spread wider as the light from a passing car filters into the back seat. I hold one of her thighs down, stroking the inside so she isn't distracted from what I'm doing to her. I continue pumping my fingers into her tight pussy.

I don't want to think of any man who was here before me, but I'm sure as hell going to destroy her for every man after. A woman like this deserves to be worshipped.

She tastes like everything I thought she would and more.

And now I have a problem. I want more.

I need fucking more.

I'm going to make sure she breaks into a million pieces all over my tongue so I can selfishly get my fill of her sweet cunt.

Motivation aside, this woman is fucking beautiful, and I want to break her from the inside out. I want to claim every inch and patiently wait until she comes crawling back, begging for me to take her.

"Fuck," she says breathlessly as she grabs the front seat in a tight grip. Sliding my finger between her folds, I suck on her clit as I bring another finger to her entrance.

"Oh gosh," she pants as I slip a third digit inside her. She moans as I continue to pump my fingers into her. Like a good girl, she still hasn't looked away, and I get the pleasure of watching her face contort in ecstasy.

Her pussy tightens around my fingers as she grips the hand still holding her thigh. It's as if she needs to anchor herself while her slender fingers tighten around mine. Another moan escapes her as I take another deep lick.

"Oh fuck." She sounds like she's about to cry, and I eagerly stare, unblinking, waiting for her to shatter.

Lights begin to flash outside the car, but neither of us pays them any attention.

"Oh fuck." She moans as her legs try to clamp around my head. Her sharp nails dig into my hand as she comes undone. I devour her, licking up every drop, my cock pressing painfully hard against my pants, wanting to be slathered in her juices.

Fuck, she tastes so sweet.

So opposite to her scathing, poisonous tongue.

My spine tingles the moment I realize we're not alone.

"Is there an issue here?" a male's voice asks as they walk towards the car.

Posie freezes, and immediately, her knee crashes into my face as she tries to sit up. I growl in irritation, not yet having my fill as I lick my lips and adjust my jaw. She got me good, and I'll have to be mindful if there's a bruise there tomorrow.

She's frantically grabbing at her jeans, and I can't help but smirk at the once-composed Posie, who is now in a fluster because she's been caught—literally with her pants down.

She's holding the jeans to cover herself as I smirk and turn to greet the officer who interrupted my new guilty pleasure. I make sure to block his view of her, smug in the way she's clearly embarrassed. It feels like a victory in itself against this sharp-tongued vixen who's always so defiant.

"Hello, Officer." His hand is on his belt, but the moment he realizes who I am, he's floundering.

"Oh. Mr. Taylor. Car trouble?" he asks, glancing at the car, then back to me. I lean against it and hit the side of it.

I recognize him from one of my father's shops. He buys a lot of lingerie for his wife. And mistress.

"No, just a bit of lady trouble," I curtly explain.

He nervously laughs and tries to peek over my shoulder. I shoot a glance in Posie's direction. She's still on her back, holding her jeans on her stomach, eyes wide as she stares at the ceiling. I try not to laugh while keeping my shoulders where they are so the officer can't see her.

"Okay, well, this is a traffic hazard, so I'll have to ask you to move it along."

Still looking at Posie, I smile, and I can tell by the expression on her face that if she had a gun, she would've shot me more than once already. I can't help but antagonize her further.

"You heard the man; put your pants on and get back in your seat," I tell her.

She gasps, mortified, and tries to wiggle her pants on.

"Goodnight," the officer says and walks back to his patrol car. When I turn back to Posie, I see her climbing into the front seat and buckling up quickly. When I'm behind the wheel, I adjust my cock and then triumphantly drive her home while she gives me the silent treatment.

I'm surprised that I want to uncover more about this woman, including her past and connections. Still, I seem to be failing miserably because instead, I get distracted by wanting to punish her for her smart mouth and the curiosity to feel her every curve.

Fuck, I have become no better than an ordinary man.

I'm not usually susceptible to these things.

But, fuck, she tastes fantastic.

TEN
POSIE

My face is red with embarrassment; I know that much. No matter how much I had to drink, it was not enough to dull the humiliation of what just occurred. How can I go from not having had sex for six years to getting caught by the police, half naked, and being eaten out by my boss in the back of a car? And Dutton—the fucker who barely ever smiles—has the audacity to smirk about it.

I will admit, he sure knows what to do with his mouth. This isn't surprising, considering he owns a strip club, and his dad pretty much sells sex for a living. When my ex used to go down on me, it would take him a very long time to get me anywhere close to my goal. It got to the point where he just didn't bother trying, blaming it on me, so eventually, I started lying about getting off because I was bored with his head between my legs.

I've never been with a man who asserts such complete domination, and the intensity of looking into his eyes the entire time was both intimate and shattering. It felt like he was seeing every part of me, not just my body, and that type of connection is something I definitely avoid.

He gives off the vibe that he knows exactly what to do with a woman's body.

I'm so glad I tested that theory.

Even if I'm going to regret the aftermath.

"Goodnight, Posie," he drawls as he approaches my house. I'm already grabbing my bags and opening the door before he even comes to a complete stop. Before I step out of the car, I look back at him, willing that knowing fucking smirk off his face.

"This"—I wave a finger between us—"will never happen again."

"If you say so." His arrogant smirk never even twitches. I don't bother arguing with him as I get out of his car and enter the house.

I find Amy asleep on the couch and throw a blanket over her. She prefers to go home most nights, but I don't like to wake her when she's sleeping. She's young and in college, so I think any extra sleep she can get is a bonus.

I lean against the doorframe of Bentley's room, taking a moment to watch him as he sleeps. He's cuddling the new teddy Amy bought him for his birthday. I smile as I tiptoe into the room to kiss him on the forehead and lift the blankets over him. He's a restless sleeper like me, so the blankets end up in every direction.

I head to the kitchen, trying to do anything to block out what unfolded in the last thirty minutes.

As soon as an image of Dutton's head between my legs pops into my mind, my core starts to throb, and I immediately shut the image out and try to focus on something else.

I pull out my new phone. My current one is rundown and has been dropped one too many times. I'm surprised it still works, but it covers the essentials like making appointments for Bentley. I don't have any social media accounts, not since I fled from Bobbi. I didn't want to risk any chances of him finding us or keeping tabs on me.

But for some reason, I think that's about to change. I'm not going to post a bunch of photos of myself and Bentley or anything, but I want to feel like I'm a part of the world again. If I've learned anything since working at the club, it's how stagnant I've become. And I thought I was okay with that. For the most part, I am. But it doesn't mean I can't have a few moments to myself, even if it's scrolling on social media.

I change over my phone, and I can't believe how easy and quick it is. I assumed it would be difficult to install. I then open my new laptop and, feeling inspired, download the software program I used to enjoy graphic design.

Although I've never studied graphic design, I've always enjoyed it and seemed to have a knack for it. I made money doing it until I sold my laptop. When I worked at the café, I took over their social media account, and I miss it—not the small amount of pay I received for it, but the design aspect.

When I look at the time, I realize it's already two in the morning, and I stifle a yawn. I strip down to nothing on the way to the bathroom, pausing to swipe the clothes piled on my mattress onto the floor. I haven't bought myself a bedframe because it doesn't feel essential. As long as Bentley has everything he needs and I have cash saved, I'm happy.

I yawn again, and then something purple on my inner thigh catches my attention in the reflection of the mirror. I look down and gape at what I find. The fucker marked me with a hickey.

I scrub my hands over it as if that will help remove it. When it doesn't, I click my tongue, irritated. He should know better than anyone not to leave marks. *Not that I was complaining at the time.*

I'm going to have to cover it with makeup to go on stage. *Fuck.* He's the asshole who stipulated in our contracts that we refrain from receiving love bites to give the illusion that we're not taken. It builds into our clients' fantasies. If I had his number, I'd sure as shit be giving him a piece of my mind right now. I sigh, realizing he'd probably enjoy it. I don't know what the fuck my boss is thinking... ever. But antagonizing me seems to be a hobby of his lately.

Stepping into the shower, I stand there for what feels like ten minutes. Closing my eyes, all I see is his head between my legs. *Damn it.* The memories are flooding back with a vengeance.

I hate that I feel like I've been missing out on something. I could go another five years without fucking another man if it means my son and I are safe. But a small part of me feels like I'm being seen as a woman for the first time in a long time. Not just as a sexual object at work. But for me.

And that's fucking terrifying as much as it is unwanted.

So I tuck it away as a one-night fling, appreciative of the orgasm.

ELEVEN
DUTTON

The manager at Honey, one of my father's lingerie stores he co-owns with my mother, is piling the lingerie over her arm as I point to the pieces I think will look best on Posie. Whether she doesn't have the time or chooses not to take advantage of access to my father's stores, I'm not sure, nor do I care.

The store has yet to open for the day, and I haven't stepped foot in it for over eighteen months as I have focused all my efforts on expanding my clubs.

"That will do for now," I say as I take almost a third of the store, including sets that haven't yet been launched. She looks like she's struggling under their weight as she carries them over to the register to start wrapping them. I put a hand on the one I most want to see her in. "Put this one in a separate bag."

"Yes, sir." She smiles and tucks a piece of her hair behind her ear. I don't mingle with employees... usually. Posie is the first. Most likely because she's the first woman—employed by me or not—ever to tell me no and who gives me a piece of her mind. For some reason, I want to force her into submission because of it. What better way to do that than sexually so I can rid myself of this fascination with her?

I initially took an interest in her because of her potential association with the Boston Delinquents, but I'm already wavering on that. Intuitively, I know the only sinister thing about that woman is her temper. Then again, perhaps I've become so fixated on her in other measures that I'm not thinking logically. But I convince myself that wooing her sexually might be in my favor. If the Boston Delinquents have planted her into my business on purpose, she won't expose herself. So I'll make sure she'll come to trust me, tell me her secrets, and I can determine whether she's a threat to my family once and for all. So, right now, keeping her close is the most practical course of action. A small part of me, ever so small, and I'd rather ignore it, tells me it's because of personal intrigue instead.

Amongst it all, I want to punish her over and over again for being the only woman ballsy enough to tell me 'no.' So until I uncover the truth of her dealings with the Boston Delinquents, I'll play with her as my own personal toy. She made the mistake of catching my attention.

I check out the sex toys, contemplating which ones might excite her the most. I immediately step into the bondage section, my cock twitching at the thought of all the ways I can tie and gag the little vixen.

Although Honey is a franchise with locations all over the country, this particular store is the largest lingerie and sex toy store in New York. It has a very specific and sophisticated clientele. The building itself has belonged to my father for almost thirty years, even after it caught fire when Will Walker's wife, Alina, was renovating it. I'm still certain there's more behind that story, but it happened so long ago that I don't really care for the details, and if it had been a problem, I know my father would've dealt with it.

"Didn't expect to see you here." My father's voice carries through the empty space.

I was hoping not to run into him here because that always raises too many questions. My parents are far too curious about my life, and I'd much rather keep to myself.

I turn, offering the perfect smile—how I always act to ensure they don't ask any questions or raise concerns that I'm 'working too hard' or not 'living enough' by not taking a leisurely break. Instead, I give them no reason to doubt me. My father hugs me and then glances over to the pile of gifts being wrapped.

"Shopping for someone in particular?" he asks curiously.

I shake my head. "No, I wanted to bring some of the new collection for my dancers at Pearl. They've been working hard, and business is good, so I wanted to incentivize them."

His eyebrows furrow. "Don't you already offer them ninety percent off everything here? Last I checked, almost all of them come here to update their wardrobe when the new collections come in."

"Not all of them." I do my best not to grit my teeth.

His eyebrow raises as if he's not entirely convinced, but he says nothing. My father is strikingly handsome, and I've inherited most of his features. However, our demeanors are very different. Where my father is better at dazzling people, I struggle to show anything but indifference.

"Your sister was upset about a classmate recently. Said you had something to do with him going to jail. Because he asked her on a date?"

I pick up some of the rope and casually say, "She

assumes I had a part to play. And besides, isn't it best she not date a soon-to-be convicted felon?"

He smirks. "I entirely agree."

My father and I have circled the topic of Billie's poor luck in love a few times. I've never been discreet regarding my overprotectiveness of my sister, and my father has never reprimanded me. In fact, he's always encouraged it.

"I don't mind you expressing yourself through... alternative methods," he begins. When he says "alternative methods," he means violence. "Just make sure you're careful, especially when conducting business with Eli."

My father has always shown an interesting reverence when it comes to the Monti family. It's always been an option for me to step into the role of Eli's advisor, and although I do at times, it's not official. I much prefer the industry that my father built his entire fortune on.

Pleasure is something to be sold and exploited as much as it is to be experienced.

Everyone has a fantasy.

Everyone has a vice.

Bring both together, and you'll make a profit.

And when someone can't afford something they

deeply desire, they're willing to do anything for it. It makes them dangerous. And I very much enjoy lulling them into a false sense of safety because then I can use them in any way I want.

Where my cousin might prefer torture as a means to get what he wants, I prefer exploitation.

Promiscuous lies can start small, but in the end, I'm always waiting to benefit from them.

"I haven't seen much of my cousin lately since he's preoccupied with his new wife," I note, placing the rope down. That's when I notice half of the lingerie is already packed up.

"Has that perhaps made you curious about marriage?" he asks, following me to the front counter.

My jaw tics. For the last two years, my parents have become quite vocal with their concerns regarding my lack of bringing any partner home. But it's because I've never had a partner... Well, one that wasn't only sexual.

I'm certain their main concern is whether I'm a heartless psychopath. My mother got it into her head that I need someone full of sunshine and rainbows to balance my distant personality. In other ways that they've explained, they're concerned that I only ever focus on my career, but I don't understand what having a wife does to resolve that. Just because the two of them were fortunate to find love and joy, it was not something I actively looked for myself. Because I am far from a ray of fucking sunshine.

If that made me appear a recluse, then so be it.

"Not in the least," I say, snagging the black ribbon handle of the bag containing the lingerie piece I most like.

"It might—"

"No." I'm adamant as I square up with my father. "Just because you and Mom found a serene, happily-ever-after marriage does not mean I want or need the same thing. Marriage is a liability. Why would I bother building everything I have to give someone the opportunity to take it? To give someone access to *our* family? It's not worth the risk."

"Son, you say it's to protect your family, but the only one you're trying to protect is yourself."

"Of the matters of the heart?" I scoff. "Mom's already used that line. If you want grandchildren, it won't be from me," I say as I turn to walk away.

My father calls out, "Well, we aren't going to get them from your sister either if you keep intervening."

I smirk at that because I know he's not at all upset about it.

It's the same thing every time: their sudden fixation on me being "cold and twisted" to use Billie's words.

I understand it, theoretically.

I'm too calculated to be reckless.

So why have they been pushing this issue so fucking much lately?

Am I not the definition of the perfect son?

TWELVE
POSIE

I'm dreading going to work today because I might see him. I find this funny because I went months without even running into him, and now I can't seem to escape him. I don't know if there is another reason why he's been around more often recently, but I wish it would go back to normal.

Whatever normal is?

I'm actually on time for once, and when Paula sees me, she looks at her watch in shock but then smiles. She follows me into the back room, where I start to get changed.

"You have a present," Paula says, revealing a black bag. I immediately know from the emblem what store it came from, and I'm slightly confused as to why she's giving this to me.

"Why am I getting this?" I ask, my brows pinching in wonder.

She begins to walk away but looks over her shoulder with a mischievous grin. "I don't know. You'll have to ask the boss himself."

I pull a box out of the bag. Opening it, I tear away the tissue paper to find a set of hot-pink lingerie.

It's beautiful.

Expensive.

But no gift comes without strings attached.

Especially from a man who is used to owning everything and everyone.

Turning to Samantha, I smile and hand her the box.

"I got the wrong size. Want it?" It's a lie because it looks exactly like my size.

"Oh my gosh, are you sure? This is stunning!" she gushes, admiring it. She immediately tries it on. It's stunning and sexy, and I'm grateful we're the same size so someone can wear it. She's not arguing with me about the fact. She knows we're the same size, but she obviously loves the beautiful material.

"I'm wearing this tonight. I'll look smoking in it. Thanks, girl!" I smile as she gets ready to go on stage. I remain seated and begin to touch up my makeup. I don't think much of the gift because I don't want to spiral into questioning what that gift is supposed to mean, if anything at all. All I know is any kind of gift or help from a man you've had sex with usually has strings attached. And I definitely think Dutton is the kind to have possessive entitlement issues.

I hear the crowd cheer as Samantha steps out onto the stage, and I smile. She does look pretty hot in that lingerie set. I comb out the tight curls I prepared my hair in, letting them hang loosely over my shoulder.

Just as I finish applying my mascara, the door opens and in walks Dutton. His gaze immediately finds me, and I pretend not to notice him as he stalks up beside me. "You give away all gifts like that?"

I try to ignore the fact that his cock is at my eye level as I look up at his face. Then he leans against the table, and I try my hardest to be unfazed by his proximity. "I assumed the gifts were for all the women in your employ. Turns out it was the wrong size for me anyway. It looks great on Samantha, though," I say with a sweet smile as I turn back to the mirror. I carefully apply the last of my mascara and do my best not to squirm under the cold calculation of his gaze.

I will not crumble under this intimidation bullshit. However, if I were a wiser woman, I'd do as advised. Unfortunately, obedience isn't a strength of mine.

"Was there something else I can help you with?" I

stand and undo my dressing gown, revealing my green lingerie, which he clearly thinks is not good enough for him. "Boss?"

His jaw clenches so hard, I think he might blow a vein from how irritated he looks about things not going his way—such a spoiled man, used to getting everything he wants.

I daringly reach for his chin and tilt it up. "This is very unprofessional," I remind him.

"My office. Now," he growls, stepping out of reach as he turns and strides to his office. I make no move to follow him. When he notices, he looks back at me. "I said *now*."

"Not happening. I mean, unless you're firing me." I arch an eyebrow at him.

"No, I'm going to fuck you into submission," he states.

I laugh at that. Definitely not someone who can stand being told no. I'm just grateful all the other girls are out working on the main floor right now, so no one can hear him.

"Yeah, I'm going with a no. I don't jump just because a spoiled rich kid tells me to. So, if you'll excuse me, I need to make some money." I grab my heels and slide them on my feet. I can feel his stare raking down my body, so I make sure to bend over just a little bit farther. It's not like he hasn't already seen what's between my legs.

I'm intentionally teasing him because my boss needs to learn a lesson that although he thinks he's in charge of me, he's not.

I sigh at the purple mark on my inner thigh and reach for the makeup sponge and concealer to try and cover it.

"You know, it's against policy to have marks," he adds with his eyes on my leg.

"Yeah, some dickhead gave it to me, but you won't have to worry about it happening again because it was a one-time thing. Although, he was good at giving head," I say, as I tap a finger on my chin. "I have bills to pay, so I'm gonna get to work." I saunter past him but am very aware the moment his footsteps sound behind me.

Does this fucker have nothing better to do than antagonize me?

Is he that unfamiliar with the word "no" that he gives chase because it's like a fucking phenomenon to him?

I try my best to ignore him as I sweep a gaze around the room and approach my first customer, who is smiling as he stares at my legs. Before I can say anything, Dutton's hot breath is over my shoulder as he says to the customer, "Touch her, and I'll kill you."

The man goes pale, and I can't help but gape as I swing around to face Dutton. He's staring down at me with those cold blue eyes. There's no fucking soul in there, I swear, because the moment he wants complete obedience, he turns into this asshole.

My fingers curl into my palms as I try to ignore him and approach the next man, but no words are exchanged because he sees my looming shadow. Is this fucker going to follow me around to make sure I can't make any money all night just to make a point that he has the power to do so? For what? Disobeying him?

"You're being a petty fuck," I grit out over my shoulder. He doesn't reply; he just continues following me. When I'm at my breaking point—it only takes a few minutes to get there—I spot his friends from the other night, the twins, who seem to be enjoying the show. Well, mostly the muscular twin, as he stares in awe as Samantha dances.

So I go to step in their direction. "I wouldn't if I were you," Dutton growls.

I smile, flicking my hair over my shoulder as I now have a pep in my step. "And has you telling me what to do worked out for you so far?" I whisper under my breath.

"Hello, boys, are you enjo—" Before I can finish the sentence, I'm thrown over Dutton's shoulder. He carries me to the back as I try my hardest to wriggle free. The twins stare at us, eyebrows raised and mouths agape.

"Let me down, asshole!" I push at his face. It's not until we're in his office and he kicks the door closed that he lets me down. The moment he does, I go to slap him. But he quickly catches my wrist.

"I'd be careful if I were you. It might worsen your punishment as I spank the brat out of you."

"Are you out of your fucking mind?!" I yank my wrist out of his grip. "Do you know how much money you've cost me tonight? All to prove a point?!" I'm getting angrier by the second. At this point, I don't even fucking care if I keep this job.

He circles me as I lose my fucking mind, which makes me even more furious because the pompous prick is still acting like he's in control. "You're just so fucking used to people being at your beck and call, and that isn't me! I fucking refuse."

The slightest hint of his smirk snaps my final thread of sanity. He's pushing me on purpose. He wants crazy? I'll give him crazy. That way, he might stay the fuck away from me.

"This might be some novelty for you, but I *need*

this money!" I grab the stapler off his desk. "I wouldn't be working in this shithole, trying to sell my fucking body otherwise." I throw the stapler at his head, and he dodges it. It puts a hole in the door instead. That smirk never leaves his expression. *This fucking asshole!*

"Fuck one of the other girls for all I care," I shout as I grab the keyboard and throw it at him. This time, he has to raise his hand to block it. It falls to the ground at his feet. I'm so fucking mad I can't even handle it. This man is too easily pushing my buttons, and I'm detonating.

"And you're just fucking smiling like a dickhead!" I yell as I throw a stack of pens, then a glass half full of whiskey. He dodges those as well, and his smile only grows wider. I pick up the scissors. "You won't be smiling if I carve up that pretty face of yours, will you?"

I raise the scissors, my heart beating erratically. He catches my wrist again, but it's not like when I went to slap him. This time, the mood in the room immediately shifts. His smirk remains, but his gaze is penetrating and outright predatory.

A shiver runs down my spine as I realize I crossed a line. "Have you ever cut someone open before?" His voice is chilling, unlike the perfect mask he presents to the world. No, this is violent and unhinged, and I'm terrified to realize it runs deeper than I could've ever imagined. "It's easy, really," he says emotionlessly as he admires the scissors. "But not with a blunt blade like this. No, you want something sharper to really carve out a message."

He plucks the scissors out of my hand. I yank my wrist free, surprised that he lets me. And it's like in the blink of an eye, whatever dark corrosion I just touched disappears, and the pretty boy is back in the room.

"You're a fucking psycho," I whisper.

He seems to consider that. "I don't think so. Besides, my sexual partner inflicting cuts on me isn't my thing. It might be my cousin's, but contrary to belief, I only enjoy carving messages onto other people," he says lazily as he circles me and then leans against his desk.

My mouth opens and then closes, and I'm not sure if he's saying all this to strike fear into me or if he's serious. Probably both.

I still do my best to hide the unsettling fear swarming in my gut. I feel exposed in my lingerie when I usually use it as a weapon. But this part of Dutton I just saw isn't human. I wonder how many people see beneath his mask and, if they do, if it's too late. I do my best to keep my body from trembling as all the buzzing adrenaline saps out of me. The office is a fucking mess from everything I threw at him.

And here I was, judging his mask for slipping.

This asshole knows how to wind me up.

"I told you the other night was a one-off. Didn't think you'd be the type to get attached." I cross my arms over my chest. "Or display such a lack of professionalism."

He sighs, exasperated. "I never thought you'd be the type who needed to be wined and dined."

"Excuse me?" I demand.

"Go on a date with me so we can get to know one another better."

My face scrunches up in disbelief. This fucker undoubtedly isn't used to being shot down by a woman. "No. And if you ask again, I'll throw this thick book at your fucking face," I say, grabbing the closest book off his shelf. I hide my intrigue at the heavy tome of bondage instructions. I raise it as if to throw it at him.

"One date, and I'll provide you with a different job."

I scoff. "What, as your sex bunny or something? Hard pass."

He smirks. "Oh, you'll do that for free. I will never pay you to have sex with me."

"I don't want to have sex with you!" I remind him.

He kicks up an arrogant smile. "Sure you don't. You could work behind the bar."

"I suck at pouring drinks!" I yell because all I want to do is wring this unreasonable fucker's neck. This man is as insufferable as I pegged him from the moment I met him. I had a fucking lapse in judgment in the back seat of his car, and now I'm paying for it.

This asshole thinks he can throw around money and own people. I'd come to terms with working for him, but I won't let him own me.

"You can work in my office, and I'll pay you double what you make on the floor."

I hesitate to throw the book. I want to because, again, the dickhead thinks he can buy me out. But I start doing quick math in my head as to how much I could earn, how it could set Bentley and me up if I could bear with it for even six months. Dancing wasn't meant to be a permanent thing, but if I agree, it'd be working closely with the devil himself.

"Why are you doing this? Is it because I told you no? No offense, fucker, but I don't know if you'll stick to your word considering how crazy you're acting right now."

He arches a perfect eyebrow. "I'm the one being labeled crazy right now?" He scans the room with his gaze, then gives a pointed look to the book I'm holding in the air, ready to throw at him.

Okay.

Good point.

I lower the book.

"One thing you can trust me on is my word. Always. Despite how much you think of me as an asshole, I'll never jeopardize your safety or force myself on you. This is a legitimate deal."

I roll my eyes. "But I have to go on a date with you?" That's the stupidest fucking thing I've ever heard. Has this man ever actually been on a date before? I imagine he gets the luxury of skipping even the name exchange before women are on their backs for him.

"A date doesn't equate to sex. But preferably, will end with it."

"I'm not sleeping with you," I reiterate. "Why are you offering this? It's unprofessional."

I don't understand Dutton Taylor. There is no rhyme or reason to him, and that sharp intellect is always running some type of scheme in the background. What could he ever want from me to make him go so far?

"Because I have an issue with other men touching you. It would appear I don't think rationally when you're on the floor, and I find it awfully distracting. I don't want it to jeopardize my business if I accidentally kill one of my clients, so this seems like the most practical approach." His words are straightforward, his tone emotionless.

I'm shocked by his honesty, and all I can say to derail the intensity of that possessive statement is, "They don't touch me; I touch them."

His face glazes over with a lustful expression. "Hmm. I suppose you did touch me when you gave me that private dance, and I don't usually let that happen. But I touched you more that night in the back seat of my car," he says, pushing off the edge of the desk and stepping closer. "And I want to touch you again. You might be used to being in control out there with your clients, but I promise you, you're very much out of your depth if you think you can control me and my desires."

His intense aura is stifling, but I refuse to look away as he picks up a piece of my curled hair. This guy is giving me whiplash between his possessive asshole and charismatic playboy personas.

"You don't fuck those you work with," I point out as I slowly push away his hand.

"I don't fuck the girls who dance," he clarifies. "And you no longer dance."

I bite my bottom lip, trying to consider my choices,

but it all feels too rushed right now. And I still need to decide whether it's worth the hassle of dealing with this asshole. Then again, earning double what I'm earning now is not an opportunity a single mother is given every day.

"If I agree, I want a sign-on bonus as well," I demand defiantly.

His blue eyes darken as he looks down on me and takes another step forward. He encroaches into my space, and I inevitably take a step back. He barricades me against the door, and I feel his intensity dancing along my skin, creating a heat at my core that I wish I didn't acknowledge. His body suffocates mine, and when he leans down, I can't help but hold my breath.

I shouldn't want this.

I should push him back.

But my body wants to pull him in. This fucker has a magnetism that I've never known or dealt with before. And I want to defy it with all my might so that he doesn't think he's won.

His lips brush my cheek as he says, "What's your price?"

My heart is pounding as his lips linger against my cheek and then move to my jaw. I try not to move, not trusting my body in its heated desire.

I blurt out the first thing that comes to mind. "Ten thousand?"

"Is that a question?" he says, lifting up a piece of my hair again. His nose grazes against my neck as if he's smelling me, and I can't help but lean into him. *Fuck.* If he pushes any further right now, I'm not sure if I'll be able to say no.

"Did I hear twenty thousand?" I say.

He chuckles as he steps away from me. I lick my lips as I glance down quickly, realizing his cock is straining against his pants.

"Done." He nods once as he rounds his desk and gets money from his top drawer. He rejoins me at the door and offers me what looks like a few thousand dollars—certainly not ten or twenty thousand.

"This is payment to cover tonight since I cost you your earnings. Once you figure out your job description, the bonus will come through with a new contract. I do have one condition. When I message you, I expect a reply."

I'm gob smacked. "You don't care what job I do?"

"No. I just want a date and to get you off the floor."

I'm so confused by the situation that I don't know where to start, but I know better than to shoot myself in the foot. It might be crazy, and my boss is certainly unhinged, but I can't say no to that type of money.

I offer him my hand. He looks at it, confused, but then takes it, and we shake on the deal. "I'd like to say it was a pleasure doing business with you, but we both know that's a lie. I still hate your guts."

The corner of his mouth tilts up, those blue eyes seemingly staring into my soul. "I look forward to our date, Posie."

I release his hand and swallow. I feel like I've just made a deal with the devil. I turn and go to open the door, holding up the book. "I'll be keeping this as well."

As I open the door, I pale when I see the twins leaning against the wall with their hands in their pockets. They look me up and down, and Dutton's voice growls over my shoulder. "Inside, you two."

The bulkier one chuckles as he dips his head in greeting. The other one seems to be assessing me as if I'm some kind of threat.

How long were they standing there?

Were they listening?

I don't give a fuck.

I head to the back to collect my things to go home. I need to figure out if I've just done the right thing or if I've signed my life away to a psychopath.

THIRTEEN
POSIE

"Snap!" Bentley giggles as he beats me in another game of cards.

"Oh no! You're too fast! But I know who's faster at..." I raise my hands in the air. "Tickles!" He squeals as I launch a tickle attack on him. He's kicking back and forth as he tries to make his grand escape.

"Stop, Mommy! I'm going to burst!" he gets out in short breaths. I scoop him up into a hug and press kisses to his cheeks. This kid is just too cute. He snuggles into me, and I enjoy the peace as I sit on the living room floor and lean against the couch as I hold him.

"Can we play the new game you got me for my birthday?" he asks excitedly.

"Go on!" I encourage him, and he squeals in delight as I clean up the cards.

Today is my day off, and I plan to spend it with my favorite little boy.

I go to make myself another cup of coffee while Bentley is preoccupied, most likely cleaning up the board game from the floor of his room so he can relocate it to the living room.

I turn the kettle on, and my mind immediately drifts back to the same thing it's been dancing around since last night. Dutton Taylor. I don't like the idea of owing him anything. But I can't deny the attractive package.

I've done my very best getting everything together so Bentley and I can enjoy our lives here in Manhattan, but there's no denying its expense. I consider the sign-on bonus I'll get from Dutton and how I could spend it.

I'll save most of it, but perhaps I'll finally be able to buy myself a bed frame. The thought opens my eyes to all the things I could add to the house to make it feel homier.

I pour the instant coffee into my mug and stir. Hell, I couldn't even get the espresso machine I've been eyeing for two years. But none of it seemed to matter as long as Bentley had everything he needed.

I tip my head back and sigh.

What job could I do for Dutton? I don't want to be his personal assistant because that would involve way too much time with the asshole. I glance to my left at my laptop, and an idea springs to mind. I've recently gotten back into graphic design, and my interest in social media has again been sparked. Perhaps I can offer something there? I mean, I'd much rather not have to deal with clients, so maybe an office job that's creative is something I could enjoy.

My mind starts racing with a bunch of ideas. I grab my coffee and go back into the living room, where I open my new Instagram account. I only opened it so I could check out what other people were doing. My eyebrows dip as I take a sip of my coffee and look at the new friend request.

Amy is the only friend I have on there. My profile is blocked and isn't under my real name, but I have one new friend request. My jaw unhinges as I see Dutton Taylor has tried to add me as a friend.

Oh, fuck off.

Over my dead body.

I pocket my phone, ignoring the friend request as I have all the texts he's sent me throughout the day. I'll reply to them eventually when I decide how to handle this situation on my terms.

"Look, isn't this cool," Bentley says as he sets the game up in the living room. I take a seat on the floor despite us having a kitchen table. There's always been something cozy about playing games on the floor. Or maybe it's because it takes me back to my childhood with my parents. We used to play games every Christmas. I stuck to the same tradition but decided any time was a good time for games.

"It's so cool!" I say with a smile. "Did you play this with Amy last night?"

He nods. "Yeah, she said I'm way too clever for a five-year-old," he says proudly. "I asked if we could ask the girl next door to play, but she said it was too late."

I smile, but something lodges in my throat. I always feel bad for not giving Bentley more opportunities to be social. He doesn't really have friends, and I haven't been able to afford any type of schooling. I know he would thrive in the right social environment.

I swallow as I place the coffee down. "Are you excited to go to school with other kids your age?" I ask him softly.

He looks up, his big brown eyes sparkling. "Yes! But I hope everyone will like me."

My heart falls and shatters into a thousand pieces. "How could they not? You're like the coolest!"

He giggles as he looks back at his board game. "You have to say that because you're my mom," he says with a slight blush. I hide my smile.

It's only a few weeks until he starts kindergarten,

and I'm terrified as much as I am excited for him. I'd planned on getting a part-time job during school hours to save more money, but with Dutton's offer, I'd be earning almost triple anything I could earn anywhere else. Maybe I could put Bentley in a private school the following year if I'm able to put enough funds away.

"Will I be able to bring my new board game to school?" Bentley asks.

"We could ask the teacher."

"What's the teacher's name?" he asks.

"I don't know yet. We'll have to find out together," I say, and he giggles as if we're in cahoots, and his laughter does everything to relieve my worries.

My priority has been and always will be this boy. I'll do whatever I can to save the money he needs for his future.

Suddenly, Dutton's offer doesn't look so bad.

It's only one date, and he never stipulated when it had to take place.

FOURTEEN
DUTTON

"I heard you're going on a date," Eli says as he sits behind me. I choose to ignore him.

A row of ten women and four men stand before me in lingerie. I assess each of them to make sure they're in sellable condition.

"Does your father know about this date?" he asks.

"Does your father know about all your activities?" I ask pointedly. I look away when I realize I bit at his antics. "Remove the bra," I tell the last woman.

She gulps but does as I say. I don't move on to the next in line, I stare at the woman in front of me who barely stands five foot two. I loom over her, and it's obvious she's intimidated. Usually, I feed off that, but not here. Not in this place.

"Are you sure about this?" I ask the woman. She

looks up at me, her freckled features young and inno-cent. "You'll all receive an abundant amount for these services, but it's okay to back out."

The virginity auctions have been something my father has run for over thirty years now. He came to an agreement with Anya and Alek Ivanov to conduct business in their territory because they host all the other black-market auctions in Manhattan. In return, they get a small cut. The virgins earn the most.

We safely conduct the auctions with vetted clients who have specific fantasies. Security is provided outside the room, and by tonight, these fourteen people will leave with their virginity taken. They range in age, but I'm always quick to pluck out the ones who aren't quite ready, no matter how desperate they are for the money.

The girl swallows.

"Leave us," I say to the other candidates. The girl in front of me is confused but doesn't move. Only Eli remains in the room.

"Please. I need the money," she says, almost tearing up. She had only just turned twenty-one, but the girl was as frightened as a fledgling. It means she'll sell for more because the innocent types always sell for the most.

"Are you sure you're prepared for the money to

come at the expense of someone taking from you and using your body in the process?" I ask clinically. She flinches. I try my hardest to soften my tone.

"You don't have to do this. This is not the only option to make money," I tell her, and her bottom lip wobbles. "If you don't feel like you'll be empowered by this decision, then you should leave. You're safe here, but we won't force you to do anything." I bend down and pick up her bra from the floor.

When I hand it to her, tears begin to spill over her cheeks. "I n-need the money to h-help my little sister. She n-needs chemo. If we don't... then—" She can't finish the sentence.

"Corinne," I call loudly for my assistant, who schedules all of my virginity auctions. "Please escort her to gather her things."

"No, please—" The girl's mouth immediately snaps shut as my cold stare lands on her.

I continue. "See what jobs we have available. Perhaps we can manage an advance that's paid off over the duration of her employment."

The woman seems surprised but tries to keep her sobs in as she says, "Thank you," and hurriedly leaves the room.

"Yes, sir," Corinne says. I wave her off and face my cousin again, who raises his scarred eyebrow.

"Well, well, well. Isn't someone becoming soft," he says, following me into my office.

"I don't need to hear that from you," I berate as I sit behind my desk. I have many offices but have only recently found the one at Pearl to be my favorite. Most likely because it brings me entertainment in the form of a particular little monster who thinks it's appropriate to throw things at me.

"Touché." He glances at his ring and smirks as he takes the seat across from me. I try not to roll my eyes at the lovesick fool as I pour us a glass of whiskey.

I'm not convinced by anyone who tries to tell me that marriage is anything but a contract where you lose your fucking mind and ambition.

Fucking pussy-whipped asshole.

Though, he'd pull a gun on me if I voiced that.

"How's married life?" I don't care about it; I'd rather avoid having the focus on myself. I look at my phone, pissed, as I see she still hasn't responded to my friend request on Instagram. I'm hardly on the fucking app and only use it for PR purposes that a team manages for me. But the fact that she won't add me has me wildly irritated for some reason. It's like she goes out of her way to fight me on every little thing. The closer I try to get to her, the more she resists. And it's driving me insane. I've never had this issue with a woman.

"Fucking amazing. I'm obsessed with her," Eli says without hesitation.

"I can tell," I reply, distracted by my phone as I look over my last text message, waiting for Posie to respond. I sent her a text an hour ago, telling her to meet me tonight for dinner, and she still hasn't replied. That's when I notice Eli's silence and look up. "What?"

"Are you jealous?" he asks, leaning forward in his chair.

I can tell when he's intentionally trying to push my buttons. In fact, I'm incredibly gifted at it myself. Pissing people off is what we do best. I don't like it when the woman I've set my eyes on is doing it to me.

"No."

"Interesting. Because I heard rumors about a blonde girl at a certain club..."

I raise a brow at him. News travels fast.

"What did the twins say?" I growl.

"That you were acting weird around a dancer."

"I told you; I'm keeping an eye on her and her association with the Boston Delinquents club."

"Is that all, though?" he asks. "Because you haven't mentioned hiring Will yet for intel about her. And

that's very unlike you. You usually go for the most efficient route, so why are you looking into this
personally?"

"Shouldn't you be thanking me for looking out for
you?" I ask.

He shrugs. "I don't think the Boston Delinquents
are going to be a problem. I met with their new president, Waylon Striker, a few weeks ago, and we're in the
midst of negotiations. Nothing's solidified yet, though,
and if I were them, I'd definitely be putting spies in
where I can. But I think we've come to an understanding."

"Which is exactly why I have to get to the bottom
of this," I say, glancing back at my phone.

Eli doesn't seem convinced. "Hawke said she's a
looker."

I clench my jaw as I attempt not to play into his
hand and give him a reaction. "Hawke will fuck
anything with a hole, so tell him to back off this one," I
deadpan.

"That sounds awfully possessive of you." He gives
me a humorless smile.

My phone pings, and I immediately look down
at it.

Posie: No

Two simple letters rolled into one powerful statement.

Her favorite fucking word.

I quickly reply.

> Me: You agreed to one date.

"So, yeah, I sucked cock the other day," Eli says, but I'm not paying attention.

"That's nice," I say, concentrating on my phone. The dancing dots appear, then disappear.

"Or maybe it was you who wants to suck cock," he adds.

> Posie: I didn't agree to when. I'm busy tonight.

Busy? With what? Or whom? I go to reply but then blank on what to say. She doesn't do as I tell her, and this time, I actually asked... sort of.

"Let me guess, it's the blonde." This time I look up at him.

"Why are you talking about someone's fucking cock?"

"So you were listening." He shakes his head.

"She agreed to go on a date with me, then backed out," I tell him, finally throwing my phone down. "I'm genuinely at my wits' end on how to deal with this woman. My usual tactics for obedience don't seem to be working. What do you do when intimidation doesn't work and you can't resort to torture?"

"Hold up. Rewind. So you *did* actually ask a girl on a date?" He sounds baffled. "When was the last time you did that?"

"Never."

"Exactly."

"Well, she wouldn't let me fuck her. So I figured dinner would be the next best option so I could extract information."

"Hmmm." A knowing smirk crosses his features. I want to wipe that arrogant smile from his face.

"I'm doing this for you, remember?" I remind him as his phone rings.

"Of course. It's definitely me you're thinking of and not your cock." He laughs as he stands to take the call. His tone changes immediately, and I know who it is on the other end of the line: his wife. While I wasn't the biggest fan of Jewel initially, since she's a hitwoman who had Eli as a target when they met, I now respect that she loves him. Though I still don't like that she's a better shot than all of us.

"I have to go," he tells me absentmindedly, still holding the phone to his ear. "Why don't you send her flowers?"

Jewel's voice comes through the phone. "Or a gun. I love guns as a present. Wait. Is Dutton dating someone?"

"I'm not sure most women would like your type of gifts, Kitten."

I roll my eyes at how quickly gossip spreads in this family. It's like wildfire.

And yet, I find myself grumbling to make a point. "She would throw out flowers if I got them for her."

"Okay, so take dinner to her if she won't meet you somewhere," Eli suggests as he leaves.

A smile blossoms on my lips because although I'm definitely not taking dating advice from Eli or the twins, his suggestion isn't a bad one.

Guess I'm bringing her dinner.

FIFTEEN
POSIE

I'm doing the dishes when there's a knock on my door. My eyebrows furrow because eight in the evening is way too late for a delivery driver. There's another knock, and I curse. I'd leave it if the person weren't so persistent, and I wasn't worried about it waking Bentley.

I collect the bat beside my door, bracing myself for the third knock. I open the door, and my left eye twitches when I see Dutton standing there, looking like he's just stepped off the runway, holding a big brown bag that I'd much rather be over his head. Because, fuck, he looks too good for an insufferable asshole.

I swear the scowl is permanently etched onto his face unless he's purposefully trying to rile me up.

Does this man ever smile?

I've only ever seen him smirk.

I guess I can't expect too much. I'm sure he's a psycho.

"What are you doing here?" I ask, making a point to show my bat.

He holds up the bag in his hand, and a pleasant scent of food hits my nose.

Persistent motherfucker can't take no for an answer.

I narrow my gaze on him. "I never asked for this. I told you I was busy. Were you so spoiled as a child that the mere thought of being told no becomes like a kink to you or something?"

The corner of his mouth tilts up. "You don't know anything of my kinks yet, sweetheart. But I'd gladly elaborate if you're open for the discussion."

"I'd like to skip to the short discussion of you getting the fuck off my porch."

He might not laugh, but I can see the moment humor twinkles in his gaze. I don't understand this enigma of a man. Is his ice shield so fucking high he doesn't want anyone to know he has a personality? Then again, it's highly possible he genuinely doesn't have one. Not unless it's being a pain in the ass and pissing people off, which he's very good at.

"Let me in to feed you," he encourages.

"No." I close the door further in case Bentley hears or pops his head out of his room.

Dutton cracks his neck from side to side and licks his lips as if trying to remain calm.

Oh no, someone used the big "no" word again. Psycho.

"I'm being nice here, and nice is not something I'm overly familiar with," he says.

"Good, neither am I." I step back to push the door shut, but his foot stops it. I let out an irritated sigh. "I told you; I don't want your food. I already ate, and you aren't allowed in my house."

"Take the fucking food then," he snaps. He then clears his throat and looks away. "I'm sorry."

My jaw drops. "What was that?"

His gaze remains on the ground for a moment before he looks back up at me as if willing the confidence to apologize to my face. "Please take the food."

I glance at the bag. If I take it, he might actually leave.

"Did you poison it?"

"No." He scoffs like he can't believe I even considered it.

"Okay, did you spit in it?"

"Just take the goddamn food," he says, thrusting it at me.

"Okay." I take it from him, and our fingers brush as he passes it to me. I hate the spark it charges me with. It floods me with memories of him between my legs. Him pressing me against a door.

I can see in the way he's looking at me that we're thinking the same thing. As I go to pull the bag toward myself, he holds onto it.

"I want dessert," he says.

"And I want a million dollars, but we can't all get what we want," I reply, yanking the bag from his hand. Fuck. Every time I touch this man, or I'm near him, my wires get crossed. "Goodnight, boss."

"You can call me Dutton." I roll my eyes as I try to kick his foot out of the doorway. "Wait. One more thing," he says, keeping his foot wedged in the door's opening.

I sigh, exasperated, and raise my eyebrows expectantly.

"Why won't you add me on Instagram?"

It feels like the world stops at the absurdity of that question. Is this fucker for real? Why does he look like a disheartened child who I told I won't share my toys with? I kick his foot out of the way and slam the door as I say, "Goodnight, Mr. Taylor."

"Or that works," I hear him mumble on the other

side of the door. "This doesn't count as the date. That involves two people."

"Yeah, well, tonight it can involve you and your hand," I call back as I walk away from the door.

I peek out of the living room window and watch as he turns and walks back to his car.

If there were a manual to deal with Dutton Taylor, I'd read it from front to back so that I can figure out how the fuck his brain works.

When I open the bag in the kitchen, the smell hits me *hard*. Yum. I cooked chicken nuggets the last few nights, so something other than that is a win.

I pull out each container and find food I know is from a five-star restaurant. I wonder which plate was for him. Actually, who cares? They're both mine now.

Dutton messages me consistently over the next two weeks. The only ones I reply to are work-related. I choose to only focus on Bentley when I'm with him. I know that's probably not a healthy way to be, but he's been my everything and only family since my parents died. With their death anniversary coming up, I've been feeling sentimental. It's been over six years since I've gone to their graves, and I can't help but want to go and spend time with them. I'm not a huge spiritual person, but there's something comforting in knowing there's a place I can go to update them on my life, even if no one is listening. I want them to be proud of what I'm building for Bentley and me.

It's why I've always been so present for Bentley. Life is too short, and I want us to have as many memories together as possible. Men can come and go, but family... that's life.

I walk into the club during the daytime, which I can attest I have never done before. Amy was free today to babysit, and as of next week, Bentley will officially start kindergarten a few days a week, so I thought it might work perfectly for work.

I might not need Amy as much for evenings now that I won't be working them, but maybe I can go out a little more. Perhaps a dinner a week or something, now that my pay has increased.

Dutton and I agreed on one thing among the various messages I've been ignoring. I've now been officially hired to run the club's social media and website. I also manage the private bookings. Because this club is exclusive, there is a barrier to promoting it because it's not open to just anyone. But then I started to enjoy the challenge, and my brain has been going into overdrive with ideas.

Today is officially my first day in the new role. I received my sign-on bonus this week, and let's just say I almost toppled over when I saw the multiple zeros. It might not be a lot of money to some, but twenty thousand is a lot to me.

I've sat with the new bedframe in my shopping cart, idly wondering whether I'm being impulsive with the purchase. I'm so used to buying for Bentley that it feels strange to splurge on myself. I did, however, buy the coffee machine.

I don't plan to move any time soon. I like my little home, and it works for both of us right now, so I'm convincing myself that buying the bedframe is totally justified. It feels silly, but I haven't done anything for myself in so long.

"You're here early," Paula says with a smile. "Congratulations on the promotion. I can't wait to see what you come up with."

Paula came into my life at the right time. She might've badgered me about my tardiness, but I've always been grateful for her bringing me in and providing me with this job.

"Thanks. You aren't mad I left you for the new position?" I ask.

She waves a hand at me. "Gosh, no. I was doing that job and failing miserably. I told Dutton I couldn't do everything, so thank you for your help."

"I wanted to run a new idea by you. I'd like to do a photoshoot of the girls to post on the socials. It'll be for an exclusive subscription that is available only to regular members. Maybe we could not show the women's faces, so if it's ever reshared, the girls will be protected despite the privacy clauses. We could use the socials as a teaser for that."

"You know nothing raunchy would get approved," she reminds me.

"Yes, no nakedness, but I was thinking more along the lines of no faces, just their bodies and lingerie or some sexy clothes. And it'll promote the new lingerie line at Honey as well. It'll be to tease until they access the portfolio to buy. A lot of our customers are into feet and other kinks."

She laughs because it's the truth. We've had many strange requests during private dances. Honestly, I don't mind being paid for a man to massage my feet. Some of the girls have even considered going onto an app for it, but because of the contract Dutton has the women sign, they can't join any other site where they sell their bodies or anything of the sort—this way, they can do it safely.

Paula scratches her chin, thinking about it.

"Most of our audience is men anyway," I remind her. "So we have to do something that appeals to them. Our current posts don't do anything for them; they're text posts and boring pictures."

"I get it, I do." She nods her head. "And usually, I would say run this by Mr. Taylor, but I think you're onto something, so organize what you can, and we'll present it to him when he's in next. And I have the credit card to pay for it." We smile at one another mischievously.

I walk into the office she said I can use when I'm here. I'm mostly allowed to work from home, but I'll have to come in for some things. The only other office is Dutton's, and I don't plan to use the boss's, although I've heard he has better cell reception.

I'm not sure how to take him.

Or even what he wants from me.

He eats me out—which he gets an A+ in—basically fires me from my other job and puts me in a new position, then demands I go on a date with him and instead shows up at my door with food when I say no. And now I haven't seen him for two weeks.

Which doesn't bother me all that much, but the whiplash is a lot.

But it's expected from a man who is used to the entire world revolving around him.

I hope he leaves me alone so I can do my job.

I'm going to prove to him that although he changed my job role on a whim, I'm the best person for the job, even though I'm equally as fantastic at shaking my ass.

I've been gone for almost two weeks. It's the final evening of my trip as I bring a new business venture to a close. After taking my new business partner to the most recent gentlemen's club I opened, he seems impressed with the opportunity to traffic drugs through it.

In Italy, I work closely within the Monti family's reach. Although Crue and Eli are stationed in New York, business is booming here from their influence and the work my grandfather put in before them. I make these trips to ensure those we've put in place to run the businesses are efficient enough to maintain the family's reign and keep the profits at an all-time high.

Realistically, I should move here to run things more

personally, but I have an attachment to my family in New York, so flying here every so often will have to do.

Paulo, the man who runs everything here for us with an iron fist, stands behind me. Coming in at six foot six, he's a tattooed Italian demon that everyone fears.

We're in my office, which is attached to one of my three-story mansions. Although I enjoy conducting most business meetings in my clubs, this is a double-edged deal tonight.

I shake my new business partner's hand and wait until he leaves before I pour a whiskey for myself and one for Paulo. He never drinks on the job but thanks me for it anyway.

"Are they here?" I ask, a lethal buzz cascading over my skin. One thing we take very seriously is our staff's safety. The sex industry can be a dangerous place, and although I'm not above certain nefarious dealings, the safety of my staff is absolute. It's the foundation of everything my father taught me. Having primarily female employees, and with a younger sister, I take all acts of misconduct seriously.

"Yes," Paulo says as we head to one of my favorite rooms in the house. One of my other security guys opens the door expectantly. I take a sip of the whiskey as he presents the two naked men gagged and tied to chairs. Plastic tarps have been stretched out beneath them. Their eyes go wide as I enter.

"Gentlemen, it would appear we have business to conduct," I say conversationally as I place my whiskey on the small tray to my left. Beside it are three knives of various sizes. After giving them each a moment of consideration, I choose my favorite.

Paulo places both of his hands behind his back as he stands behind the door, watching with keen interest. The men try to speak through their gags, but I don't care for their apologies because what they did was inexcusable.

They're both shaking with fear. One has pissed himself already.

I roll up my sleeves.

I never considered myself an artist, but I never looked back when I discovered the joy and creativity in carving messages into flesh. I was fifteen years old when I carved into the chest of an eighteen-year-old who had tried to usher my sister into his car when she was only fourteen. It was the first hunt Eli and I had done together, right before we were introduced to the twins.

While Eli enjoys outright torture, I prefer a more clinical approach to my art. I leave them with something that will shame them even after they're dead. Not that anyone ever finds the body afterward.

"I've learned that you drugged one of our dancers and sold her to a client for the night." Paulo brought it to my attention the moment the girl broke down to him about it, and we've been dealing with the clean-up ever since. The only reason it was able to happen in the first place was because these two were the hired security. I know this is fact because I already carved into and got rid of the client who paid them handsomely for the act. I vet all of those I hire, but sometimes cockroaches like these fall between the cracks.

I tap the edge of the knife against my chin thoughtfully. What should I carve on their chests? I begin with the letter "R," carefully slicing into the first man's flesh. He screams as I deeply carve into his chest while explaining to him how he brought this on himself.

I find this relaxing. I'm always running at high tension levels, and a release is necessary. Being in the sex industry, the act of having sex has become fundamentally not essential for me. This, however, satisfies me.

I pause on the second letter—an "A."

Then again, that was before a certain blonde dancer came across my stage. I try to shake off the lingering thought of Posie because she has no place in what goes on here.

After finishing the "*A*," I start with the letter "*P*." The man is sweating and screaming, blood running down his chest.

I'm curious how she'd react if she saw this savage side of me. I wouldn't even allow my little sister to see me like this. Although I know she suspects, she's definitely heard rumors. She might still love me, but I can't imagine any woman loving a monster. But it's too much of who I am. It is too heavily ingrained in my twisted pursuit of justice.

I carve the letter "*I*."

When I realize he's about to pass out on me, I backhand him across the face. He keels over in the chair, blood splattering everywhere. I roll my eyes with a heavy sigh at having to pick him up from the floor and reset him. "Stay with me," I say to him, slapping his face again.

The chest is my favorite place to write messages. The skin and muscles are thin enough for clear, detailed lacerations. I experimented with other body parts, such as faces, arms, legs, and even genitals, but the chest was the optimal location.

An "*S*" comes next.

Posie seems like a strong enough woman, but I

notice the switch in her when she becomes wary of me as she should. As any sane person should, but some are too distracted by my charming personality to have such caution.

And finally, a "*T*."

I curse under my breath as I realize I'm still thinking of Posie. She's all I've been thinking about since I've been away. And I *never* have hang-ups when I travel overseas.

I focus on the man's screams, trying to drown out all things Posie. Because I don't want to acknowledge that my deadly obsession might be shifting toward a sassy little blonde who revels in telling me no and has no interest in fucking me. My cock twitches at the thought of tasting her only weeks ago, and I curse again, knowing I'm fucking starved. But the idea of touching any other woman physically revolts me. I have no choice but to ride out this curiosity.

IT'S ONLY RECENTLY that Posie has been replying to my messages more frequently. That's to say, she still doesn't respond to them all. So, I'll purposefully do things to interrupt her day. If she's at home, I'll send lingerie, with the knowledge that she'll most likely give it to the girls at Pearl. Or food. I know she'll keep that.

The one thing that's gotten me everything I've wanted in life is tenacity. So I'm not going to give up.

She's a mystery to me. I know I should hire Will Walker to do a thorough search into her background, but for some reason, it feels like I need to do this myself in the old-fashioned way. I want to figure out the woman who adamantly says no to me so much.

I just didn't think it'd take me so long. I've been unsuccessful in getting her to respond to me, let alone forcing her into submission. So I send her gifts so she's constantly thinking of me.

It's three in the morning, and I look out at Rome from the balcony of my room as I sip whiskey. I finalized all my business endeavors and checked up on the new gentlemen's club, which is earning me a fortune. I've expanded the virgin auctions here as well. While my father preferred to keep his auctions strictly in Manhattan, I've been focusing on branching out to other locales.

I've hired a select few who I can trust, or who at the very least fear the consequences of betraying me, to keep everything in order.

I should shower and get a few hours' sleep before

my flight departs, but instead, I find myself picking up my phone. As I do, the screen lights up.

Finally, she replied.

I've noticed that she only replies to things that are work-related, which is irritating. How am I supposed to figure out this little monster if she's as short and curt as I usually am?

It's about nine in the evening back in Manhattan, and she's complained about the cold snap. She's also sent a link to the platform she's been working on. I scroll through it, admittedly impressed.

I didn't care what type of role she chose for herself as long as she wasn't dancing. I just needed her within my reach to monitor her. I throw back the whiskey and then grab my coat as I hit call.

It rings out, and I grit my teeth as I step out of the elevator and into the main lobby. It's cold here, too, but I quite enjoy the winter months over the warmer ones.

I call again.

On the sixth ring, she finally answers.

"What?" she growls.

A sliver of amusement runs through me. "Is that how you should answer your boss's call?"

"I'm not at work at the moment," she replies.

"No, I suppose you're not. So what are you doing?"

"Is this work-related?" she grumbles.

"Yes, it's regarding the link you just sent me. I'm impressed. You've done well."

She's quiet for a moment, and I check the phone to make sure she's still on the call. When I put it back to my ear, she says, "Thank you."

"When does it launch?" I ask to keep her on the line. I don't know when this unique obsession began, but from the moment I tasted her sweet pussy, I haven't been able to get her out of my mind. And all I want is to do it again.

Money has always bought me anything I want. For the things it doesn't, I've used intimidation. But this woman is different, and I refuse to pay for sex despite making my living from it.

No, Posie must come to me willingly.

A strong breeze whips by me, and I welcome its frigid touch.

"Where are you anyway? In a hurricane?" she asks. She must have heard the wind.

It's the first time she's asked about my where-abouts, and I can't help but smile as I walk adjacent to the Colosseum that glows with light from within against the early morning darkness. There aren't too many people out at this hour, but I spot a few restaurants across the road and notice a gelato store that's still open with a small line. I have no doubt that the line only consists of tourists.

"Do you miss me, Posie?"

"You wish," she bites back.

Ah, how I miss that sass.

"I'm in Rome. I'll be back tomorrow."

"Rome? What time is it there?" she asks, and I can hear rustling in the background but can't decipher what she's doing. At the very least, I know if she's talking to me on a Friday evening, she's not with anyone else. I've been so tempted to have her followed. For security purposes, of course, in case she is connected with the Boston Delinquents.

I try not to envision Eli rolling his eyes at me. Okay, even I acknowledge how far of a stretch it might now be that she's associated with them. But it's all I have to blame this obsession on.

"Three in the morning."

"Wow, you really are a robot. Do you not sleep?"

"Not if there's money to be made."

"That's so like you. I've never been to Rome. I've heard it's pretty, and they have the best gelato," she says. Then, there's a clattering sound, as if she dropped the phone. "Shit."

I look back to the gelato store, and my legs move across the road before I know it.

"What are you doing?" I ask.

"I'm painting my nails. I'm not sure if I like the red, though."

"Change it," I immediately say, not understanding why it irritates me. Knowing that it's my cousin's favorite color, I suddenly can't stand the thought of her wearing it.

"Pfft. As if I care what you think. Is the gelato good there?"

My jaw tics at her disobedience, but I swallow my pride, which is painful. "So I've heard."

"You don't eat it, do you?" I can imagine her eye roll from here. I stand in line at the gelato store with only one customer in front of me.

"No, I don't worry about things that don't offer nutritional value." Unlike my mother and sister's fascination with the culinary arts, I've never much cared for food. However, I only dine at the finest restaurants. I believe in good quality but have never been one to enjoy food as much as others.

"I suppose you don't get a body like that from eating carbs all day," she says under her breath.

"Have you been thinking of my body, Posie?" I ask, very interested in her answer.

She seems to realize her mistake as she says, "No,

obviously not, because we aren't going down that road. I just... it was an observation."

Observation, my ass.

When it's my turn to order, I look over the flavors. I don't fucking know which to choose. I point to the one marked "most popular," which happens to be pistachio.

"We can revisit the back of my car anytime you'd like, Posie. Just give me the word." A blush crosses the server's cheeks as I hand over cash and take the cone.

"And with that, I'm hanging up, bossman."

"So quick to run." The moment I realize she might hang up, I find myself adding, "Have you ever wanted to travel to Rome?"

"Get some sleep, bossman," she says, then hangs up.

Fuck.

I stand there holding a gelato that I have no interest in eating. I look back at the Colosseum and raise the gelato in front of it. I've seen Billie do this on numerous occasions when the family traveled together.

I go to send the photo to Posie, and my thumb hovers over the send button. What in the ever-fucking hell am I doing? Messaging a woman when she doesn't even want to fuck me? That's a lie. I know she wants to fuck me. I can sense it in the way her body reacts to me. I have to treat Posie differently than any other... conquest isn't the right word.

Fuck it. I hit send and immediately throw the gelato in the trash. The server's jaw drops as if I'd just committed blasphemy.

But perhaps Posie was right about one thing. I should get a few hours of sleep.

I go to pocket my phone, but a new notification lights the screen.

Posie hearted my message.

I'm uncomfortable by the unfamiliar emotion that stirs within me at that.

It's similar to the effects of being praised as a child for doing something right. I haven't required that from people for a very long time. So why am I feeling it now?

I stuff that right down with the unknown emotions that don't serve me. But at least I know she's finally being more responsive to my messages, and for the first time, she actually answered a fucking call.

Hallelujah! We're making progress.

EIGHTEEN
DUTTON

"Do you like the texture?" Billie asks our mother, referring to the tiramisu she made. We'd just had dinner and were sitting around the table, the two of them enjoying their dessert while my father and I each sip a glass of whiskey.

"Oh, sweetheart. You've done so well!" My mother applauds. Billie takes a scoop of the tiramisu with a smile on her face.

I only just returned today, but as is tradition, we try to have a family dinner at least once a month. A few years ago, my mother made a rule that there should be no business talk at the table, so we often talk about trivial matters.

"Eli seems happily married," my mother says, which is her way of starting a very specific conversation that my parents seem to be focusing on a lot more lately.

Billie rolls her eyes. "I love Jewel, but Eli is so pussy whipped. He always gets mad when we're hanging out over there, even though Jewel says it's okay."

They've always invited themselves, and Eli has, in fact, always had an issue with them being there.

But now that the topic has changed, I can expect what's to come.

Eli is married, so it's my turn.

"Marriage isn't for everyone, but I think it might suit you nicely, son." My father is many things, and persistent is absolutely one of them. He likes to say it's how he won my mother over. If that's true, then I don't know why the same thing isn't working for me.

However, I don't require further details about some of the stories I've heard about them—especially the one about my mother being part of the virginity auctions. Nausea rolls through me. Nope, I definitely don't want to hear more about that.

"Or even dating," Billie presses with a suggestive raise of her eyebrow. "Weren't you supposed to be going on a date with a blonde stripper?" she asks, placing the spoon on her tongue with a smug expression.

My hands ball into fists. This entire family is nothing but gossips, I swear. I don't even have to ask her who she heard that from because I know without doubt it was Hawke, who has the biggest fucking mouth.

"Dating?" my mother questions, this obviously news to her. "Who are you dating? What is she like?"

"I'm not dating anyone," I grit out. "I understand everyone here is excited by Eli taking a wife, but might I remind you all that I have never had, nor will I ever have, any intention of marrying."

"It just means you haven't met the right person, sweetie," my mother says softly.

They act like running the type of business I do, and being associated with the Monti family is easily accepted by most women. It's only because my mother was raised in the mafia that she was so accepting of my father's businesses. I've never once had the urge to tie myself to another person, ask for permission, or have them wait for me to return home every night. I'm not a man who answers to anyone.

"I don't think there's someone out there for every-one, Mother."

She looks sad, and I hate that I offend her with that belief, but she's building her hopes up on something that will never happen.

"Well, any woman cut from the same cloth as you must be an ice queen. Hello? Personality, where are you?" Billie jests.

"Billie!" my mother chastises, and I can't help but smile at that one. It was pretty good. She mirrors my smile.

My father, however, is watching me from the corner of his eye. Not that I explain myself to many, but I do to him at times. He is my father, after all. "I run a fucking sex empire, an even bigger one than you did at my age. There is nothing but my work. And, yes, I am married to that and will stay married to it for the rest of my life."

My mother's expression falls further, and it pains me to know I'm making her sad, but I don't understand why they're pressing the matter so much.

"I can find you a wife," he says. "I know you don't like the idea, but Crue's father found Crue's wife, your aunty Rya, through an arranged marriage. And look at them. I can do the same for you; it might give you something else to focus on besides sleepless nights and long working hours."

"No, And I don't want to talk about it again. Leave it." I down the rest of my drink and stand, ending the discussion

"Sweetheart, you don't have to leave," my mother says apologetically. "We're just worried, that's all."

"You have no need to be," I say coolly. "Thank you for dinner. I'm tired from my travels, and I'd like to excuse myself." I press a kiss on my mother's cheek. My father stands and hugs me, but it's Billie who follows me out.

When I'm collecting my coat, she leans against the wall and crosses her arms over her chest.

"You know they're just worried about you being too focused on work, right? That, and they're not entirely sure if you're a psychopath or not," she says casually.

"And that will never change," I grit. I fish a gift box out of my pocket and toss it in her direction. It's not a matter of if I'm a psychopath; I'm certain I'm not. But my cold, calculated nature has always been unsettling, even to my family. And I have no idea why they think me having a wife will fix that.

She catches the present, and her expression lights up. "See, I knew you weren't a psychopath." She beams as she comes up to hug me. Her voice quietens. "But in all seriousness, you can't only focus on work and this family. We're all living our separate lives and doing our own things. Are you sure you want to be left behind? I know you're busy, but are you fulfilled?"

I kiss her forehead. "My work is fulfilling. As long as you're all safe and provided for, I have no issue or complaint. Goodnight, Billie. Stay out of mischief."

She rolls her eyes as I open the door. "But if I do that, how will you get to flex your knight-in-shining-armor muscles? Which I despise, by the way. Also, can we talk about the last time you—"

I close the door, cutting off Billie's temper, which is about to snap at any moment. At times, it reminds me of a particular little monster who enjoys throwing things at my face.

"And you are?" I turn in my chair to find a man standing at the door, looking at me expectantly. I've been coming into work for the last two weeks without anyone else being here. Usually, by the time I leave, a few of the staff working that evening are coming in. But that's the extent of it. Sometimes Paula is in earlier in the afternoon, but those days are few and far between.

I was so focused on scheduling the social media that I didn't even hear the man enter the office. I'm assuming he has keys—I fucking hope so anyway. He's far too attractive to be a thief.

How rude of him to ask for my name before he offers his own; it reminds me of a certain asshole boss.

"Sorry. Do I know you? I didn't know anyone else

was here," I say cautiously because I was supposed to be the only one in today.

"You're in my son's office. Does he know this?"

Ohhh. My eyes widen, and I stand from behind the desk, gathering my things and roping in my sassy attitude.

"I'm sorry, I didn't know anyone would be coming in here. This office has the best internet connection, so I thought I'd work from here since he's out."

"And he allows that?" he asks.

I take a moment to really look at him. While he looks a lot like Dutton, with high cheekbones, eyes that seem to stare straight through me, and dressed impeccably, he also gives off a warmer vibe than his son. Dutton is cold, even when his head is between my legs. And that's saying something.

I want to slap myself. I have to stop thinking about that night. It happened over a month ago.

"Yes. I received his permission while he was in Italy. He's not here today if you're looking for him."

"He told you where he was? Interesting." His expression turns thoughtful. "You don't have to leave on my account." He waves at my belongings as he takes a seat on the other side of the desk. The chair looks far too small for his bulky frame. Much like his son, he has an aura around him that seems to suck in everything and anything within its reach.

I stare at him in confusion. He crosses one leg over the other and leans back. "And your name?"

Okay then... I start putting my things back down and sit across from him.

"Posie." I offer him a smile.

"And what is it exactly that you do here?" he asks his gaze just as penetrating as his son's.

"I do admin and handle the social media accounts," I tell him.

"And your relationship with my son?" My hand freezes on the piece of paper I was about to pick up. His gaze flicks to it quickly before focusing on my face again. I don't like how much he notices; he's just like his son in that way. Notices fucking everything.

"Relationship?"

"Yes, what is it?" he asks.

I hear a loud noise coming from outside the room, and my gaze darts to the open door.

"He's my boss," I reply, returning my attention to him.

"That's good to know," he says, standing again.

We both turn at the sound of footsteps stopping at the door to find Dutton standing there. Comparatively, Dutton is slightly taller and more muscled than his father. I can tell where Dutton gets his immaculate taste in clothing from now.

"Son, you kept me waiting."

"I wasn't aware we had an appointment." Dutton gives me a quick glance. His father notices, and a slight tug of his lips indicates he sees more than he lets on. "You weren't meant to be in today," Dutton says, and I realize he's talking to me.

"Yes, sorry. I had to finalize a post and was just getting ready to leave." I finish grabbing the papers and look back at Dutton's father. "It was nice to meet you."

"Likewise. I'm sure I'll see you again." He gives me a warm smile, and Dutton seems wildly pissed, his gaze narrowing on his father. A palpable tension fills the room, and I decide it's best to ignore whatever is going on with these two. I walk past his father, but when I reach the door, Dutton hasn't moved to let me pass. His cold eyes look down on me, and I don't understand why he looks pissed. I'm not sure if it's directed at me or his father. He steps to the side wordlessly.

Well, okay then.

Finally escaping the suffocating energy in Dutton's office, I find Paula walking in. She smiles at me, and I give her a wave.

"I'm just heading out. Also, Dutton's father is

here," I inform her, pointing a thumb over my shoulder. "Tension is high in there, so I'd avoid the room."

Her eyes go wide. "Strange. He never comes here, but thank you for the heads-up. From what I heard, Dutton has a good relationship with his family. "Oh well, not our problem," she says with a casual shrug.

I head to the back of the room to collect the rest of my things as Paula takes a call. She curses under her breath, and I look over at her worriedly.

When she hangs up, I ask, "Is everything okay?"

"No. That's the third dancer tonight to call in sick. I think there's a virus going around, but we're way too short-staffed for a Saturday night." She pulls at the back of her neck. "Fuck. I don't know what I'm going to do." She looks at me then and bites her bottom lip. I know what she's going to ask before it even leaves her lips. "Could you work the floor for one night? Even if it's only for a few hours. One dance and the rest on the floor?"

I groan, not at all wanting to do that. Nor am I obliged to. But I know Paula wouldn't ask unless she was desperate, and I'd rather not say no to the woman who's helped me so much.

"There's no one else?" I ask. I'd have to call and see if Amy's available.

"I wish there was, unless you want this old hag

dancing on stage." She waves a hand at herself with a laugh, but there's no amusement in it.

"I'll do it. But only for tonight. Let me check with my babysitter."

She grabs both of my arms. "You're a lifesaver, Posie. Thank you."

I roll my eyes as I make the call—Amy is more than willing to help out since her plans for the evening were canceled.

"Only this once!" I tell Paula. "I'll see you in a few hours." I wave to her before I finally escape.

IT'S BUSY, which only means one thing. My efforts in my new role are working, which makes me proud.

I told Paula I would only stay for one dance and then work the floor for two hours. She was just happy that the empty slot had been filled.

"Haven't seen you for ages," Samantha says as she comes off the stage. I smile at the pink lingerie she's wearing—the set I gave her. It's obviously her new favorite.

"And you're looking amazing. Thanks again for agreeing to do the photo shoot," I reply. She gives me a wave as if it's nothing.

"You didn't even include my face, so it's a win-win. And you photoshopped my tattoos. So even those closest to me won't know it's me." She winks. The music changes and I know that's my cue to go out onto the stage. "Good luck," she yells as I hurry past her and stand behind the curtains. I wait a few breaths as the music drops to a lower beat, then I make my move. Relaxing my jaw, I saunter out, one foot in front of the other.

I'm wearing a lingerie set Dutton gifted me. I didn't know what to do with the pile of skimpy items. And even though I don't like the feeling of owing anyone anything, I was very partial to this set studded with diamonds. So if I'm dancing one more time, why not wear it? I certainly feel hot as fuck in it.

Tonight, I'm wearing black leather—a short skirt and a top with a cutout at the breast area. My high-heeled boots are black to match the attire, and I'm wearing fishnet stockings. When the music picks up, cheers start, and I sashay around the pole, one hand wrapped around the cool metal, making eye contact with the men.

My gaze lands on a set of cold blue eyes, and immediately, I know I'm in deep trouble. But I don't care because I don't answer to that asshole. Okay, technically, I do because he's my boss, but not on matters where he's treating me differently from the others. There's only so much fuckery I'll accept.

Besides, I've always lived by the philosophy of asking for forgiveness over permission. My boss doesn't look happy, scowling in his seat beside the twins. I smirk, and even from here, I swear I can see his left eye twitch.

I can't help but fill with mischievous delight at pissing him off as a friendly reminder that he doesn't own me.

Dropping down to my hands and knees, I crawl to the edge of the stage. The twins are warily looking at Dutton. The bulkier one, who I've come to learn is named Hawke, can't help but stare, and I smile. His brother punches him in the arm, and he curses, rubbing it.

Dutton looks like he's about to burn him alive.

He better tip me.

"Hey." I wink as I get up on my knees. Lifting my hands to my shirt, I pull it open and expose my lace bra, which gives hints of my nipples underneath. This time, I only look at Dutton. His gaze dips only once before coming back to my face. He's seriously pissed.

"Stop," he grits.

"Sorry, sweetheart, I only answer to tips," I smirk.

I keep eye contact with Dutton as I throw the shirt onto his lap. Usually, I would never do that, but I know I'll get it back from him. His fists close around it, and I feel too smug at how he looks like he wants to teach me a lesson.

I switch positions, grinding down sensually until my back hits the floor.

"Get off the stage, and do not remove one more piece," he growls.

I smile sweetly, and that's when Hawke nudges him.

"You still haven't tipped her," Hawke whisper-shouts.

See, his friend gets it.

I bring my heels together and pulse a few times before sensually standing up again. I sway my hips as I walk to the pole and climb it, gripping my legs around it and flicking my hair over my shoulder. When my feet hit the floor again, I'm about to readjust my grip and position, but I'm grabbed around my waist and pulled backward.

"Hey!" I scream as I'm flipped over a broad shoulder.

"I warned you. Do I not pay you enough that you have to resort to dancing again?" Dutton says as he carries me out. I kick and scream as he drags me off the back of the stage. I'm having serious déjà vu right now. I take a glance back at the audience, who seem baffled. The twins appear to be the most stunned of all.

When we reach the backstage area, Paula looks mortified and shocked. She can't speak as he charges us toward his office.

"I'm a woman; we love money," I say as I kick and elbow him. Okay, I knew this would piss him off a little, but this is some stupid macho shit.

He enters his office and slams the door shut behind us. As he slides me down over his shoulder and onto my feet, he snaps, "Cover up. And you aren't allowed to find the nearest weapon and hit me with it. Do you understand me?"

The moment my heels touch the floor, I shove him hard enough that he has to take a step back. "I don't hit you," I seethe, fuming. I know I antagonized him, but I didn't think he'd literally drag me off mid-performance. *Again.*

"No, you just grab things and chuck them at me," he replies. And although his tone is neutral, I can tell he's livid beneath the surface. It's evident in the way his blue gaze turns shades darker. "You enjoy pushing your luck, don't you?"

I scoff at him as I turn away and move to his desk. I scan the items littering the surface, contemplating what I might enjoy throwing at him. "You just cost me heaps of money," I accuse, leaning against the desk and crossing my ankles. He can't help but look now that we're in private, his gaze roaming up my legs appreciatively.

"I don't appreciate you displaying the gifts I give you to other men."

"I thought this was for work," I say sassily.

He kicks up a humorless smirk as he crosses the distance between us. He's in my space, looming over me with a hand on either side. I have the urgent desire to grab the stapler and smash it over his head. I don't like how he fills my space and consumes me. But my core floods with an entirely different type of urgency and need.

Fuck my treacherous body.

Sometimes, I wonder if I do these things because I want to see his reaction.

Because I want him to want me.

And that's toxic as fuck.

"I'll pay you whatever you want in tips for that little stunt out there, but you only show your body and lingerie to *me*."

He opens a small box on his desk, barely moving around me, and then sets a stack of freshly printed bills in my hands.

That heated liquid sensation churns in my stomach. I try to do everything I can to push his effect on me away. Is it because I haven't seen him for two weeks that the magnetizing pull feels intensely epic tonight?

"Aww, you love me. Shall I call you sugar boss?" I taunt, fluttering my lashes.

"No."

Tension ripples between us, and I can't move, don't want to move, because I'm scared of what I might do. There's a good chance I'll grab for him.

I hated it when he first started texting me. I ignored most of his messages, but now I find myself laughing at his responses and know that the relationship with Dutton is anything but a professional one.

"Okay. Now that I've made my tips, I'll just go home." I try to move past him, but he doesn't budge. I fall back against the desk and notice how tightly he's holding the edge as if doing everything in his power to restrain himself.

"You're not going home in that," he growls. I daringly dip a gaze to the front of his pants because I can feel the effect I have on him. He's on his fucking last nerve, and it rattles me with desire and need I haven't felt for a *very* long time. Well, not since we were in the back of his car.

I think about the orgasm he gave me, and my pussy starts greedily throbbing.

"I'll wear my jacket," I tell him. "I've done it dozens of times."

"Posie." His voice is like gravel, and a vein bulges in his neck.

"Yes, boss?" I tack on the "boss" because one of us needs to say it. This is to remind us of the precarious situation we're clearly putting ourselves in. And I'm not entirely sure I have the self-control or desire to push him away. After all, I *enjoy* getting under this powerful man's skin. I love defying him in every way. And all I've been thinking about for the last month—no matter how much I try to deny it—is how I can get beneath him again.

"I want to taste you again," he states, but his tone is a mixture of that earlier frustration and barely-there discipline to not touch me without permission.

I go to speak, but my mouth closes again.

I'll regret it, won't I? Nothing good can come from submitting to a man like this, but fuck me, how I want to.

I can't look away, and as I stare into his eyes, all the memories of that night come flooding back. I was drunk then, but I'm not now. I'm dead sober, and yet the electricity crackling between us feels the same.

"I think I can arrange that," I whisper, shocked by my honesty. His blue eyes darken, and this time, his frustration is replaced by voracious lust. His gaze is so intense that I'm certain I'm going to crumble beneath it. But, fuck, is he good with his mouth. My gaze dips to his lips.

"Good. Tonight?"

Amy said she could stay all night since I haven't used her much lately. She'll also be looking after Bentley tomorrow because I've made other plans. So, I could go with him tonight, but what will that mean? Will our dynamic change more than it already has? And will I be okay with that?

I know it might ruin me, and his tendency to dominate might kick up a level. Or he might get bored of me once he has another taste, and I can just get a wild fucking night out of it. The risk is high, but I'm not thinking straight when my body is screaming for his cock.

"Just a taste?" I whisper.

Wrapping his arm around my waist, he pulls me tighter against him. His mouth lowers to within a breath of mine as he says, "No. The whole fucking thing. Top to bottom, with my mouth, then my fucking cock. And you will take it all."

"Will I?" I question, not able to look away from his lips.

"Yes. And you'll enjoy it."

"The possibility is there," I reply with a tilt of my head.

He smirks, and before I can say another word, he leans down and touches my lips gently with his, no tongue, just his lips. They're soft and firm at the same time as he applies pressure. And just before I can push for more, his lips disappear, and he pulls back.

"First taste complete."

Motherfucker. When did this dominant fucker turn into a little tease?

"Here in your office?" I ask.

He shakes his head. "Not here because the noises you're about to make will make anyone think I'm killing you. Let's go. I live close by."

"To your house?" Surely not. I don't like the idea of anyone thinking I'm being treated differently than them, even though it's true at the moment. But also, I'll do whatever is necessary to better my situation and Bentley's when an opportunity presents itself. Me fucking the boss is an entirely different matter. I almost wish Dutton was a middle-aged, balding man because it would be much easier to say no to him.

"Do you have an issue with that?"

"I just..."

"It's okay, Posie. I'll make sure your body remains intact. Well, mostly." He grins as he backs up, grabbing my hand and dragging me out the door.

TWENTY
DUTTON

Her hand is small and soft in mine, except for the few calluses on her palm from gripping the pole. The only reason I'm holding her hand is because I'm afraid that at any moment, she might change her mind and run.

She's like a scared cat, ready to scamper away at any second, and I'm not taking any chances this time. Before we reach the exit, Hawke cuts us off. His gaze moves to Posie before sliding back to me.

"You're leaving already?" he asks.

"Yes."

"You suck at guys' nights," he accuses, shaking his head before he turns to Posie. "Did he at least tip you?"

She shrugs. "Could have been better."

"Well, at least he didn't pull a knife on you. He likes to carve things into people's bodies." He waggles his fingers in what I think is supposed to be a spooky gesture.

I glare at him. This fucker never knows how to read a room, and he always says the first thing that comes to his mind.

"Sorry, what?" Posie scrutinizes him.

"He's trying to scare you," I interject as she raises a brow. She doesn't have to ask if it's true. Posie is a smart woman, and she's certainly seen the less attractive side of me, what with her constantly pushing my buttons.

"Ignore my brother," Ford says, his attention glued to his phone screen as he comes up next to Hawke.

I don't like how often they've been visiting the club lately. They're obviously bored since Eli is married and always sending them away. I also don't appreciate my father's sudden appearance here either. And I'm certain they're all far too curious about the blonde standing beside me.

"I'm sure I'll see you again, Posie," Hawke says.

Her brow furrows, and I know she's remembering when my father said the same thing in the office. And I understand why they both said it. They think there is more going on between the two of us than I'm telling them. And that couldn't be further from the truth. I need to get her out of my system. And besides, they know she has a possible connection to the Boston

Delinquents, although I'm sure they're not falling for that excuse any more than I am.

As Paula approaches us, she looks at my hand clutching Posie's but speaks directly to her. "Thanks for filling in as best as you could."

"That reminds me. Posie is banned from the stage," I say. Paula's eyes widen but she nods in agreement.

"You can't do that! I'll dance whenever I want to," Posie argues, trying to pull her hand out of mine.

"Not in this club."

"So you want me to quit, then?"

"No."

"Then don't try to tell me what to do."

"I'm your boss; it's my job," I remind her.

She finally gets her hand free, only to defiantly cross her arms over her chest. She won't agree with me openly, but I know she's come to an internal agreement with my last statement.

"I've been told it's time to go home, but I'll see you through the week," Posie says with a smile, and Paula offers a sincere smile in return.

I don't want the women thinking differently of Posie, which is why I made a point to take her out now, but I'm sure me pulling her off stage might tip some of them off about how interested my cock is in this particular blonde. But I couldn't help myself. I was moving before I even registered what I was doing.

"Call me if there're any issues," I say, grabbing Posie's hand again and pulling her away from the twins —those nosy fuckers—and toward the exit.

I don't like anyone snooping around in my business. And right now, Posie is my business. I need to flush her out of my system so I can start thinking straight again.

I left my car at the club, and now I'm sitting in his passenger seat as he rounds the hood to my side to open the door. I'm not sure what I expected when I agreed to go back to his place. I knew he had money, which is evident from the car he drives, but the brownstone I'm currently staring at proves it. Not only is it in a good area, it's far from my subpar house. The neighborhood oozes wealth, the type I'm not used to.

Shit, I would've felt better with an average hotel, so the reality of what I'm about to do wouldn't be so unnerving. I'm about to sleep with my ridiculously wealthy and attractive boss.

"Do you plan to get out?" he asks, holding the passenger door open for me.

"Why am I here?"

He doesn't need to flaunt his wealth around me, but I think it's more so the fact that once we do this, there's no coming back from it. I want to fuck him. Just once. But it might change everything going forward, even if it's just sex. I can't help but have my guard up around this man and the unknown way he might react.

"You know why; we both do. Now, please get out."

Just get out of your head, Posie. Not everything and everyone is out to get you.

I nod decisively and step out. I'm still wearing my stripping clothes. The jacket covers all but the high heel boots, but if anyone saw us, they might assume I'm a hooker. I have no issue with the profession, but it makes me wonder how many women he's brought here. Perhaps I'm just one of many.

He escorts me up the staircase, his hand resting on my lower back as if he's afraid I might run. When he unlocks the door and opens it, I'm shocked by the beauty of the interior. If I thought the neighborhood was pretty, it has nothing on this. Rough brickwork acts as a feature wall against the deeply polished wooden walls and floors. A circular staircase goes to the next floor, with room on either side of the entryway. One has a piano and chessboard. The other has what looks like a living space with a library and fireplace.

It's more... homey than I expected, but it feels like

it's missing that personal touch. Maybe because its owner doesn't necessarily have a heart, but it smells like him—all-consuming and rich, with a light hit of citrus.

He locks the front door behind me.

"Would you like a drink?" he asks as he removes his jacket. He then rolls up the sleeves of his button-down, keeping his gaze solely on me.

"No."

"What would you like?" he inquires arrogantly, bending over and dropping onto one knee to undo his shoes and remove them.

I think about that while he looks up at me through thick eyelashes.

What would I like?

Well, I am here for a specific reason.

Because I've missed having his mouth on me, and I would greatly like it back there. Once just wasn't enough.

I remove my jacket, letting it slip off my shoulders, and fall to the floor. We remain in the entryway, him staring at me, his throat constricting as he swallows. I lift a booted foot and place it on his chest, dirtying his white shirt with the footprint.

"Undo it," I order. His hand slides up my knee-high boot until he reaches the top, then he unzips it slowly and pulls it from my leg, discarding it to the side. We repeat the process for the other boot, and he doesn't once look between my legs. If he did, he could easily see my panties due to the shortness of the skirt.

"What would I like?" I say as he pulls the boot off. When I put my foot back on the floor, he doesn't move, remaining on his knees expectantly.

Ladies and gentlemen, Dutton Taylor is on his knees.

I'm so shocked at first that I can only stare down at him. Then he reaches up my skirt, grips the top of my stockings, and slowly pulls them down my legs and off each foot.

"Posie."

"Hmmm."

"I'm hungry now, and you'll behave, right?"

"Behave?"

"Yes. Keep your hands to yourself, and I'll reward you. And the word 'no' does not exist in this home."

I raise a brow at him. "As long as you don't give me a reason to say no, and your hands are on me, keeping me distracted."

"They're already on you," he reminds me as he squeezes my legs.

It feels like electricity runs up my body. The intensity of this man's gaze devours me, but I don't look away, learning from my last experience with Dutton that he doesn't like it if I don't remain purely focused on him.

"Hands to myself. Noted." I clear my throat.

His palms glide up my legs painfully slowly, as if he's memorizing the feel of my skin. When he reaches my underwear, he tears them from my body, shredding them at the seams before grabbing my ass and squeezing the flesh there.

His gaze finally dips to the juncture of my legs. He squeezes my ass again and pulls me closer until his face is directly between my thighs. He kisses my clit, then moves lower, between my folds, his tongue tasting. I almost immediately melt into him.

It's scorching hot, and I can't help the moan that leaves me. My hands lift of their own accord as his tongue flicks, and I, at the last moment, remember his order not to touch him.

Do. Not. Touch him.

But that's a challenging instruction to follow when I don't have anything around me to grab onto but him. The wall is too far back, and the door isn't within reachable distance.

He removes one hand from my ass and wastes no time sliding a finger inside me.

It's so sudden and purposeful that another moan slips from me.

My hands are clenched at my sides, dying to touch him as his tongue works even faster and more persistently.

"Dutton." His name slips from my lips, and he pulls back for a moment. I'm confused, and I look down at him expectantly.

"That's the first time you ever called me by my name instead of boss or asshole, *Mostriciattola*."

My brow furrows in confusion because, although I've overheard him speaking fluent Italian, I have no idea what he just called me.

"I told you not to give me a reason to tell you no," I growl; I don't want him to get sentimental or show he has a slither of emotion in him just because I finally used his name. It'd be a total buzz kill to the hard fucking I expect.

He smirks and plants his lips back on my clit, the suction pacifying me and pulling out a deep hunger. I fall back as much as I can into the bliss. Small whimpers escape me as I let him worship me and let all my worries and concerns fall by the wayside. This man breaks me apart in ways I never thought possible.

Then he pulls back and stands, and I instantly miss the feel of him. My eyes snap open, and I expect him to reprimand me for not staring at him like he had last time, but instead, he begins unbuttoning his shirt. I follow his lead, reaching behind to unhook my bra, leaving me in just the leather skirt.

When his shirt hits the floor, I have a moment to appreciate his muscles. He's fucking stunning. Lean with six-pack abs and arms that easily carry my weight over his shoulder. But there are also cuts and scars all over his body. A sensation of danger tingles through me, a reminder that this man is not someone to be trifled with. I, more than anyone, should know better than to mingle with a man like this. And yet I gravitate toward him like a moth to a flame.

I realize then that Dutton has done his best to try to be professional, except for, of course, when he's acting like a caveman and dragging me off stage. Because in all the times and ways he's looked at me, his gaze has never lingered at work. But now it's all-consuming.

He admires me, which I appreciate. I'm very much used to men admiring my naked body. It's how I earned money before Dutton gave me my new job. But having a man admire me after he was just between my legs? Well, that's a new experience for me, and I really fucking like it. Especially how his gaze greedily takes me in, like he's seeing more than just my body. *It's like he's seeing all of me.*

My boss might be an asshole, but right now, he looks as if he's under my spell, and I want to see what might happen if I try to break the cool intensity of his control. He's so used to having everything go his way. I want to make him break apart.

"My turn," I purr as I drop to my knees and pull his belt free, discarding it before I unbutton his pants and lower the zipper. When I do, his straining cock springs free, and I can't help but admire it. He's bigger than Bobbi, who was the last person I was with. And that was before Bentley was born. I wonder if it will hurt. I've only used toys during the previous five years, and they've done the job well enough, but I know they haven't prepared me for this man. Not with a sizeable cock like that.

"I don't need you to please me. I told you, I'm here to taste and consume all of you, Posie."

"Yes, but we take turns," I say charmingly, looking at him in a way that most men can't deny. "Do you not want me to touch you?" I whisper. I put my hands behind my back and lean forward to kiss the tip of his cock. He mumbles something under his breath, and I look up at him.

"No touching." I throw his words back at him. The tendon in his neck looks like it's about to snap. He must fucking hate me when I tell him what to do, but he permits me to touch him with one curt nod of his head.

Leaning forward again, I take his cock in my mouth and suck while swirling my tongue around the tip. He groans, and I move my head up and down, pleased at the sounds vibrating through him.

I keep eye contact because I know how much he needs that, and the intensity of it is staggering. Tears well in my eyes, but I continue taking him to the back of my throat. He speaks in Italian, and I'm sure it's mostly curses. His arms and pecs flex as if reminding himself to keep his hands behind his back.

"Stop." I'm surprised at the harsh demand, but I sit back on my heels. He steps out of his pants, now completely naked. "Stand."

I try to hide the smile begging to bloom on my lips. Of course, this man can only give away control for a few minutes. But I do as he says, and I'm curious to see what else he might do to me.

When I'm on my feet, he circles me, his fingers sensually caressing my bare skin as if appraising me. As if wondering what to do with me.

"What do you want?" I ask when I can't handle the

tension anymore. I swallow hard when I get another glance at his massive cock.

"You, *Mostriciattola*."

"Then why aren't you taking me?"

I can sense his smirk as he comes to a stop behind me, and I'm surprised by the warm touch of his lips on the back of my neck. He trails kisses along my shoulders while one hand snakes around my stomach to pull me against his hard cock, causing it to poke against my asshole. He cups my breast and then squeezes, and I shudder at the stimulation of his aggressive hands and marking kisses. I'm not used to this type of attentiveness.

"Do you want me to stop?" he growls.

"I've been told I can't use a certain word in this house," I reply huskily.

His mood shifts as he comes around to face me. "Do I intimidate you?" he asks. I think about that question as I glance at his hand possessively gripping my hip. I can sense the moment he puts that ice wall between us. I don't mind it because I'm so used to doing it myself with everyone else. But right now, it feels easier to speak truths than lies.

"Maybe a little," I confess.

"You hide it well," he says, then spins me to face

him. He picks me up, and my legs automatically wrap around his waist. When he walks me up the stairs, I notice a lounge area with a large black couch and a TV mounted on the wall. He's staring at me, and it's hard not to stare back at him. Words unsaid. Intensities matched. A fire that I want him to put out between my legs, but I'm positive it'll only create an insatiable craving instead.

I would never admit it, but I like the way he carries me. It makes me feel small, almost protected, something I haven't felt in a long time. Instead of a mother or a stripper, I'm simply a woman being carried in a man's arms. Not just any man's arms either.

I lean back and meet his gaze. "Do *I* intimidate *you*?"

He turns left and strides into a dimly lit room, which I'm assuming is his bedroom. When he lowers me, my ass lands on something soft, and I realize it's his bed. He doesn't bother turning on a light as he reaches into the drawer and pulls out a condom. I almost think he's not going to reply to my question as I watch him rip it open with his teeth and then slide it on. When it's in place, he looks back at me.

"More than you could ever understand."

My eyebrows raise, but before I can digest that, he's

on me, kicking my legs apart and positioning himself between them. He doesn't immediately push inside. No, instead, his mouth finds my nipples, and he does as he told me he was going to do—he tastes me. Biting my nipples before he sucks his way down to my belly and back again. Each time he gets to my neck, I reach my hands behind him and try to pull him closer. It's a game of teasing, and he's an expert at it. The pounding of desire is a living, breathing, feral creature beneath my skin, and if I don't have him soon, I may just claw his fucking eyes out.

"Dutton," I growl, irritated by his purposeful teasing.

"Yes, Posie?" he answers, and although I can't see him clearly, I know he's intentionally fucking with me.

"Fuck me already," I grit.

He chuckles. And it's the rawest version I've seen of this man. Not the monster beneath the mask. Not the boss. Not the perfect businessman. Simply Dutton.

"As you command," he says, and his mouth comes back to mine. He still hasn't kissed me fully. Yes, his mouth has tasted my lips and my skin, but his tongue has never tasted mine. So when our lips meet, I open my mouth in invitation, and he slides his tongue inside. And as he does that, his cock finds precisely where it needs to be and slams straight into me. I gasp, but he doesn't stop kissing me, doesn't pull away, as if needing to devour my every hitched breath.

I focus only on him as I thread my fingers through his hair, pulling him deeper into me as if he's my only anchor to this moment as I relax around the size of him.

His hips start moving, and I drag my very sharp nails down his back. He grunts and begins to fuck me harder with each thrust and kiss. The shadow of his beard tickles me as he ravages me, and I don't know where he begins, and I end as I match him thrust for thrust, the loud slapping of our skin echoing through the room.

I moan and wince under the pain and pleasure. His hand comes up to my throat as if keeping me in place while he hits that spot inside me over and over again. I can barely squirm beneath him, brought to new heights every time he slams into me.

I squeak—an unusual sound for me to make—as I greedily try to cling to him as he constricts my airflow. *This fucking man.*

The pressure begins to build, and I whimper, so close to climax.

Oh fuck.

How is this possible?

"Dutton," I whimper, almost scared of what this climax will rip out of me. It's been so long. My body is in overdrive, and tingles rise along my legs as I cling to him for dear life.

"Scream for me, *Mostriciattola*." He grunts.

I grip his hair and pull, but it does nothing to deter him from taking my lips as he completely cuts off my air. A moment of panic strikes me but mixes with the high of teetering on the edge.

I yank my face to the side, a breathless moan passing through me as the pressure builds. His mouth then shifts to work on my neck; his cock keeps pounding into me, and his hand slides down where his fingers circle my clit.

How can he...?

Oh my God.

What in the ever-fucking hell is he doing with his hands and his cock?

"See what a good girl you are?" he croons, and I nod my head, unable to do anything else.

He leans back and pulls me to the end of the bed by my knees. He's now standing, looking down at me as he fucks me, releasing his grip on my throat ever so slightly so I can gulp for air. But it's not enough. Not enough oxygen in the world will save me from drowning in the sea of pure bliss I'm experiencing right now. I grip the sheets, unable to stop what's happening.

No one I've ever fucked before comes close to Dutton.

No one.

And I'm afraid he's ruined me for this life and the next. When I come, I see stars. And I mean, I come so hard that when I open my eyes, even in this dark room, bright pinpricks of light flash in my vision.

In the middle of my orgasm, I feel like I've pissed all over him. That's when I shockingly realize that I'm squirting. I've heard other women describe it, but I've never experienced it. I didn't even know my body was capable of it.

Until now.

He jerks into me, and I watch his silhouette, his powerful form going from rigid to fluid as he gives himself to my body entirely, and it fills me with a satisfaction I haven't had with another lover.

"Fucking perfect," he says with a sigh as he slowly pulls out and repositions himself so his face is between my legs again, licking everything, tasting, and eating. Devouring my sensitive clit. I have the urge to push him away because of how sensitive I am, but it's not so intense that I can't handle it. It's a lazy type of aftercare, but it's one that's already slowly building my desire all over again.

Urgently demanding my fill once again.

Oh fuck. This man really has ruined me.

I'll forever compare any other lover to him.

I can't speak, so I roll my hips into his face, languid with his lazy control.

And I realize this man is going to break me apart all over again, and the only thing to keep me here is... him.

Last night, when I entered the bedroom after taking a shower, I saw that she had passed out on my bed. Sleeping so fucking peacefully, I was unsure if she was still alive. She literally sleeps like she's dead. The blankets had been thrown across the bed in what looked like a violent tantrum. Forever a little monster, even in her sleep.

I'd planned on using her body and doing many things to her last night, but I couldn't get enough of tasting her. I just continued putting my head between her legs, taking her over and over again, breaking her until she had nothing else to give.

Sex is easy.

Sex is transactional.

But never had I lost myself so deeply to someone else's rhythm and rhyme.

I've always been considered a generous lover, but I've been told I'm too cold and intense.

Not with Posie.

I was going to catch up on some work last night, but instead, I came to sit next to her to watch her sleep, curious of the woman when she left herself unguarded.

Before I knew it, I was lying beside her, stroking a piece of hair out of her face repetitively as if petting her. And then I must've dozed off into a deep sleep, something I haven't had in a very long time.

But she'd vanished when I woke and reached for her because I wanted her again. I went downstairs to find all her clothes gone.

By how peacefully she was sleeping, I simply assumed she'd still be here when I woke. In fact, I'd always had women try to overextend their stay. Not that I ever brought them to my home.

She's always throwing some type of curveball at me. Like this job I gave her. I never expected her to do it so fucking well. And she has. She does an amazing job; too fucking good, actually.

And people are taking notice. More specifically, my family is taking notice.

Finding my phone, I press call. She doesn't answer. So I text her.

> Me: Do you like to ignore your boss's phone call?

I see that she reads it. And her reply quickly follows.

> Posie: The boss who I also fucked?

I can't help but smirk. Yes, we fucked. And I would very much like to do it again.

I ignore the multiple messages from Eli and Hawke inquiring about my business last night.

I check the tracker I put on Posie's car to see if she picked it up from the club this morning. If she hasn't, I'll have someone drop it off at her house.

When I check the tracker, my brow furrows; she's currently located outside of New Haven.

New Haven? What business does she have there? Unless that's not the final stop.

Unless she's going to Boston?

An alarm goes off in my head, one I've never ignored. Perhaps I was right all along, and her ties with the Boston Delinquents club are stronger than I thought.

I jog up the stairs to get changed, and within

minutes I'm pulling out of my garage on my motorcycle. I've been riding it less frequently lately, finding it easier to accommodate a certain little miss and my fantasies of having her in the back of my car.

The motorcycle is faster, though, and I need speed right now. I need to catch up with her and find out what that little monster is really scheming. I also have to ensure she isn't running away because I'm not yet done with her.

TWENTY-THREE
POSIE

Last night had been the distraction I needed for what was to come. However, it had also become a dangerous intrusion into my thoughts as I drove to Boston to confront some demons.

After collecting my car from the club, I went home to shower, change, and spend breakfast with Bentley and Amy. Before I left again, I promised Amy I'd be home by early evening.

I hadn't been in Boston since I ran away. I wasn't willing to risk taking Bentley to the same city where his father is more than likely still living. It saddens me that I can't yet bring him to his grandparents' graves.

I've told him a lot about them, but I'll never be able to bring him to this place. It'll never be safe. It's a gamble even for me to come, but I had to pay my respects to them on their anniversary. Six years has been too long.

I keep to the outskirts of Boston on my way to the cemetery, and it brings back so many memories. I've come a long way from the lost girl looking for validation. I had Bentley, became a mother, and found purpose beyond myself. I never understood the sacrifices my parents made until I became a parent myself, and even then, it didn't feel like a sacrifice, just a change.

I take a moment to center myself as I get out of my car. Moving between the headstones, I carry a bouquet of lilacs because they were my mother's favorite. I come to a stop at their graves and let out a shaky breath.

It feels strange being here after all this time. It's been eight years now since their boating accident. It was only because I was adamant about staying at a friend's house that night for a sleepover that I wasn't with them.

For months after I got the news of their deaths, I found myself wishing I'd been with them. I'd never have experienced that gut-wrenching feeling of losing everything all at once. Of not knowing left from right or regretting all the stupid fights or horrible things I called them.

I was a spoiled brat.

I guess it's why I was so susceptible to Bobbi's influence shortly after their funeral. I'd made mistakes in my grieving but snapped out of it quick smart for Bentley's sake.

I smile sadly, thinking about that as I crouch to put the flowers down. They'd always told me I had a fiery temper but a heart of gold. And they constantly lectured me about the fights I'd get into at school if someone was disrespectful to my friends.

I'd forgotten all those things about myself as if they'd happened in another life. It's only recently that the temperamental bratty part of me has come to the surface again, and I blame that on a certain asshole who intentionally draws it out of me to wind me up.

My mind immediately flashes to last night—his hands on me, his lips on mine. I try to push the thought away as I sit down and prepare to update my parents on the last six years.

"He's five now. Can you believe that?" I tell them. So much of me wishes they were here to spend time with him, to play with him, and to have Sunday meals with him. I wish my father could teach him things like fishing and my mother could spoil him with sweets.

I wrap my arms around myself. Sometimes, I wonder if I'm as good a parent as they were. I can't help but feel like I'm failing at times. I can't fill every role Bentley needs in his life. But I still try to be all of those things for him. I'm a good mother, but what if one day I can't answer his questions or guide him in the best way possible?

I sigh. My parents made parenting look so easy.

"You were right about one thing," I say. "Paying bills sucks." I laugh sadly, remembering our last argument a week before the accident. I'd announced I was going to move out and live my life the way I wanted to. I didn't realize in a few weeks I'd be doing exactly that... without them being there as a safety net.

I stayed with my aunt for a few weeks after my parents died, but she and I never got along, and soon, I fell into the wrong crowd with the Boston Delinquents. She practically disowned me when she found out, and I became a part of their family instead. My aunt passed away from cancer when I was eighteen, and I was too caught up in my own business that I didn't so much as visit her when she was sick.

I'd been selfish.

I'd been grieving.

But eventually, I found myself.

And I make sure not to hold any of those things too deeply. Because I know too well how crippling the weight of grief and regret can be, so, it doesn't serve

Bentley or me to be living in the past when all I have to do is look forward to our future.

"I can't believe you actually came," a voice says behind me.

I furrow my brow, turning around as I stand. I don't recognize the man. I do, however, recognize the leathers and patches he's wearing. I immediately start scanning the cemetery, making sure he's the only one here.

"Oh, he's not here. But he told me to hang out here for the day in case you showed up. And you did," he says smugly.

"What are you, Bobbi's lackey or something?" I ask snidely.

Fuck.

This is not good.

I didn't want to run into anyone here, but I didn't think he'd actually remember what today meant to me. When I found out I was pregnant with Bentley, he threw cash at me and told me to get rid of it, and I never saw him again. It's been six years since then. I thought enough time had passed that he would've moved on.

The error was in my own sentiment: I needed to come back. Digging into the past never brought anything good.

"I'm not his lackey!" he shouts, offended. "I'm one of his really good friends." This guy looks like he's barely twenty.

I scoff. "Bobbi doesn't have good friends. He has people who he uses and takes advantage of."

"What was that, bitch?" he says, squaring up.

Fuck, this is bad.

I don't carry guns with me, and I can't hide behind the bat that's stationed beside my door at home.

I'm not scared of men, but I know when standing alone in a graveyard with one who's double my size and potentially on something, I'm not going to win that fight. Not without my bat, anyway.

My fiery temperament aside, I don't take chances of never returning to my son.

So I make the split-second decision to run to my car.

"Hey! Get back here!" he yells.

I run as fast as my legs will take me. I pass through the metal gate, grabbing my keys from my pocket. As I round the big oak tree, I run into someone in leathers.

My heart pounds from fear and the exertion of running. I shove at them as they try to grab me. Terror grips me like a vise, and I punch them in the face, the key scratching them across the cheek as I shove them off. They grab me again, and I thrash in their arms until a familiar voice cuts through the haze of panic.

"Posie." Dutton shakes me, and I stare at him wide-eyed, and terrified.

He looks over my shoulder as the man comes around the corner, and he immediately shoves me behind him.

"Who the fuck are—"

Dutton's so fast that I take another step back, tripping over the roots of the tree and falling on my ass as I watch in horror.

Dutton punches the man, causing him to fall to the ground, and within seconds, Dutton is on him, laying into him so the man can't even get back up. There's no fight from the man when Dutton's pure, unleashed rage overpowers him.

Blood spatters as Dutton hits him again and again. It takes me a while to stand on shaky legs, and I am completely surprised by the last few minutes. The shock of the situation begins to lessen, and I find my fire once again.

"Dutton! You're going to kill him!" I lean against the tree. "Dutton!" I yell. Not because I care about the other guy—I've seen a handful of men killed—but because of the repercussions it might have on Dutton.

I understand he has connections, but the motorcycle club is savage, and no matter the reason, they will defend their own, especially if an outsider kills one.

Dutton kicks the guy's face in. The guy chokes on blood, barely conscious.

"Dutton!" I scream, picking up a rock and throwing it at his back. He turns then as if noticing me for the first time since his rage took over. His hair is a mess, and his eyes shine so brightly in the day that they're a vivid, icy blue.

He blinks once and then twice. He glances down at the man who's barely moving and then takes two long strides toward me. One hand cups my cheek, and his other hand rests on my hip. "Did he hurt you?"

I'm shocked by the concern in his voice. It's so different from his usually controlled and clipped tone. I'm shaking my head before I can speak.

"No, he didn't touch me."

"Good. Get in your car and drive back to Manhattan. I'll clean up here." He goes to pull away from me, but I grab his hand.

"No, you can't kill him. You don't understand the repercussions."

"Oh, I understand the repercussions," he says savagely. "I'm going to make an example out of him."

"Please, Dutton." I bring his hand back to cup my cheek as if that might be the only way to stop him. To anchor him. I'm not one to beg; the adrenaline is running so high right now that I don't even know what I'm doing or saying. All I know is we must leave in case someone else is watching. "Please. Leave this as it is."

"What are you even doing here?" he whispers accusingly. I flinch at his tone and take a step back. Then I really look at him for the first time since he miraculously arrived. He's wearing leathers. When I glance at my car, I notice a motorcycle that might be his parked behind it.

"Did you follow me here?" I ask.

"Yes. And had I not, who knows what might've happened," he all but growls. He's bleeding across the cheek from where my keys cut him.

"What the fuck?" I shove him back. "Are you out of your fucking mind? How did you even know I was here?"

His expression darkens, and I can sense his ice wall erecting between us once more, pissing me off. All the fear, adrenaline, and emotional shock of the day spills over. I shove him. "Are you fucking kidding me?! You don't want to answer me when you stalked me all the way here?" I shove him again, and he barely budges.

"You should be thanking me," he grits out.

I scoff. "Thank you? For tracking me? How are you

any different from the asshole on the ground over there?"

"First of all, I'm not on the ground with a broken face," he says pointedly.

Smack. His head swings to the left as I slap him across the face. He grinds his jaw, and I'm sure he most likely could've stopped me. "Oh, you'll release that temper on me, *Mostriciattola*, but not the asshole you were just so fearfully running away from?"

"Stop calling me that!" I growl. I don't know what *mostriciattola* means, but whatever it is, I don't like the way he can use it on me while we're fucking *and* when I'm losing my shit at him.

"What are you scared of? Or who are you so scared of?" he asks pointedly.

I turn to walk away, but he grabs my wrist. "Let go of me," I grit out with so much rage that I'm unsure what I might do if he doesn't. As if sensing my anger, he lets go of my wrist.

"We're not done here," he says, but I'm already striding quickly toward the car.

"I swear to God, if you kill that man, I'm quitting right now. I mean it," I tell him over my shoulder. Because if Dutton does kill him, the motorcycle club will hunt him down by any means necessary. And I refuse to draw close attention to my place of work or myself because that would lead them to Bentley.

It was a mistake coming here today.

I get into my car, slam the door, and scream as I pound the steering wheel.

I thought six years would've been enough to escape Bobbi's reach, but I feel no less trapped now, knowing he's still looming over me in some way. I'd become too comfortable, and letting my emotions bring me back here was a mistake. And I hate Bobbi for having this power over me when there's nothing I can fucking do about his influence in these parts.

All I can do is run again and make sure to keep my son safe.

No matter the cost.

I take a breath and push my hair back, trying my hardest to rein in the trapped fire that's spilling out from my seams. I start the engine. I hate Dutton for tracking me, but a small part of me is glad he was here. I'm mortified to know he saw that fearful expression on my face as my demons caught up to me.

But I'm not going to stay to confront them.

No, there are some things that are best left in the past.

And I'll face the new ice monster when I get home because that motherfucker has a lot of explaining to do.

TWENTY-FOUR
DUTTON

When someone advises I don't kill a particular person, I usually do the opposite and kill the fucker. However, the threat of Posie quitting seemed too high of a risk because she was deadly serious.

If Posie was at a cemetery, it's likely she buried someone she cares about there, and I need to know who it is. So before leaving Boston, I call Will Walker. My desire to figure her out myself no longer matters. I want and need to know everything about her because I never want to see that level of fear in her eyes again. I've seen so many sides of Posie—sassy, sexy, intelligent, mischievous, and flashes of her monstrous temperament. But I've never witnessed fear in her, and I'm willing to hunt down every fucker who ever made her feel that way.

I trail behind her, weaving between cars, making sure no one is following her and she's safe. When she pulls onto her street, I keep driving because I don't trust myself around her right now. Not because I think I'll hurt her. I know no matter the circumstance, I could never hurt her. I'm giving her space because, with how she looked at me, I'd most likely only make matters worse until she cools down and processes what happened today. That, and Will has already sent me the information on her, which leads me to believe that perhaps my little blonde monster isn't so much of a mystery at all.

I'm not surprised to see Eli's car sitting outside when I arrive at my brownstone. I curse under my breath as I park my motorcycle on the street and take my helmet off. Hawke, Ford, and Eli step out of the car.

"You've been busy," Eli states after taking one look at me.

"I didn't kill him," I say matter-of-factly as I unlock the door and open it. They follow me inside.

"No, you didn't kill him, but you put the kid in the hospital, and I got a call from their president asking why you were even on their turf. What the fuck happened?" Eli asks expectantly.

I go into the living room and grab my laptop so I can open the files Will sent over. I haven't come down from the adrenaline high from earlier, and I didn't get my release by carving a message into his chest, so I need something to grasp onto to make sense of all of this.

"Dutton," Eli says, and it draws my attention. "Jesus, you've got blood all over yourself." He goes into the kitchen and comes back with a wet cloth.

Hawke goes into the pantry and grabs a bag of chips and a bar of chocolate, throwing the sweets to Ford, who's taken a seat across from me. *They're just making themselves right at home, aren't they?*

Eli throws the wet towel at me, and I notice my face in the reflection of the laptop screen as I dab the cloth over it. Damn, she got me pretty good on the cheek with that car key, and yet I couldn't be fucking prouder of her. Next time, I'll have to tell her to go for the eyes. Hopefully, they won't be mine.

"What happened?" Eli presses. "You know we're on the verge of closing a deal with their president, and then you do this? Why were you even in Boston?"

I sigh, frustrated that I jeopardized Eli's business negotiations. It's not like it'll completely derail them, but they might not go as smoothly after this. I hadn't even thought of that at the time, which is very unlike me. I'm always prepared. But when I saw how frightened Posie was I just snapped.

"It has something to do with the blonde, doesn't it?" Hawke asks around a mouthful of chips. I glare at him, fucking hating how much the twins have been lingering around the club lately. Usually, I wouldn't mind, but when they're being observant, nosy little fuckers, I want them out.

"I put a tracker on her car," I begin, and Ford rolls his eyes.

"Says the man who swears he doesn't have a thing for her," Ford says.

"Sounds pretty serious to me. Isn't that what everyone does when they're infatuated with a girl?" Hawke adds around another mouthful.

"Obviously," Eli adds, looking at me expectantly again.

"I'm not infatuated," I grit out, in massive denial, but I'm not admitting it to these fuckers. "But, yes, I followed her to Boston because, as I expected, she might have some connection to the Boston Delinquents."

"And does she?" Eli asks.

It goes without saying that I'd started to doubt the seriousness of her connection with the club, but now I'm not so sure. I'm not thinking clearly when it comes to Posie.

"I don't know. But when I got there, one of their

members was chasing after her through the cemetery, and she looked terrified. I beat the shit out of him and didn't worry about asking questions until after."

They're silent, and I can see them thinking it over. I open the folder Will sent me and scan over the key parts, a picture quickly forming in my mind.

Her parents died at sixteen. Got involved with the motorcycle club thereafter. Left Boston two years later. Then, a birth certificate for her son.

I pause on that.

Her son?

I click on an image.

A recent photo of Bentley Quinn appears.

I frown.

I'd enquired multiple times who Bentley was, but when she reassured me she wasn't married, I figured if it were one of her lovers, I'd deal with him soon enough. But this... was not at all what I was expecting.

"What is it?" Eli asks.

I lean back in my chair.

She has a son.

How did I not know that?

How has she kept that from me?

I look around the room at the other men.

"She has a son."

"And do you think the son has something to do with the connection?" Eli questions.

A protective energy comes over me. I know Eli would never do anything to harm a child, but it catches me so off guard I'm not sure what to do with this information. I only thought about Posie. I was only having fun with Posie. Yet, somehow, this feels like it changes things.

"I don't know," I reply.

"It could be that she just pissed the wrong person off and got out before things got too serious. Could've had a one-night stand and *tada*—baby," Hawke says, tipping the remainder of the chip packet into his mouth.

"So glad you actually know how babies are made," Ford says, gaze locked on his phone screen.

"Please. Anya gave me the birds and bees talk almost as soon as we moved in, and I started fucking the neighbor's daughter."

Ford furrows his brow. "Wasn't she twenty-four, and you were like sixteen?"

"Yeah, but apparently, I could still get her pregnant even then." Hawke casually shrugs. "Neighbors were pissed."

Ford nods once. "I always wondered why they suddenly up and left."

"Anyway..." Eli says, glaring at them both, but mostly Hawke. "I'm going to smooth this over with Waylon Striker. You sort out your situation with the blonde and determine whether she's an actual threat. If you're going to go barreling in like that again, give us a heads-up."

"As if you ever give me a heads-up whenever you're about to do shit," I remind him.

"Touché. But I'd rather not lose the potential of profit here. You, of all people, should understand that."

And I do, completely.

I continue reading the file after they leave, reviewing it more than once. But every time I see the recent photos of Posie and her son, I think what a great mother she appears to be, and I can't truly grasp what this shift within me is.

Somehow, it changes everything.

But nothing at the same time.

One thing I have to figure out is whether I have to protect my family from her or if she needs to be protected like my family.

TWENTY-FIVE
POSIE

A knock comes on my door at dinner time. Bentley runs to open it, and I call him back. I immediately grab for the bat, jerking Bentley behind me with such fierceness that I'm certain I startle him. I don't mean to, but I'm rattled after the events of earlier today. The main thought going through my mind being, what if someone followed us?

"Who are you?" Bentley asks, and my heart freezes.

"I'm Dutton."

Shit. They were never meant to meet. I've always been cautious about who Bentley meets. He definitely doesn't need to meet the guy I'm fucking, or just fucked once. My mind runs through a million different ways to get out of this situation.

"That's a weird name," Bentley says. I somewhat hide the bat behind my back, more so for Bentley's sake.

"And what's your name?" Dutton asks him, and though I imagine it's difficult for him to break away from his cool demeanor, I can tell he's trying to be slightly gentler, as if he's unsure how to handle himself around a child.

"Bentley," Bentley tells him, holding out his hand.

"Dutton," I say. Bending down to Bentley, I whisper to him, "Go back to the table and finish your dinner while Mommy talks to her friend, okay?" He drops his hand but nods before he offers Dutton a wave and runs off.

When I'm sure he's gone, I stand, only to find Dutton watching me. Stepping outside the door, I leave it ajar behind me and position myself in front of it, still with the bat in hand, blocking the view into my home.

"That's new." He nods in the direction of where Bentley went.

He's changed into a gray suit, and the gash on his cheek still looks red and angry. Though he's clean and freshly shaven, he looks tired, and I can't help but think I'm the cause. A pang of guilt ripples through me. I was so caught off guard in the grave-yard, and my emotions were at an all-time high. I'd never been one to run, much to my detriment, but this time, I did, and I blame it on the emotional roller coaster of visiting my parents' graves for the first time in years.

"Why are you here?" I ask, crossing my arms over my chest.

"I wanted to check up on you and make sure you're okay," he says earnestly, and his sincerity rattles me. This is all kinds of fucked-up. When I glance at his big hands, I notice the busted knuckles and a speck of blood on his gold ring.

I sigh. "You have blood on your ring."

He raises his hand to check it himself and swears. He tries to remove the ring, but it's stuck.

"Here." I step forward to grab his hand, removing the tea towel over my shoulder. I rest the bat beside the door, then wipe the ring with the towel. I feel guilty because the only reason the blood is there is because of me.

"Did you kill him?" I ask quietly. I can't even look at him; the guilt is too much. I hate that he followed me. But had he not, who knows what might've happened?

"You asked me not to, so I didn't."

I freeze for a moment before I continue cleaning the ring, and then I look up at him, still holding his hand. I never thought Dutton Taylor would do anything because I asked him to.

"I would've preferred carving a message into his chest and then leaving his body on the doorstep of the Boston Delinquents to make a point to never come after you again."

My mouth opens and then closes again. There's so much to unpack in that one statement. What a fucked-up knight in shining armor indeed.

"Who even talks like that?" I ask, dropping his hand and stepping back to put distance between us because I never trust myself in his proximity.

"Don't act like you don't know who I am, Posie. You knew exactly who you were letting between your legs."

I bite the inside of my cheek. Yes, I knew he was connected to the mafia. But to come to my home, where my son sleeps, with blood on him...

That I will not accept.

"Why are you looking at me like that?" he asks.

I don't know how to express my feelings because I still haven't entirely processed it. Dutton is a monster in his own right. I'd never seen him snap like that, never seen that violent side of him. But in that moment, amongst the ugliness, I knew immediately that I was *safe*. And yet, I know I should step away from him; magnetism be damned, because I should be scared by a powerful man like him.

But how do I express any of that? I want to be mad at him for following me, but I'm grateful he did. I want to thank him for last night and how he brought me to life for the first time in what felt like years, but I also want to reprimand him for assuming he can arrive at my doorstep whenever he wants.

My gaze lands back on the cut on his cheek, and guilt floods me once again. So, I settle on a simple apology. "I'm sorry about your cheek," I say, grateful he didn't follow me all the way home after the incident. I didn't want to explain to Amy or my son why a man on a motorcycle was on my doorstep, splattered with blood.

I'd closed that chapter of my life.

At least, I thought I had.

"Why were you in Boston? Are you a part of that motorcycle club?" he questions, all his softness now gone.

I grow uncomfortable, knowing too well a man like this could probably gather all sorts of information on me. And I hate that about him. I hate that because of his power, money, and influence; he can so easily place me in a box that he can dig into my past, to a version of myself that I'd rather leave hidden. But I suppose, at the very least, I can give him an honest answer.

"I'm not. I got caught up in the wrong crowd when I lived in Boston after my parents died. I returned today to grieve the anniversary of their deaths. I didn't expect someone would be there waiting."

His eyebrows furrow as if not sure whether to believe me. I don't give a flying fuck if he does. I have no loyalty to him.

Tension ripples around us, but I refuse to look away. A million unasked questions seem to pass between us and then it's my turn to question him.

"Why did you follow me? How did you know where I was?" I've already strangely come to accept that Dutton is an enigma; he's everywhere and nowhere all at once. But why is he so fixated on me?

"You left my house without saying goodbye."

I narrow my gaze. "Yeah, newsflash. Most guys prefer that. They don't haul ass for a four-hour drive and miraculously somehow know where I'm at. That's stalker-level shit."

He casually shrugs a shoulder. "I'm attentive. And don't ever compare me to other men. *Ever.* I might be so inclined to uncover the names of every man you've slept with and then remove them permanently so you have no one to compare me to."

"You really are a psycho, aren't you? Dutton, stop talking in circles. I'm not a stupid woman. Answer me outright."

He's not a man who often answers to others, and I imagine he's not used to revealing his hand. But I'm also one to keep my cards close to the vest.

He rubs his jaw—something I haven't seen him do before—as if seriously considering what he should say.

"I put a tracker on your car. I'd like to say I take security for my employees very seriously, but I'd be lying if I said you're not the only one I've done it to."

My jaw drops. "What the fuck?"

"I believe you once called me a possessive asshole; there may be some truth to that, and I'm not going to apologize. Also, you might call it foresight. Because it's lucky I did track you, or who knows if you'd be coming back in one piece after today."

I want to argue with him because I know he's not telling me the entire truth. I feel like Dutton is hiding a motive I don't entirely understand. He might also be so overbearing that he just tracked me because he has the money and time to do so.

I want to throw every fucking piece of furniture in my house at him and maybe use the bat on his sparkly fucking bike parked in front of my house. But also... he's right. As if realizing the weight of his words, his expression softens ever so slightly, and he seems lost, as if unsure how to comfort someone.

"Posie, who was that kid?" Dutton asks suddenly, immediately ripping me away from my spiraling emotions. I just needed a night to sleep on it and process it so I can get my shit together.

"My son," I tell him.

"You never mentioned you had a child," he says quickly, and I don't know how to take that. It's not like I have to answer to him. And, frankly, it's none of his business.

"You never asked. And to be honest, you and I are nothing serious, Dutton. You're my boss, and we have sexual chemistry. The sex was good, so let's leave it at that, and we'll continue working like nothing ever happened." He looks like I've slapped him. "Okay, cool. Now that we've discussed that, I should go inside." I turn to slip through the door, but his front slams into my back, his hand barricading me in and preventing me from opening the door any farther.

"Are you telling me you don't want me to fuck you again?" His lips brush my ear lobe, and I immediately sink into him. Fuck, I could do with a release after today. He bites the lobe before he sucks it into his mouth, and warmth floods my core as I lean back against him, my body constantly betraying me around this man.

"No," I say, not sure what I'm answering. Because now I'm flustered.

How can this man so easily make me melt this way? I hate that he can do this to me.

"Mommy!" Bentley calls: I can tell he's coming toward the door. I freeze, then shove backward, but Dutton doesn't budge.

"So help me God, Dutton, if you don't move, I will get that bat and shove it so deeply up your ass it might actually reach farther than the pole you already have up there."

"I might like it," he says, then kisses the side of my neck and backs away. I pull open the door to find Bentley standing there.

"Are we having dessert?" he asks me. I scoop him up into my arms. "Do you like dessert?" he aims this question at Dutton.

"Dutton was just leaving," I say, then slam the door in his face without so much as another glance at him. Bentley asks why I did that, and I tell him to finish his food. I sit next to him, staring at my own meal, unsure how to manage this non-relationship with my very dominating and possessive boss.

And that should be the least of my worries, considering what happened at the cemetery. Though I'm certain Bobbi has nothing to go off of to find me. But maybe I should reconsider everything I've done recently. Maybe I should delete the social media accounts I created. I didn't use my real name, and he shouldn't be able to find me, but I didn't think he'd have someone watching my parents' graves just in case I appeared, for fuck's sake.

I was stupid. I'd been wary all this time, and I gave into a moment of weakness, hoping that I could have this small moment of peace to visit their graves. But Bobbi ruins even that.

We eat in silence, and I'm thankful Bentley doesn't ask any more questions. Taking our plates to the sink, I start to wash them when there's another knock at the door. Bentley runs to it, and that immediate fear spikes again as I call out and chase after him. When he pulls the door open, Dutton stands there, holding a bag in his hand. I narrow my gaze on the insufferable man who can't take a hint.

"Ice cream," Dutton says to Bentley.

"Oh, I love ice cream." Bentley reaches for it, but I grab it before he can, shooting an accusing glare at Dutton.

"Dessert," Dutton reiterates as if I'm the one being unreasonable.

"Bentley is allergic to nuts. Did you check if there are nuts in this?" I ask, making a point because he knows nothing about me or my son.

"Yeah, I could die," Bentley adds, and Dutton's blue gaze flicks to him.

"Well, that got dark really quick."

I sigh as Bentley gives me puppy dog eyes. Opening the bag, I see Dutton grabbed five different tubs of ice cream. One has nuts, made evident by its name, so I scan the ingredients of the others.

"You can have this one." I pull the tub out of the bag and hand it to Bentley. "What do you say?"

Bentley looks to Dutton. "Thank you. Want to come in and watch *Transformers*?"

"No," I say at the same time that Dutton says, "Yes." I glare at Dutton, but Bentley is already running off to get a spoon.

"Anything you're allergic to that I should be aware of?" Dutton asks.

"Overbearing assholes."

"Last time I checked, you rather enjoy choking on those."

Heat rises up my neck. The nerve of this man. "Why are you still here?"

"For dessert," he states, and I know he's not talking about what's in my hand.

"I can't, not tonight. And I don't bring men around, my son."

"Where is his father?"

"Dead for all I care," I say nonchalantly. He raises a brow at my words and then nods. Oh my fucking God, this man might be learning social cues and how to take a hint.

"Tomorrow night?" he asks.

"No, I have no one to watch him." He looks past me but can't see Bentley.

"You really are his mother."

I roll my eyes. "Yes, I am. And I would like it if you leave."

"I'll leave when you tell me when I can have you again." I put the bag on the floor and swap it for the bat. "There she is." He winks.

"You really want this shoved up your ass, don't you?" I whisper-shout, hoping Bentley won't hear. But I know he's most likely already glued to the TV.

"Have a good night, Posie," Dutton says with a smirk as he turns to leave.

I work from home that week, and two deliveries come. Both are desserts that have no nuts in them.

A text comes after the second delivery.

> Dutton: I'm waiting for mine…

I've tried my hardest to ignore him but can't help but smile at the message even though I don't respond. I don't need to give him answers when men have avoided doing that for me so often in my life. And I'm still unsure how to handle Dutton. He's crossed the boundary I set that separates sex from becoming something more. It terrifies me that Bentley has met him because he's asked about Dutton more than once. I don't want him getting attached to someone who will unquestionably not be around for long.

I've come down from the high of going to Boston. The reality is, there's no way Bobbi can track me back here, and that offers me some sense of security. But it doesn't make me feel any more comfortable with the fact that he's still there, keeping an eye out for me. I know it's not out of love but rather his need to control people and situations.

At times, he'd even use physical force to get me to agree to things. It's why I have such an issue with Dutton being so bossy. The difference is that I know Dutton would never physically hurt me, and although he intervenes at times, I still very much get my own way on many things. Dutton provided me with a job that included a pay rise and promotion, whereas Bobbi would only take and take, so I had no choice but to depend on him.

The men, in that regard, couldn't be more different. And I hate that I even compare them. As furious as I am with Dutton putting a tracker on my car, which is the wildest fucking thing I've ever heard, I'm also grateful. I don't believe in coincidences, but I definitely think there's something to the timing of when certain people appear in your life. Dutton literally appeared when I needed someone most. And maybe that's why I hated it so much: because he saw my weakness and my fear.

He saw my vulnerability in an old life that I no longer live. What if he pities me? What if he thinks less of me?

Then again, I don't care what Dutton thinks of me in that regard. And with the number of messages he sends, I know we're far from done, even when I try to push him away.

He's as tenacious as he is patient.

When I ignore a few more messages and only answer the ones regarding work, he sends a bold demand.

> Dutton: Either you hire a babysitter tonight or I will. You've been avoiding me at the office, and I will come to your door and collect you myself.

I wring my hands in the air, wanting to choke the life out of the determined fucker. I've enjoyed that he's been respectful enough not to arrive at my door again since that night, but now he's pushing my buttons. But I know he'll stay true to his word and most likely arrive on my doorstep.

And if I'm being honest... I've fantasized about Dutton ever since the night we spent together before I went to Boston. How can a girl not when a man gives her that many orgasms?

I bite my bottom lip as I check in with Amy. She's available to watch Bentley tonight.

I tap the edge of my laptop as I sit at the kitchen table, finishing up my work for the day.

I'm out of my fucking mind for considering meeting him tonight. But my toy can't compare to the way my boss knows how to make my body come undone. I wanted to do more things for *me*. To have fun. And as much as I try to ignore him, I'm a glutton for punishment. Literally.

I reply.

> Me: What time?

He replies immediately.

> Dutton: I'll pick you up at six.

> Me: Don't get out of the car. I'll come to you.

> Dutton: Wear the blue lingerie set I got you.

I roll my eyes. I know I shouldn't be attracted to him, but no matter how much I remind myself of that, I can't seem to stay away from him. And I'm not sure if I'm entirely ready to let go of the fun we might have. It is, after all, the best sex of my life. Don't I at least deserve this one thing?

TWENTY-SEVEN
DUTTON

"I assume most women would expect me to arrive at their door with flowers," I say as she runs out to my car, looking more like a teenager sneaking out of her home.

She closes the door behind her. "Not a mother who doesn't want to expose her young and impressionable son to a dangerous man."

I smirk as I put my hand on her inner thigh, curious about what she looks like beneath the loose, light-blue dress. I pull away from the curb.

"You think I'm a bad man?" I ask.

"Would you say the things you do to my body are good?" She arches a brow at me.

"If I recall, you beg for it at times. Isn't that why we're here right now?"

"You're the one who mentioned flowers and weird

shit, so you best remember that I'm only here for the bad man to do what he's very good at."

"And what's that?" I question, my cock already twitching at her proximity. It's been a whole week since I've seen her, and I feel like a starved man. Her floral scent hangs in the car as if touching every fucking thing I own and sinking into it. I welcome it.

"Your mouth on my pussy, of course," she says with a demure smile.

I can't help but smirk.

When we arrive at one of the many estates I own, we don't even make it through the door before I'm on her—devouring her.

She jumps into my arms, straddling my hips as I slam her against the wall. I try for the light switch, but at this point, I don't even care as I take her to the bedroom.

Her moans bring my cock to attention.

I love how inexcusably fucking needy she is.

"Did you wear my color?" I growl.

"You'll have to find out," she says between kisses, and I smirk as I kick open my bedroom door and throw her onto the bed. She bounces, and I see a flash of light blue under the dress.

I remove my shirt and tear at my jeans. She stares at my veiny cock hungrily as I order her to remove her dress. She smirks but does as she's told. When she reveals the blue lingerie set I bought her, I swallow. Hard.

The bra snugly accentuates her perfect tits. And I salivate at the crotchless panties as she leans back, giving me a full view.

"You've been very disobedient this week," I say as I crawl over her.

She grins. "Can't be too bad if I'm getting special treatment."

I squeeze her cheeks and stare down at her. "This mouth is the fucking problem."

"Or the solution," she tries to say. I grab one of her hands and place it near the headboard.

"What are you—" Her eyes widen as I cuff one wrist to the headboard. I grab her other hand and cuff it to the other side.

"You've been wreaking havoc in my mind, *Mostriciattola*."

"And you've been making promises all week," she bites back, but her mouth snaps shut the moment my finger slips inside her pussy.

"So you have been reading my messages." Her eyes roll back in her head, but I remind her, "You will look at me, or I'll have you cuffed to this bed all night, denying you orgasm after orgasm. It can be torture."

Her gaze snaps to attention, and I like how quickly her obedience shines through because this little monster is starved for the attention she deserves. *Attention she will only be getting from me.*

I grab the chains at the end of the bed and lock in both of her feet. She tests out the restraints, finding she has minimal movement.

Satisfied at having her entirely to myself and with nowhere to run, I circle her clit with my thumb and then insert another finger. A greedy little whimper escapes her as her legs twitch. I smirk knowingly. "You said you like my mouth on you? How else do you want me to break this perfect body of yours?"

"I want you to fuck me into oblivion," she replies breathlessly. I slam my fingers into her again, pleased by how soaked she already is.

"And are you going to choke on my cock like a good girl while I tongue fuck this sweet pussy of yours?"

She licks her lips and swallows. I stretch over her to open my bedside drawer, revealing the toys I bought specifically with her in mind.

"What are those?" she questions, unable to see what I'm pulling out of the drawer.

"Do you trust me?" I ask, mischief tingeing my voice.

She nods adamantly, and I lean down and kiss her.

Her body arches into mine as a little moan escapes her. I'll never get sick of hearing her begging noises.

"Then take my cock like a good girl, and don't ask questions," I growl as I flip around and nestle her face beneath my cock. I shove the tip toward her mouth and watch as she greedily tries to reach it. I stare at her sweet pussy, loving that she wore my color. I lower myself so she can lick the tip of my cock as I lap her cunt with my tongue.

I suck on her clit, then grab the small vibrator and rub it against her folds. She tries to squirm but can't, the restraints holding her in place. Her warm, wet mouth envelopes me, and she chokes as I slowly roll my hips, pushing myself into her throat.

I insert the small vibrator into her pussy, and her body arches, pulling at the chains as I suck on her clit. She whimpers around my cock as I shove it in harder, hitting the back of her throat. I stroke her time and time again, and whenever I think she's about to come, I back off, only allowing her to hungrily suck my cock.

By the third time I deny her climax, she bites my dick. Hard.

I chuckle, my cock twitching and wanting to shoot down her throat. But I plan on stretching this out all fucking night. I want to ruin her for any other man. I want her crawling to me on all fours, pleading for me to stuff her every hole with my cock.

"Be careful, Posie. I might just force you to swallow my cock all night."

Even if it breaks her jaw.

She won't get an orgasm until I think she's deserving of one.

I lift my hips high enough for her to gasp for air.

"Dutton, just fuck me. *Please.*"

I grin evilly as I grab the lube and squirt it on her asshole, then rub the cool liquid in circles around the opening. "Has anyone had this ass, Posie?"

It's a dangerous question, especially if she says yes.

She's panting, a sheen of sweat covering her skin, as she says, "No."

"Good. Tonight, I'm going to make you mine in every way," I say and shove my cock back into her mouth before she can reply. Her throat accepts me as I suck on her clit and press the toy against her asshole. And, ever so slowly, I begin to edge it inside. Hungrily licking between her lips and sucking on her clit, lapping up every fucking drop of her.

The vibrating toy is stretching me, and I feel like I'm being fucked senseless. Overstimulated by choking on his cock, his tongue on my clit, and the invasive toy at my ass. I moan as he inserts a finger between my legs.

"Relax," he croons, and I immediately do as he says, letting him fuck me in every which way he wants.

I'm so frustrated. He's had me teetering on the edge of an orgasm three times now, and every time I've been denied. I just need a fucking release. My jaw aches, but I'm being used like a fuckable doll, and I fucking love it.

I love that Dutton takes what he wants and uses me to get it. I love it because of the small kisses in between, the reminder that, although this man might be a monster, one with a voracious appetite, he's also checking on me throughout. However, tonight feels different. It feels like he will take and take and, in equal measure, give me an experience I've never had before and most likely will never have again.

The toy stretches my asshole as I squirm, resisting it.

"Relax, Posie. Accept it." I do as he says. The moment I do, I feel it enter me. And then he pulls it out and pushes it back in. *Oh. Ohhh.* I moan around his cock. Fuck me. A new kind of pleasure washes over me, and my eyes roll into the back of my head. Oh wow.

The sucking on my clit intensifies, and my body charges up, ready to explode in a way I haven't felt before. Then his mouth is gone, and I groan, frustrated, as he removes his cock from the back of my throat.

"What?" I gasp desperately. I was climbing, so close to coming.

He shifts so he's hovering above me, the toy still buzzing in my ass, putting me in a state of heightened pleasure, but not enough to get me anywhere. I thrash against the restraints.

"I swear to fuck, Dutton, you better make me come, or I'll fucking slit your throat in your sleep tonight."

He smiles, staring down at me like the devil himself. "There she is," he says as he strokes my cheek, his gold ring brushing my skin, and he pushes away a hair that's sticking to the perspiration on my throat.

His hand caresses down my neck and chest, his gaze trailing every inch of me in admiration. "So fucking perfect," he murmurs, as if to himself. But it fills me with pride. His hand comes back to my throat, and he squeezes as he says, "So delicate. So fiery."

"And now he's a fucking poet," I bite back.

He beams an arrogant smile as he casually leans back, and I can feel the moment he switches the toy in my ass up another level. I squirm under the heightened pleasure, and he seems pleased that he's made his point.

"You only make it worse for yourself, Posie."

"Not... if..." Fuck, I'm panting like a dog. I try to clear my throat. *"Please,"* I beg because I know it's what he's after.

He grabs a condom and rips it open with his teeth. I watch with heightened expectation as he rolls it over his thick cock. I try to move my legs, but they're like Jell-O. My arms ache from the lack of blood circulation. My wrists and ankles hurt from how tightly he's restrained me, and yet it brings me a pleasure I've never tasted before.

He lines his cock up at my entrance, rubbing it against my pussy. "Fuck, you're so wet."

"For you," I say quickly, hoping he doesn't tease me anymore.

"You're a quick learner."

He slowly and painfully shoves his cock into me, stretching me.

"Oh fuck." I moan at his size and the overstimulation of the toy buzzing in my ass. He stays there for a moment, impaled inside me, as he reaches up and grabs the headboard. He pulls, somehow managing to get deeper inside me, and I watch as the muscles in his arms flex.

He dips his head so his lips are hovering over mine. "Tell me who owns you, *Mostriciattola*."

"You," I breathe, without doubt. I'll tell him anything he wants to hear right now as long as he makes me fucking come. "Oh my God." He pulls out of me and then pushes back in. I don't break eye contact as he rolls his hips back and forth. It's a torturous pace, but not enough to immediately send me over the edge.

"You're going to soak my cock, aren't you, Posie so that I can have my dessert after."

I shake my head, and he smirks. That beautiful, devilish fucking smirk that's all sin.

He leans back slightly, and I scream, the vibration of the toy lodged in my ass growing in intensity.

"I can feel it too, Posie," he grits as he pumps into

me a little faster. "The toy is brushing against my cock through the thin layer between your ass and cunt. All of your holes belong to me."

"Yes." I can't even think. "Yes, it's all for you."

I'm out of my fucking mind, but I'm rewarded as his thrusts pick up speed. His blue eyes are the only thing I can focus on as my body goes into overdrive. The pleasure is so painful that I think I might break apart at any moment, and yet I can't seem to fall over the edge. But I pray for it. Beg for the release.

One of his hands slips between us, and I dip my gaze for a moment to watch him slamming into me. His finger circles my clit, and my body convulses with the stimulation.

I pull at the restraints, wanting to grab him, to cling to him for dear life. I'm exposed as he watches me come undone, drinking me in as I beg and cry, tears streaming down my face until that final climb.

His hips are slamming into me, and the shift is so sharp and sudden that I scream, my body arching off the bed as I explode into a thousand pieces. I want to hide away from the toy in my ass, the vibration too intense, as I come wave after wave after wave.

Dutton jerks into me, the circles on my clit turning into a leisurely caress as he slowly turns down the intensity of the toy in my ass to a gentle buzz.

I'm panting and coming, and all of me is a fucking beautiful, broken mess.

He chuckles as he pulls out of me and cups my pussy. He licks his fingers as he stares at me, looking more like a predator than a man.

"You didn't think we were done, did you, *Mostriciattola*?" he asks, a devilish glint in his eyes. And that's when I realize we haven't even scratched the surface of his stamina and depravations, and I'm already spent. But being tied up, I have nothing to do but to take it.

Oh no, what's a girl to do?

The man is a monster.

A monster with a hunger and sex drive I didn't think possible. When Dutton and I fuck, the most unhinged and rawest version of him comes out—tonight is the perfect example. And I'm sure I haven't even scratched the surface of his desires.

It makes me feel inexperienced, especially when comparing myself to a man who runs an empire in the sex industry. But I remind myself there's clearly something I have to offer him that keeps him coming back.

My head is on his chest as I lay there limply. I don't plan on sleeping over for the night, but I need at least an hour or two so I can feel my fucking legs and arms because right now, their official status is dead weight.

He's rubbing an ointment into my skin where the

restraints cut in, leaving red, raw marks. He doesn't seem apologetic for putting them there, and honestly, I quite like the way it stings.

Am I as twisted as he is and don't realize it? Sure, I earned money by putting my body on display for men and their fantasies, but I never let anyone have sex with me. Let alone... *this*.

I watch as he massages my wrists, the gold ring shining in the light coming in from the window. He's since turned on the electric fireplace, which crackles across the room. The sheets and blankets have been discarded on the floor.

"Where did you get this ring?" I ask. I don't know much about Dutton, and I don't plan on having heart-to-hearts with him since this is just sex, but I've always been curious about the square-shaped ring.

He raises his hand to look at it. "It's a painful addition for a right hook." I roll my eyes, and he chuckles, something I've noticed he's doing more lately. "My father gave it to me when I turned sixteen. The same night he divulged secrets of his past, I imagine he never shared with anyone. I was surprised he even told me. But my father's sly in those ways. He gives merit to everything he does, and it only hardened my resolve that, no matter what, I'll always protect my family. The wealth, power, and influence are who I am... entirely. But I'd be none of those things without my family. They wouldn't serve a purpose if I didn't have anyone to share it with."

My eyebrows wrinkle as I adjust myself to see him better. "So why haven't you started your own family, then?"

He chuckles again. "You sound like my parents." And there's more ammunition in that statement than I care to acknowledge.

"Do you not want marriage and children?"

"No," he simply says.

"Why?" Why wouldn't he want that if he cares so much for his family? Especially with the type of family he comes from. Legacy and all that shit?

"I make calculated steps in everything I do. I'm a man who lives and breathes my work. I won't let someone take that from me or lure my attention away.

"I'd be a terrible husband. I travel often and answer to no one. My wife would end up despising me, and my family would pity her. I'd suddenly look like an asshole for simply doing and being who I've been all along. Marriage is not for everyone. Especially for an asshole like me."

"Wow, you're surprisingly self-aware," I say, resting my head against his chest again. He chuckles, but I find it sad.

I think about my parents' marriage. My father traveled often for his sales job, but he and my mother always made time for each other. But I don't disagree with Dutton. Marriage isn't for everyone.

"Do you want those things?" he asks.

I sigh because it's been a loaded question for some time now. I didn't want to step into any relationship after how Bobbi treated me. I've watched so many unfaithful men come through Pearl, and yet, deep down, there's still the glimmer of a fantasy that there could be someone special out there for me. Someone who will love me for me and treat Bentley like his own son.

"I think so," I confess. "One day, I'd like Bentley to have a father, maybe even a sibling or two. I was an only child and loved my independence, but Bentley loves people. I think he'd thrive with a little sister to protect," I say with a smile.

Silence fills the room at the strangeness of the situation, of telling my boss about my desires for marriage and children after fucking him.

Especially when that fantasy man is so obviously not him.

A palpable tension wraps around us.

"Is Bentley's father dead?" he asks. I look up at

him, those ocean-blue eyes penetrating in their intensity.

I sigh, defeated. "No. I don't think he is. But I won't give you his name."

"Why not?" Dutton asks tightly, and I can see the vein in his neck bulge as he tries to angle himself to see me better.

"Because you're an unhinged asshole who apparently likes to do weird shit with knives. And I don't need you fighting my battles."

"You know, the moment you ask me to, I will fight them for you."

His sincerity catches me off guard, and so I sensually wiggle up his body. "You don't have to do anything for me other than fill every one of my holes. I don't need a knight in shining armor; I need you to keep me satisfied."

"Are you not satisfied?" he growls as he scoops me into his arms and slowly flips me onto my back. I can feel his very hard cock pressing against my inner thigh.

"I always think there's room for improvement." I'm punishing my bruised and swollen pussy right now, but I can't seem to get enough of this insufferable man.

"Your boss is very good at receiving constructive criticism," he says into my ear, and I laugh because

Dutton Taylor is anything but open to the opinion of others.

"I've managed to get into good favor with Striker again, but if we pull another stunt like you did in Boston a few weeks ago, I don't think I'll be able to save it twice, and that could cost me a lot of money," Eli tells me.

It was a miscalculation on my part to severely beat one of Striker's men, so perhaps Posie did me a favor by swearing me not to kill him because after I saw the fear in her eyes, I was about to.

I try not to smirk, thinking about all the delicious positions I put her in last night, pushing her past her limits. I thought I'd fuck her so thoroughly that she wouldn't be able to move for days, but somehow, she was still able to silently sneak out in the early hours of the morning while I slept.

I don't often sleep that deeply, but having her there

offers a comfort I don't entirely understand. It's terrifying as much as it is intriguing.

"Fuck off, Jewel!" Hawke snaps.

Eli stands abruptly from his seat at the back of his cinema room. "Watch how you speak to my wife," he growls, and Jewel is laughing as she completely obliterates Hawke in the video game they're playing.

"Down, Eli. I can handle myself. And besides, this is very satisfying," she says, smirking at him over her shoulder. Hawke sulks as he rolls his shoulders.

"It's about time we got a woman in here who can kick your ass, you big oaf," Billie says as she snatches the controller out of his hand to take her turn to play. If only my sister knew how accurate of an aim Eli's wife was in real life. She's a hitwoman and equally as dangerous as most of the men in this room.

Ford sits quietly with Ivy Walker, playing a game of chess. He's eating a slice of the cake Billie baked and brought over, and I swear the glutton eats every last piece every time; he has the biggest sweet tooth here, yet he's smaller in lean muscle mass than his brother.

"It's good that the deal isn't affected because of my miscalculation," I say, ignoring the others and taking a sip from the glass of whiskey in my hand. I look over the contract Eli is considering presenting to the MC to exchange weapon contacts and shipping for drug distribution in Boston. The deal could be highly profitable for us and silently extend our reach into the Boston area. He wouldn't even have to put much security or labor there since Striker's men would do most of it for him.

"It looks manageable and attractive on both ends," I say thoughtfully. Eli is a clever businessman. Granted, sometimes he's reckless, but only when he's thinking emotionally. The few times I've seen that happen mostly happened after Jewel entered his life. "I'm going to have to start charging you for looking over these." I smile as I put the contract down.

"As if being my cousin isn't payment enough," Eli says. "Besides, it's the least you can do after almost fucking this up for me."

My teeth grind, but I don't reply.

He takes a sip of his whiskey contemplatively. "So, any update on the blonde? I've heard you've promoted her from stripper to some social media role."

I glare at him because nobody seems to be able to keep their mouth shut in this family. But, at the very least, I owe him some explanation since I almost ruined this deal for him.

"Will found out everything about her. She lost her parents at sixteen. Fell in with the wrong crowd after. Ran away at eighteen and had a child."

"And how do you feel about that?"

"About what?"

"Her having a ki—"

"Fuck, you are too good! Are you sure you weren't a sniper in a previous life?" Billie exclaims, interrupting what Eli was saying. Like Hawke, she throws the controller, and he laughs and makes fun of her.

"I'm sorry, guys. That'll be fifty bucks," Jewel says, holding her hand out with a smug smile.

"Double or nothing!" Hawke yells.

"Fuck that, I'm out," Billie states. She comes over to me with her hand out. "Can I have fifty? I don't carry around cash."

"And you think I do?" I reply with a raised eyebrow.

She narrows her gaze on me. "You own strip joints. Of course, you do. You wouldn't want me to go back on my word in a bet, would you? That'd look so bad for the family."

Eli chuckles. "Remind me why I come to you as my advisor and not your younger sister."

Hawke and Jewel continue playing as I roll my eyes and pull a hundred-dollar bill for Billie because it's all I carry.

"Speaking of the blonde, why don't you invite her to my birthday party tomorrow?" Billie asks.

"She has a name," I growl, irritated that my sister was obviously eavesdropping. "Posie will not at all be interested in meeting my family."

She shrugs. "Yeah, but if you've invited Striker to this thing, why not invite her and see if they recognize each other? You'll see how deep their connection runs by their reactions. Surely, if the president of the motorcycle club recognizes her, she was a lot closer with them than just chilling with them for two years."

"I don't disagree with her," Ford interjects.

Eli grits out, "Have you all been fucking listening?"

Ford looks up at him then. "You usually discuss business in your office. You were the one who decided to talk in here. We're not to blame for your lack of discretion."

My jaw clenches. The only reason we're in here with them is because Eli refuses to let Jewel out of his sight, and Jewel has been inviting everyone over for more of these "gamer afternoons" to bring everyone together.

"It's not a request. It's a demand. Bring her to the party," Billie says with a smile. "You were the one who taught me not to ask for permission or forgiveness. It can be part of my birthday present. I'm kind of curious about the woman who has my ice king of a brother pussy whipped."

"I'm not pussy whipped," I growl.

"No? Then it should be easy to invite her. It serves as a means to an end, doesn't it?" she challenges, and I hate how much she understands how I think and work because I've used that exact same line on her numerous times.

"If she's only someone you're fucking, and there's no attachment, I somewhat agree with your sister," Eli adds.

A strange, twisted uncertainty torments me. We invited Striker in a show of good faith, bringing him into our home and including him in the celebration. I'm not so sure about Posie. Then again, what they're saying makes sense. If I deny them, they'll think I'm protecting her. But aren't I? I don't want to share her with them. Am I passing up an opportunity to make sure that Posie isn't a threat to my family if I refuse?

"I'm certain she's not part of their antics or a threat," I say to Eli, now that my sister's dismissed herself, assuming she'll get what she wants. And usually, I indulge her.

"But do you know that for certain? You thought she wasn't connected to them, and then she went to Boston, and you lost your shit and put someone in the hospital."

I pick up the whiskey, and another thought comes

to mind. What would my mother think of Posie? I don't know why I consider that. It shouldn't matter, should it?

Posie made it very clear last night that fucking is all she wants from me. But sometimes, my mother sees things in a light that I can't. I'm too cynical, so perhaps she'll be able to provide insight as to why this woman is so easily tormenting my every waking moment.

"Perhaps I'll bring her for a few hours, but if she's innocent and things go awry, I'll intervene."

Eli raises his scarred eyebrow. "How interesting that you have the urge to protect someone outside your family. Just don't ruin this deal for me."

Dutton: You still owe me a date.
Today.

I want to ignore it, but I know Dutton has the tendency to do whatever the fuck he wants, and him rocking up to my door uninvited is a very real possibility, even though I just saw him two nights ago.

I stare at the message, confused, before I press call, and his voice comes over the phone.

"A date?" I ask just as he says, "Well, hello."

"Don't hello me. Why are you asking me on a date? This is supposed to be sex only. Why are you trying to change things?"

"I never said it was only sex. And you still owe me a date."

"We can skip the formalities since we're only fucking," I say matter-of-factly, peeking around the corner of my living room to make sure Bentley can't hear me.

He sighs. "They know about you... my family, that is. Now my sister insists you attend her birthday party, and I'm not usually able to say no to her."

"I don't give a flying fuck about your sister complex. I hate people; it's why I have no friends," I tell him.

"That's good. I hate people, too. But not you," he replies. "But you do still technically owe me a date. Remember that little deal we made when you took the new job?"

Motherfucker. I didn't think he was serious about it or that he'd want to follow through, especially now that we're fucking. That's all this is, isn't it?

"People who only have sex don't meet family," I say.

"My family is different. And I wouldn't put it past them to invite themselves to your home if you don't come."

My jaw drops. "Are you fucking kidding me?"

"Do I sound like I'm joking?" he deadpans.

Jesus. I mean, if he's capable of showing up unannounced all the time, why do I think his family would act any differently?

"Please. We don't have to be there long."

"We say please now?" I ask, surprised.

"When the occasion calls for it. But don't tell my family I begged you to come."

"Is that what this is, begging?"

"I can get on my knees and show you begging in different ways if you'd like. In fact, I'd much prefer to convince you in other ways."

I bite my bottom lip, trying not to laugh. I peek back through the living room at Bentley. Today was our day together. "I have a son; I can't just up and leave."

"Bring him."

"To what, a party where dangerous people are? I'm protective of him, Dutton."

"He'll be fine. I can assure you he won't be safer in any other house than the one we're taking him to," he says as if his reassurance is enough.

I believe him to a degree, but how can a man who doesn't have a child understand the protective nature of a parent? Part of me is curious to see what type of people Dutton's family are. I'm sure they're all cold and calculated, but I have to squash that curiosity.

"No," I tell him.

The thought of going out sounds nice, but when it comes time to leave, I don't want to. This is a real dilemma I seem to have.

"I'm at your door already."

This arrogant asshole.

"Okay, so you can also leave it." I walk to the door and pull it open to find him standing there. "How long have you been there for?" I ask, still holding the phone to my ear. He has the audacity to be holding a bouquet of roses and what appears to be a box of Lego.

"Dutton!" Bentley yells from behind me.

I hang up the phone, and he pockets his.

"Are you here to bribe me and my son?"

He hands me the flowers but makes no move to touch me in front of my son, which I appreciate. He then awkwardly hands the other present to Bentley. "I don't have wrapping paper, but when I was his age, I loved building things such as LEGO."

I can't help but snort and break my serious expression at his awkward attempt to connect with a child.

"Can I really take this?" Bentley asks me with wide eyes.

I nod, and he squeals as he takes it. I try to keep my smile hidden because I don't want to reward or approve of Dutton's attempts to wedge himself into my life.

"You shouldn't spoil him," I say as Bentley tries to rip open the box.

"I can tell the way you look at your son that you

spoil him enough as it is. A LEGO set here or there isn't going to hurt." I don't know why it takes me off guard. He's obviously been paying attention in the few interactions he's had with my son.

"Want to come to a party?" Dutton asks Bentley, ignoring everything we just discussed. My teeth grind. On second thought, this guy is still definitely an asshole.

"Party? I love parties," Bentley says as he turns to me. "Can we go?"

"Nice. Use my son against me," I say, unimpressed.

"If that's what it takes."

I lean down and kiss Bentley on the head. "Go and put that in your room for now. Don't forget to say thank you."

"Thank you, Mr. Bossman Dutton!" he says before running off excitedly.

"I don't like people," I reiterate, holding the huge bouquet. "And you know buying me this shit doesn't work on me."

"But your son sure seems to like people, and you can do whatever you want with the flowers as long as you keep the lingerie sets." He grins wickedly.

I let out a breath as I feel my temper rising. This guy just pushes and pushes. Not that I mind it in the bedroom. Flashes of a few nights ago come to mind, and I avert my gaze from him, trying not to think so fondly of this man right now while he's pissing me off.

It's true, though. Bentley loves people because he hasn't been hurt by this world and doesn't understand how cruel life can be. I certainly plan on protecting him from that as much as possible. I hope when I die, he won't be as lonely as I was when my parents died. That part kills me the most because no matter how much I want to protect him, I'm also isolating him. I can't blame it on Dutton, but he makes me more aware of the bubble we've been living in.

"What's the dress code?" I ask, and he looks me up and down. I'm wearing a skirt and a plain white shirt.

"What you have on is fine."

"So help me God, if I walk into this party and I'm dressed like this while other people are dressed up, I will kill you."

"Okay, so they may all be dressed up, but that's how they are; they love clothes."

"That's better." I shut the door in his face and head to my room. I'm pulling a few things out of drawers as Bentley runs in.

"Are we going to the party?!" he asks eagerly.

"Change into your best black pants," I tell him. He grins and runs to his room with another excited squeal. I can't help but smile. He doesn't have many fancy clothes, as he's so young, but I took him out in a new outfit for his birthday, and he's been asking me when he can wear it again. Even though it hasn't been all that long, I'm not sure if it fits him anymore—he's growing so fast. I guess we're about to find out.

I put on a simple black dress, followed by some basic black heels, just as Bentley comes running back in. The pants still fit him, barely, though I can tell he won't be able to wear them much longer. He also has his button-up shirt on, the buttons not quite matching the holes.

What am I doing? And why am I doing it?

This isn't me. I told myself not to do things for a man again. Look where it got me last time. And I try to tell myself this thing with Dutton is nothing serious. But letting Dutton around Bentley in any capacity is serious for me, and so I'll make it my mission to have a proper conversation with Dutton after this. It's not just my feelings that have to be considered; it's Bentley's feelings as well. And Dutton can't assume he has free rein to come and go as he pleases.

"Ready," Bentley says enthusiastically. I look down at his big brown eyes. I can't say no to this little guy.

I already know he's going to be talking about this for days.

"Yep. Best behavior, remember," I tell him. He

nods before he turns and runs back to the door, pulling it open to let Dutton inside. Surprisingly, he waited outside after I closed the door on him. Bentley begins telling him about the new Transformers movie he watched, and I smile as Dutton tries his best to follow along.

THIRTY-TWO
DUTTON

She hasn't stopped fidgeting since we walked into the restaurant. There is a small private area at the back for events, and the room is filled with very powerful people. Still, I don't concern myself with it because I know Posie isn't intimidated or made uncomfortable by the status or power of others.

I don't like the idea of being pressured into inviting her, but I'd be lying if I said I didn't want to spend more time with her, and a small part of me is curious to see what my mother thinks of Posie as well. Not that we're serious or anything; at least I'm telling myself that. But I can't seem to remove myself from her side as I stare down any man who so much as looks in her direction. Maybe this was a bad idea after all.

Posie grips her son's hand, and I glance down at

him. I don't hate kids, but usually they annoy the fuck out of me, so I stay as far away from them as possible. But this one seems okay... so far.

"Drink?" I ask her. I reach out to touch her, but she glares at my hand as if it's on fire. So I drop it back to my side, the message clear. *Do not fucking touch me around my son.*

"Water," she replies.

"Really?"

"Do you have a problem with my choice, or would you like to force my hand in that as well?"

My lips twitch, and her gaze narrows as if knowing I'm trying not to smile. Her fiery temper always amuses me. That's why she reminds me of a little monster when she explodes. I wouldn't give a flying fuck if she lost it at me right now in front of my family because part of me knows she enjoys acting like a brat around me; it only makes her punishments worse, which she just so happens to fucking love.

When I return with a water and an orange juice for Bentley, she silently thanks me.

A waiter walks around with food, and Bentley tugs at her hand. She grabs one of the little burgers and then hands it to him. He immediately shoves it in his mouth, and my eyebrows shoot up, surprised by what appears to be an insatiable appetite.

"He's hungry," Posie says, looking around the room and past the people standing around and talking.

"Okay." I approach the waiter and grab the whole tray from his hand. He seems confused until he notices who I am and awkwardly bows. Then his cheeks flush red when he realizes there was no need to bow, though I don't dislike it. I put the platter on a nearby table and wave a hand to Posie and Bentley.

"Eat," I order Bentley. The kid doesn't waste any time before he climbs onto the chair and sits, grabbing the first mini burger.

"Thank you," Posie says. She looks at me inquisitively now. "You haven't been around kids much, have you?"

I'm searching for my sister and parents when I say, "I speak to children in the same manner I speak to adults. I don't dumb down my vocabulary. If I do, how will they learn?"

She chuckles, and although I spot my sister, who is laughing at something one of her friends says, I can't help but turn my gaze back to Posie. "What?" I ask, confused.

"I just wonder what type of kid you must've been or if you were always just a well-polished businessman."

"Don't you prefer calling me Frosty the Snow-man?" I grumble.

"He read lots of books," my father says as he appears beside us. Posie whips her head in his direction. "And had he not, I dare say Eli wouldn't have been much rougher. Dutton was quiet, and many of the children were scared of him, especially if they tried to play with his sister, who he treated like his only friend." He smiles warmly, then adds, "It's lovely to see you here, Posie."

He then leans in and kisses her on the cheek. My jaw tics, and I know I shouldn't be jealous of my own father, but, fuck, I am. Everyone falls for his charm, and I've never cared about that magnetism he's used on people over the years until now.

"Thank you for inviting us, Mr. Taylor," she says, but I can tell by the way her throat constricts that she's uncomfortable, especially as she places her hand on her son's shoulder, as if in reassurance.

My father's gaze lands on Bentley, but my sister abrasively cuts in before he can ask about him. Suddenly, I recall how overwhelming this family can be. My mother follows her, looping her elbow with my father's.

"Wow, you actually came!" Billie yells as she throws herself at me. She's already a little tipsy, and I immediately scan the area to see how many men are here. I see Hawke, Ford, Eli, and Jewel, and the moment they spot me, Hawke starts laughing. Most likely, knowing precisely what I'm thinking.

"Dutton, introduce me!" Billie demands, hands on hips as she looks at Posie. Before I can say anything, Billie throws herself onto Posie in a hug. "I'm Billie, the better of the siblings."

Posie seems startled but awkwardly puts a hand on her back. "It's lovely to meet you, and I can't say I disagree."

I pull my sister away, jealous that she's allowed to hug Posie when I'm the one fucking her. But Posie has an issue with me touching her right now, so I'm not making exceptions for anyone else—except for her son.

"This is Posie. And the little man eating all the burgers here is her son, Bentley," I tell the group.

"Hi!" Bentley says with a big smile, swinging his legs and looking entertained. Then again, it might have to do with the bigger-than-life tray of food he has all to himself.

"You have a son?" my father asks with a smile.

"I do," Posie answers cautiously.

"Sons are the best," my mother says, reaching for my arm and squeezing it before releasing it quickly.

"I'm Honey, Dutton's mother. It's lovely to meet you. My goodness. You're beautiful."

A blush streaks over Posies cheeks. "I agree, sons are wonderful. I would be lost without Bentley," Posie says, just as my father walks off. "Happy birthday," she says to Billie, and despite the family ambush, she holds her own. "I'm sorry I didn't get you a gift."

"That's okay. Dutton plans to give me his credit card so I can go shopping," Billie says with a mischievous smile. If you and Bentley are free, we can go shopping together." She taps her fingers together deviously. "I'm sure he irritates you as much as he does me, so every year, it's become a tradition that I release that years' worth of pent-up anger toward him by spending his money. Let's just say I spend *a lot*. But then I always feel better and love my brother again afterward."

Posie laughs as she says, "I think I'd be deserving of a house on the water at the very least."

Billie brightens, encouraging her as I roll my eyes. "See, she gets it! And if you're dating my brother, I assume he owes you more than just a house. What do you think, little man?"

"I'd like a boat," Bentley says around a mouthful as he picks a bit of the meat out of the burger. Damn, even the kid's ganging up on me.

"Since when?" Posie asks him.

"Since Dutton got me a LEGO Transformer boat," he says innocently. My mother and sister look at me, and I can tell the moment my mother's gaze softens that there's something in it I don't entirely understand.

My father returns with a glass of water and hands it to Bentley. "Here. Your mouth will get dry with all that food," he says to Bentley, who smiles up at him.

Posie shoots a glance my way, and I can tell by the way her muscles are bunched that she's minorly freaking the fuck out. I've seen it before, but it's only now that I realize how protective she is of her son. Of course, it doesn't sit well with me that she feels she needs to protect him from my family... or me.

The more I feel her placing that wall up between us, the more I want to shatter it because I know mine has been lowering around her for weeks now. And there's nothing I can do about it.

I don't like that I like his family. In fact, I feel so comfortable around them that it makes me want to run. His father made me feel awkward the first time I met him in Dutton's office, and now he's getting my son a glass of ice water so his mouth doesn't go dry from the burgers.

It's weird. And they're nothing at all like Dutton.

Where Dutton is cool and calculated, his mother and sister are full of life and shine so brightly that it's almost intimidating.

Everything I've read about this family paints them in a bad light, yet I like them.

I also find it interesting to watch how other people act around Dutton. Most are wary of him, which is expected, but his family is clearly the exception. Even as his sister talks with him, he acts as if he's indifferent, but I can tell he's listening attentively. She's lecturing him about something, and he's indulging her, and when he looks at her, his eyes are filled with love. He might not understand what it's like to have a child, but he certainly isn't unfamiliar with doing anything in his power for his family. This is obvious since he dragged me here just because his sister asked him to.

"So, we meet again," Dawson drawls as he stands beside me. Honey is building a card tower with Bentley. Despite hosting a party for their daughter, it appears Bentley is getting most of their attention.

"We do," I say as we watch his wife and my son play together. I glance at Dawson and admire the way he stares at Honey. There's so much love in his gaze, and I almost envy it. It's how my parents used to look at each other.

Although their son might not know how to act around children, it's very clear his parents adore them.

"Any update with you and my son? Have things changed between the two of you, by chance?" he asks with a too-innocent smile. And I can't help almost smiling back, because I realize behind the businessman, there might be a man who has a little bit of cheek in him, just like Dutton. I imagine not everyone gets to see this, not from these powerful men who have built their reputation on being ruthless. But I've seen how Dutton cares for his employees and ensures their safety, especially the women. I suppose it's because of this man that he learned those values.

"He's still just my boss," I reply.

Dawson's smile curves wider. "Ah. Yes, of course. I was my wife's boss once upon a time as well."

Honey looks up at him as if knowing he's speaking about her. She's beautiful beyond measure. I can tell where his sister gets her looks from; she strongly resembles her mother. And while Dutton takes more after his father, I can also see Honey in him.

"It's not like that," I inform him.

"Yet here you are, at a family function. Want to know how many women Dutton has ever introduced to us?"

"Not really," I mutter, which makes him laugh. "And it was more like I was dragged here by your son. Not that I'm not grateful to be here," I add that last bit so I don't seem rude.

"He's brought none." I turn back to him to see him raise a brow. "We wanted to meet you. And although we admittedly had to apply some pressure for him to agree to bring you, it doesn't take away from the fact that he did, in the end, bring you... and your son. Dutton sometimes needs a push in the right direction."

I laugh at that. "With all due respect, Mr. Taylor, you don't know me. You don't know if pushing him in my direction is the right thing. I'm a single mother, focusing only on her son and his future."

"Yes," Dawson agrees. "Which is precisely why you're perfect for him. For all my son's achievements, he needs to focus on something other than himself and his empire. I don't think I've seen anyone take his attention like you have, and that speaks volumes, whether you or he want to admit it."

I go to speak but can't find the right words. The pressure of it makes me want to run the other way. I can't outright tell his father we're only having casual sex because it feels like it'd only offend him.

Dutton excuses himself from his conversation with Billie, and when Dawson notices, he turns to his wife and Bentley. "Now, Bentley, how about some ice cream?"

"He's allergic to nuts," I'm quick to say.

"Good to know," he replies as Bentley hops down from the chair, and Dawson offers him his hand. Out of habit, I immediately reach for Bentley to protect him. But Bentley smiles big at Dawson and practically skips over to him, then slides his hand in Dawson's. Just as they walk off, Dutton is back at my side. He makes no attempt to touch me. Slowly but surely, this man is learning to respect my boundaries.

"He's safe. My father is many things, but kids love him, and he loves them. He was a great father." I look at him then, taking my eyes off Bentley as he and Dawson go to the front of the restaurant to order the ice cream.

"You don't need to sell me on anything," I say.

"Sell you on anything?" He gives me a quizzical look.

"Yes. Why am I here, Dutton? My son is very important to me, and introducing him to strange people willy-nilly isn't okay."

His eyebrows furrow. "My family aren't 'strange people,' and I wanted to introduce you to them."

"Why?" I urge.

"You confuse the ever-loving fuck out of me. I could ask you the same thing. Why do you leave every morning before I wake up?"

I'm baffled. Is he really upset about that? I thought that's what men preferred. No strings attached or awkward mornings. "We only agreed to fuck, not tell each other our life stories." I give him my best eye roll and then look away to find Bentley again. He now has an ice cream cone in his hand, and Dawson hands him a napkin.

"Are you ever going to tell me who his father is?"

I sigh, irritated that he's pressing me all of a sudden when he won't answer my fucking questions. "He's dead for all I care."

"So he *is* dead, or you wish he were?" he pushes.

"Why are you asking so many questions but won't answer mine?" I stare at him.

He reaches for my wrist, but I pull away. His eye twitches as he nods toward a corner of the room. It looks to be a private bathroom. "You clearly need to be punished."

"You can't be serious right now. Here?" I whisper-shout.

"Your son is safe with my father. Do you really think I'd bring you to a place where you or your son aren't protected?"

I want to argue with him and tell him I never asked for his protection, but the urgency in his gaze has me stepping toward the bathroom. As we approach, a woman exits. After waiting until no one is paying us any attention, I enter, and Dutton slips in behind me. A light automatically turns on, and he locks the door behind us. It's a powder room with two toilet stalls.

When I turn around to berate him, his lips crash into mine. My brain fries as I try to register what's happening. He already has my hands behind my back, locked in a tight grip.

My body melts against him, all of my frustration rising to the surface.

"Why are you here?" he growls, pushing me against the counter. My arms begin to ache, but I appreciate the burn as I try to break free of his grasp.

I bite down on his lip as I viciously say, "Because you invited me."

"You could have said no. It's not like you don't know how to use that word." He's kissing along my jaw and down my neck. My hips begin rolling of their own accord.

"I did say no," I reply breathlessly, arching into him.

He releases his grip around my wrists, then orders, "Hands on the counter, and they don't move." I do as he says because he immediately rewards me by putting his hand up my dress. He wastes no time pushing my panties to the side and pinching my clit.

Fuck. He's mad.

"You can't demand answers when you're not willing to hand them over yourself. Do we understand each other?" he declares. His intense blue gaze has darkened with lust, and I flick a glance at his pants, where his cock is straining against the material. I lick my lips, wanting more than just his hand on my pussy.

"Are you going to put that to good use?" I ask, pointedly staring at his cock. He squeezes my cheeks and angles my head to look up at him.

"This is a punishment, not a reward," he chastises.

"Seems like punishment for you, too," I bite back.

A tic jumps in his jaw. "You'll beg for this cock like a good girl, *Mostriciattola.*"

I moan as he shoves against me, and I can feel his cock poking into my stomach. "To answer your question, I can't get enough of your sharp tongue or this cunt of yours. You can label it whatever the fuck helps you sleep at night, but let me assure you, you're not getting rid of me anytime soon."

I fucking hate him as much as I crave him.

"Do you understand?" he growls. "And don't you dare fucking say no."

He brings his face close to mine, inhaling me. My gaze jumps from his lips to his eyes, like I'm desperate for him. My appetite for him grows and grows.

"I won't play games," I say breathlessly, which is better than a no.

He smiles then, and it's anything but the charming gesture he sometimes offers others. No, this is all feral

—the monster beneath. "You're the only one who's been playing games, Posie. *Let me in.*"

There's so much loaded into that last sentence. Is it a request or a command? I don't know what he wants or how this will end, but I feel a small part of my guard slip as I breathlessly say, "Okay."

His expression softens ever so slightly as if he wasn't expecting my submission.

"Get on your knees so I can feed you my cock," he demands. "You don't get sweet nothings today. You're going to be brutally fucked to within an inch of your life for the hell you've been putting me through."

He releases my jaw, and I drop to my knees obediently, licking my lips as if grateful to be granted permission to unzip his pants and free his cock. I swallow because the size of him startles me every time.

I slide my mouth over his cock, rolling my tongue around its thick head. His hands thread through my hair, and he growls, "Look at me as I fuck your filthy, defiant mouth."

I look up at him through my eyelashes as he slowly rocks his hips into my mouth. He hits the back of my throat every time, and I choke, and then he begins thrusting almost angrily, punishing me for my defiance during the day.

This is definitely not a reward, and yet I'm getting

wetter by the second as he ruthlessly fucks my mouth. It is as if this brutal claim is the only way he can communicate something unsaid.

Tears stream down my face as he grunts, fucking my throat like it's his personal toy.

"Fuck, you're so perfect," he grits out, and it floods me with pride. "You like my cock, don't you?"

I can't nod, so I make a sound of agreement because I do. I love the way he overpowers me, the way he feeds off my defiance and turns it into something so pleasurable. I love the way he threatens to punish me but always gives me the best orgasms I've ever experienced.

Fuck. This man, in all his ruthless beauty, is so hard to deny.

"Are you going to swallow my cum like a good girl?"

I make another noise, choking on his cock.

He smirks, and it's devilish and sinister. "That's not good enough, *Mostriciattola*. I want to come in that sweet mouth of yours and mark my territory from the inside."

Fuck, I'm dripping.

"Are you ready to take me raw like a good girl?"

I nod eagerly, desperately even.

He pulls out of my mouth and tugs me up by my

hair. He immediately grabs me by the throat and hoists me onto the counter. His hand is up my dress and dragging down my panties in seconds.

He's circling my clit with heavy, firm movements, and I whimper under his bruising touch. Today, I really pushed him; I can tell by the way he's taking it out on me through sex. But I fucking love it. Thrive on it.

He kisses me—more like devours me—as he rubs himself against my folds. He yanks me toward him, and I jerk back, almost hitting my head on the mirror, but he's quick to catch me.

I scream as he impales me, the movement so fast and jolting that I don't even have time to breathe or adjust around his size. He cradles my head as he begins pounding into me, and I can only press my palms against the mirror behind me as I come undone.

The slapping of our skin is the only sound I can hear, and the music and chatter outside the door fade into the background.

I whimper as he bruises me with punishing kisses.

"Fuck, you drive me insane," he grits.

I wrap my arm around him, clawing my nails down his shirt, claiming him in the same way he often likes to leave marks on me. Because I'd be lying if I didn't admit there's some truth to whatever this is between us. That this man of ice knows how to match my inner fire.

"I'm sorry," I breathe out, not thinking straight as he rattles my brain from how hard he's fucking me.

Tingles move up my legs, and I'm startled by how quickly this raw fucking is getting me over the line.

"No, you're not!" he seethes between kisses. He's biting, sucking, tugging, and it's my undoing. I moan, clinging to him with my nails digging into his back as I wrap my legs around his waist.

"Please. Please. Dutton," I beg.

"Tell me what you want," he says with urgency as he grunts.

"You," I whisper without thought.

"Fuck!" he shouts as he breaks. This carefully put-together man comes apart inside me as he jerks and then rests his head on my shoulder. I buck under him, seeing stars as I orgasm and squirt all over his cock and the counter.

I can't breathe. I try to calm my shaky breaths as I cradle his head to my shoulder, shuddering around him as he jerks inside me again. Heavy panting slowly begins to fall into slow, rhythmic breaths as he leans back and looks at me, that intensity ever blazing in his eyes.

I'm startled when he gently cups my jaw and kisses me. It's slow and sensual, as if he's thanking me.

I melt into him, caught off guard by how something so raw and feral can turn into something so... sweet and endearing. I don't even know what we were arguing about before or how it led to now.

My legs stop shaking as he pulls away, and the moment his lips part from mine, I want to pull him back to me, but the reality of how long we might've been gone sinks in.

He's quick to tuck himself away as I adjust my dress. I look at the mess we made, unsure what to do. He chuckles as he grabs a hand towel. "Let me."

I scrunch my nose up, shocked by what we just did. "That's kind of gross."

"I don't mind you walking around with my cum dripping down your legs, Posie."

"Clean it," I deadpan, and he chuckles.

As he does so obediently, I watch him, wanting him over again. The urgency of it has become increasingly apparent the more time we spend together. And that's concerning because, somehow, this man with a heart of ice is getting into my bloodstream.

"I'm on birth control, by the way," I inform him.

I've only been with one other man, and the night I fell pregnant with Bentley was because we were both so drunk that we'd forgotten to use protection. The nurse had told me the chances were slim to get pregnant so easily, but since then, I haven't taken any chances.

"I don't fuck women without condoms. Well, usually."

"Are you fucking other women?" The question is out of my mouth before I even realize. I sounded... accusatory.

He raises an eyebrow but looks me dead in the eye. "You're plenty enough to handle. And, no, I haven't been with anyone else since you walked your tight ass into my club."

I roll my eyes. "I doubt that." Because men say shit to make women feel special. Until they get what they want, and they're done with them.

He finishes cleaning my legs and then kisses me again. It's hot and heavy and ever so demanding, just like before. Dutton breaks the kiss, and his gaze penetrates when it meets mine. "You are my only focus. So stop trying to push me away. And I swear to God, if you're comparing me to other men..." he growls.

I shove him away. "Yeah, I get it. You're going to carve messages into their chests. Well, if *I* find out you're sleeping around, I might be inclined to use my bat."

"That sounds like a jealous girlfriend," he says, following me to the door. I comb my fingers through my hair and then wipe the makeup smudged around my eyes. I'm red and raw all around my mouth, and it's obvious what we've just been doing, but there's no helping that.

I turn to him with my hand on the doorknob. "I never said I'd use the bat on the women."

He chuckles as I open the door and re-enter the lively party. I search for Bentley, spotting him laughing at something Dawson and Honey are saying to him. I can see they've somehow found him a coloring book and pencils.

I begin making my way over to him, but Billie, who is dancing with a girlfriend, grabs my attention.

"Hey, did you want to dance?" she slurs, a little drunker than when we last spoke.

"I don't dance," I tell her, and Dutton coughs behind me.

"Oh, okay. Well, what about a drink?" She holds up her glass. "I also really want to escape... but family." She gives me an eye roll.

"Hey, we're not all bad!" says a woman with short blonde hair, blue eyes, and a curvaceous figure.

"Pssh. You're the chosen ones," Billie mumbles. "This is Ivy Walker. And the red-haired one is Hope

Ivanov. And this sharpshooter here is Jewel Monti. But don't draw too much attention to her, or Eli will come and steal her. It took me so long just to get her to stand here."

"Not a dancer or a big drinker," Jewel says with a smile. There's something edgy about her, but I imagine marrying a mafia boss, you'd have to be. "I never thought I'd see the day a woman would woo Dutton."

He glares at her over my shoulder, and I can't help but want to laugh, realizing he really is just an ass to everyone. "I still can't believe you fell for my cousin's lack of charm," he bites back.

"At least he tried to charm me. You just chloroformed me the first time we met," she replies.

My head whips in his direction, and he shrugs. "She infiltrated a party."

"Don't worry. I threw a dagger in Eli's leg, so I'm not all rosy." She winks at me, and I'm baffled how casually they talk about this stuff. Definitely not your ordinary family.

"Will you come out with us next time we organize a girls' night?" Billie asks, and she looks like she's almost pleading with me. I realize then that all of these women seem to be around my age. Although all entirely different from each other, they're freely and unapologetically living their lives. It's something I'd recently been wanting to explore again—time for myself. Fun. And I know without a doubt this group of women would be a wild time.

"Maybe, if I can work it out with Bentley's babysitter," I tell her, meaning it. "Happy birthday, and thanks for letting me crash the party. I hope you get fucked up; that's always my favorite thing to do on my birthday. But if you'll excuse me, I think it's time I take my son home."

She lunges for me, wrapping me in a hug, and I'm stunned once again by how welcoming his family is. "Okay, but I'll hold you to that night of getting fucked up sometime."

"If Posie has a free night, I can assure you she'll be spending it with me," Dutton says. She pokes her tongue out at him, and I can't help but laugh as I turn to find Bentley.

He spots me first and smiles big. "Momma! Mr. Dawson said I can have this coloring book. Look, it's Transformers."

"That's very specific," I say, looking at Dawson.

"It didn't take long for my assistant to get one from the shops. I have a whole bag of other options here, too, if you'd like to take them home," he offers. Honey is smiling sweetly behind him. Okay, now I understand why I have the impression Dutton was spoiled as a kid.

"Tell them thank you, but it's time we leave," I say to Bentley.

"Close to bedtime?" Honey asks, her smile lines evidence of the bright, happy person she is.

"This kid needs more beauty sleep than I do." I chuckle, picking him up and putting him on my hip.

I bump into someone. At first, I thought it was Dutton, but then the smell of leather hits me.

I hate the smell of leather.

It reminds me of one person.

"Posie, is that you?"

My stomach drops at the familiar voice, and my gaze meets the dark brown eyes of Waylon Striker. When I left Boston, he was a member of the same motorcycle club as Bobbi.

I liked Waylon. He was nice... Well, as pleasant as a ruthless biker could be. One night, I saw him beat someone's head in for talking back to one of his men. Then he proceeded to get drunk a few minutes later like it never happened. But he always had respect for women, though I can't say the same for the rest of the men he worked alongside. What the fuck is he doing here?

"Long way from home, girl," he says.

"Do you two know each other?" Dutton asks, quick to size Waylon up. I'm ashamed of the way I use

Dutton as a shield to keep Waylon from seeing Bentley, but I know he's already seen him.

Waylon is dressed in black jeans and a long-sleeved black shirt, and his face has days' worth of scruff. I've always found him super attractive, in that perfect bad-boy way.

"Don't tell him you saw me here," I beg, and all the fire that's usually in my tone feels like it's been sucked out of me.

"Bentley, let's meet your mother outside," Dawson says, reaching for him. At first, I'm reluctant to hand over my son, but Bentley goes willingly, and I'm honestly grateful for Dawson getting him away from Waylon.

Eli and the twins stop a few feet away, looking on.

Why is Waylon here?

"He went looking for you, you know," Waylon says, referring to Bobbi.

A shudder runs through me. I bite my lip as Dutton's hand anchors on my hip, and for once, I welcome his touch, if only to feed me strength. Waylon notices, his brow raising as his gaze swings to Dutton.

"I'd suggest you listen to the lady," Dutton tells him.

Waylon raises his hands in the air and shakes his head.

"You know I don't want any bad blood with you, Dutton." Waylon looks back at me. "But, Posie, you know he'll eventually find out if that's his kid."

"He threw money at me and told me to fix the problem," I hiss. "So I did. I left."

A flash of understanding passes over Waylon's expression. "He still loves you."

"No, he loves control. Nothing more."

The tension is palpable as Waylon glances back at Dutton, who looks like he's ready to snap Waylon's neck at any moment. But the last thing I want is to start a fight between these two men. I know Dutton can hold his own, but I've seen the levels of loyalty and violence Waylon offers.

Besides, the desperate need to run is flooding my bloodstream.

"I was invited by your cousin," Waylon says, gesturing at Eli. "But it seems I might be unwelcome after all, and I hold no ill will about that." He places his drink down. I glare at him as he turns to leave. When he walks past Dutton, he offers a curt nod. Eli follows him out.

What the ever-loving fuck is he doing here in Manhattan?

"Fuck," I murmur, beelining straight for Bentley. I grab him and thank Dawson before I hurry outside. I see Waylon get on his motorcycle. Just before he slides on his helmet, he nods at me. And I know he'll tell Bobbi he saw me and where. Which means it's only a matter of time before he comes for me.

"Where are you going?" Dutton questions.

A car pulls up to the curb, and I realize it's Dutton's. Dutton tips the valet and takes the keys. "Get in the car, Posie."

I buckle Bentley into his booster seat in the back, and then I climb into the passenger seat.

With a calm voice, I ask, "Why was Waylon Striker at that party?"

Dutton seems to understand my tone. Despite Bentley almost falling asleep immediately, I don't want him overhearing us having an intense conversation.

"My cousin has business with him. It's not uncommon to invite those we're in business with to family events such as these as a gesture of goodwill." My jaw clenches as he asks, "And how do you know the president of the Boston Delinquents?"

"Waylon's the president? Since when?" I whip my head to face him but quickly glance at Bentley to make sure I haven't woken him.

"For a year now," Dutton tells me, and I sink back in the seat. I just want this all to go away. "Why are you so scared of that club? What are you running from?"

When I don't answer, he falls silent. We've come a long way from the insufferable man always demanding answers. I don't know why I don't want to tell Dutton. I know he's a powerful man and could protect us, but I don't want to ever have to depend on a man again. I also don't want anyone revisiting the past with me.

The more I tell Dutton, the more I'll come to depend on him. Won't I? And then he'll leave me. It's only a matter of time. But what if my stubborn pride is preventing me from taking advantage of the best way to protect Bentley?

Fuck.

I need to think.

My knee is bouncing out of control as we arrive at my house. We get out of the car, and I grab a passed-out Bentley from the back seat and then try to grab his booster, but Dutton stops me. "I can get that," he says, then unlatches it with an efficiency a man who doesn't have kids shouldn't have. By the time he meets me at the door, I'm struggling to get the keys out of my bag, so he helps me and unlocks the door.

"Posie." His voice is quiet. "Let me understand," he pleads.

"You can go now. Thanks for tonight," I tell him, walking inside.

I'm not ready to accept this man into my home, into my family, and my heart. Surely, I'm just a novelty to him, a season that will pass. I need to find someone who's ready to become a pillar for me and Bentley.

I hear the front door close as I carry Bentley to his room and lay him down in his bed. After removing his shoes, I tuck him in.

I've only ever thought of Bentley, and the more time I spend with Dutton, I want to be selfish. I want to spend even more time with him. But won't that take away my time with my son? I try to push back all of my irrational fears.

My heart is not ready to be disappointed, even though I've told myself for so long that I'm okay with what I have.

But I realize I'm using my son as an excuse to keep us in a bubble. I thought I was protecting us, but have I been doing more harm than good?

When I walk back toward the living room, I sigh guiltily because Dutton's silhouette is visible against the glass beside the door.

This man doesn't know how to give up, and I hate how much it's starting to wear me down. I tell him I hate it, but a small part of me is beginning to fall for it, to expect it almost. And I know I'll feel winded when he's not there anymore.

When I open the door, he straightens and turns to face me. He looks so out of place in his perfectly tailored suit, the porch light shining down on him. This exceptionally wealthy, successful, and beautiful man is sitting at my front door, just waiting for me.

"I'm sorry," I say. "I know I can be short-tempered. I... I get scared about what might happen to me and Bentley in the future. I want to make sure he's safe. I hate his father with every fiber of my being, and I don't want to give you his name so you don't get caught up in my mess."

"Do you want me to kill him?"

"What?"

"The man you seem to be terrified of. Do you want me to kill him?"

"You'd do that?" It's not much of a surprise that Dutton kills people, but this is him outright admitting it. Again, I should be terrified of him, and he should be more careful as to who he trusts with this information.

"Yes, I will, if that's what you want." And I know he means it.

I hate that the offer is appealing, which is an ugly side of me. It'd be easy to wipe this world of Bentley's father and never have to worry again. A small part of me feels protected by Dutton, knowing he'd go to such lengths for Bentley and me. But I can't help but be cautious because that would mean he would hold something over me for the rest of my life. And I never want to give another man that much power. That, and it'll direct attention to his family if he were to kill Bobbi. It could get them killed. I know his family is powerful and deadly in their own right, but this isn't their burden to carry.

"No, I don't want you to kill him." Sighing, I suggest, "You should go, Dutton." I want to slide down the wall beside him and simply lay my head on his shoulder. I want to use him for comfort instead of sex, and once I step past that boundary, I'll come to depend on him. And then he'll vanish.

I hear the rev of a motorcycle, and I tense. Dutton reaches for me, but I push his hand away.

"I can stay," he offers. "You seem unsettled."

My heart pounds as I tell him to leave. I don't like anyone seeing me like this, and this is now the second time he's seen me vulnerable and having to face the demons of my past. It's been six years, and I've become complacent.

He shakes his head as if disappointed but doesn't push the matter, which I'm grateful for. It would appear that my boss is starting to understand me a bit better. Or should I say, we're both understanding one another, which is painfully obvious.

He lazily stands up and leans down, pressing a kiss to my forehead. My gaze follows him as he walks away. I quickly close the door and lock it behind him; then I grab my bat. After making sure the house is locked up tight, I go to my room. I set the bat next to the bed and then get undressed.

I try to sleep, but it's a lost cause. When the sun begins to peek through my curtains, I know it's pointless. I get out of bed, turn on the coffee machine, and peer outside my front window. I'm surprised to find Dutton's car still parked at the curb with him in it.

He stayed all night.

And I hate him for it.

Why can't he stay the arrogant asshole I've been calling him?

Why is he ever so slowly trying to wedge himself deeper in my heart and show me that I can rely on him?

Fuck. Sleeping in the car was not as comfortable as I'd hoped.

Posie steps out of the house, tightening the belt on her robe. She purposefully strides to the driver's side of the car, and I open the door as she brushes a lock of messy hair from her face.

"I can see why you never stay the night; that bird's nest you grow on your head overnight is atrocious," I joke.

But she doesn't take the bait. Instead, she says, "You stayed all night?"

"Did you not want me to?"

"I never asked that of you."

"You don't always have to ask for help, Posie. Sometimes, people simply know when you need it."

She stares at me as if I'd just slapped her, so I reach out and grab her hand. She doesn't look like she slept much, either. I feel guilty for putting her in this position. I didn't realize her past weighed so heavily on her, and although patience is not a virtue I usually possess, I was willing to wait until she let me in a little more and trusted me. I'd fucked up by agreeing to Billie and Eli's suggestion, and I feel like shit for it.

The front door opens, and her head whips in that direction. Bentley rubs his eyes and then runs over to us. She drops her hand from mine and holds her arms out for him. He jumps into her embrace and gives her a tired hug, still looking drowsy. I try not to smirk at the similarity between them, both clearly not being morning people.

That's when he seems to notice me and asks, "Where is Dawson?"

"My father?" A pang of irritation runs through me at his question. How is it that this kid has only met my father once but still wants him more than me? I shouldn't feel jealous of my father, but a small part of me does.

"Yeah, I like him," he says, as if it's obvious.

"It's Sunday morning, so he's probably with my mother."

Bentley rubs his eyes again. "She's nice too. Can we go see them?" he asks his mother.

"Probably not, sweetie."

"Maybe we can see him at work after school tomorrow? He does go to school, doesn't he?" I ask, realizing the kid might not even be in school yet. How old are they when they usually go?

"Yes! Can we?" he says, suddenly fully alert and ready for the day.

Posie glares at me. "Promising a kid something should be an offense." Her eyes grow wide. "Oh shit. I forgot I was getting that delivered today."

A van arrives, and I'm out of the car, following her to meet it.

"Calm down, it's just a delivery driver," she scolds as she puts Bentley down. "Do you want to go and pick out what cereal you'd like for breakfast while Mommy sorts out the new big bed?"

"Bed?" I ask.

"Yeah, I got a new frame. I completely forgot about it. Want to put it together for me?" The question comes out casually, so I'm not sure if she's serious or not.

She greets the driver and signs for the bed. Two men lug large, heavy-looking boxes from the back of the truck and then carry them inside at her direction.

Put it together?

I've never fucking built a bed in my life.

"I'm kidding, pretty boy. I know you only play with knives," she says, her fingers doing some woo-woo motion. "I don't expect you to know how to use a screwdriver."

"I can put together a bed," I grumble. *At least, I hope I can.*

She arches an eyebrow. I can tell she's considering it, but she's hesitating because that would mean asking for help. But then a mischievous grin curves her lips.

"Okay, let's see what you're capable of."

And I fucking devour that smile like it's my reason to live. It's the first time she's willingly let me into her home. And I feel like, ever so slightly, Posie's letting me into her life, too.

"It would've been much easier if you just bought it prebuilt," Dutton complains as he sits on the floor in my bedroom.

I lean against the doorframe, smirking as I hold two coffees.

"That would've cost extra money," Bentley says and points to what looks like the instructions. "You just have to put it together like Lego."

Bentley is sitting on his knees beside Dutton, picking up bolts and random pieces of the bed's hardware. I bite my bottom lip and quietly place the coffees on the side table. I take a step back and pull out my phone.

"Posie, I think they sent you a broken bed," Dutton says, barely controlling his frustration. "Are you listening to me?" He looks over his shoulder, and I take a picture.

A smile spreads on his face. "You think this is funny?"

I shrug as I bring him one of the cups of coffee. When I lean down, I whisper so Bentley doesn't hear, "I find it comical that my boss, who's usually so good with his hands, seems to be at a loss as to what to do with them now."

His gaze darkens as he accepts the coffee. "You will be punished for that."

"I wonder about that," I smirk and sit beside Bentley as he tries to help Dutton. For someone who claims to not do well with children, he seems to entertain Bentley plenty.

I tuck my knees under my chin, watching them and listening to their chatter. Dutton easily bounces between the millions of topics Bentley talks about, mostly Transformers, Lego, and his teacher and friends at school.

Part of me wonders if I'm doing the right thing by letting Dutton in my home like this and giving him the privilege of spending time with me and my son. This is not just about sex now. The fact that he stayed outside my home last night proves it. And though knowing he was out there offers me some comfort, I can't depend on him for it.

But right now, I need that comfort and support to regain my strength for the storm that might soon come.

"Can I have some juice, please?" Bentley asks politely, and I tell him to get one of the little juice boxes from the fridge. It's just Dutton and me in the room now. He looks disheveled after a night sleeping in his car and then attempting what I think is his first time building a bed... or anything, for that matter.

"You're enjoying this far too much, *Mostriciattola*."

I smile, scooting a little closer to him. Simply being beside him, having him here, gives me a sense of relief I haven't felt in quite some time. I don't want to depend on him, but I submit to a moment of weakness as I lay my head on his shoulder.

"Thank you for being here," I say, exhausted because I am. My mind ran over all the different ways this could play out in the future, and I came to the realization that it's as destructive as thinking about the things I can't change in the past.

"I'll always be here for you," he says softly, not making a move to touch or grab me. He simply lets me be and take what I need from him.

I don't know what the future has in store, but I feel a little better having Dutton by my side, if even temporarily. But I promise myself to only enjoy this peace with him now because I'm certain at any moment, the rug is going to be pulled from beneath my feet, and I want to make sure there aren't too many pieces to pick up.

Dutton might've been honest once about his inability to become a husband and father. But perhaps I'm in denial as to whether I'll truly ever be able to open myself up enough at the prospect of another relationship. Because the only unconditional love I've known is the love I give my son and the love he gives me in return. Everyone else has hurt me in one way or another.

THIRTY-SIX
DUTTON

That afternoon, I barge into Eli's club, Lucy's. It's not yet open, but I know I'll find him in his office. Ford and Hawke stand outside the door, looking surprised to see me.

"Make sure we're not interrupted," I bark as I push past them and into Eli's office. He's reviewing paperwork, and part of me is disappointed that he's not punishing someone here. Not that he often does it in his club, but I could use a release.

His gaze narrows on my thumb, which is turning black underneath the nail. "What happened to your thumb?"

I glance at it. "Oh, I did that building a bed," I say offhandedly. "We need to talk about Billie's party."

His eyebrows spring up. "You built a bed? What in the fuck has happened to my cousin?"

"Shut up. It's not that difficult," I growl as I take the seat across from him.

"I'm assuming this is about the blonde and her boy?" Eli drops his pen to the desk and brings his hands together.

"Her name is Posie," I grit. He doesn't say anything, but I can tell he's studying me in the same calculating way I'd assess him. "And, yes, it is. It was a mistake bringing her."

"Oh, your parents didn't like her?"

"They fucking loved her, but that's not why I'm here, and you know it."

He sighs and lights a cigar. He offers me one, even though I've never taken up the nasty habit.

"I'm not pulling the plug on the deal," he says as he lights it.

"I'm not asking you to. But, Eli, she was terrified. I'm certain Bentley's father is a part of that club, and if they come for her..."

"Wasn't Will able to track who the father is?" Eli asks.

"No, he could only narrow it down to three men she spent a lot of time with. But whatever her relationship she had with them is unknown. She was never openly affectionate with any of them.

"She wiped her social media accounts three months after her parents passed and cut off all ties with her friends. So there are no photos. Only video footage of restaurants they might've visited."

Eli considers this. "So she might've been a dirty little secret. Or perhaps none of them are the father. Or whoever it is has ways to keep his activities unknown."

"Precisely."

"It's not definite that the kid's dad will come looking for him," Eli says.

My gut tells me otherwise. Posie was so terrified. Both in Boston and last night after the party. "She's scared that someone is going to come for her."

"How do we know she's still not a part of this?" Eli asks.

"She's not."

"Is that fact?" he pushes.

"I told you, she's not," I insist. Eli's gaze dips to my knuckles, and that's when I realize they're turning white from how tightly I'm clenching my fists.

"You're going out of your way for a woman that you're simply fucking."

I slam my hands on the desk, the chair screeching back. "I'm not just fucking her!"

My eyebrows dip as Eli's stare hardens. *What the fuck am I doing?* It's not just sex anymore. It hasn't been for me since the very beginning, but I've been in such heavy denial, confident I could never feel this way about someone. I thought it was a fixation, something I needed to get out of my system.

Eli turns his chair to face away from me, leaving me to my own humiliation. "Then make sure you protect them. I'll tell the others to watch out for anyone wearing the club's patch. This could all be for nothing, cousin. But for fuck's sake, if anything happens, tell me. Don't do anything stupid that will jeopardize my business. The last thing we want is to go to war with these fuckers."

I dig my nails into my palms, furious that my perfectly polished mask is slipping.

But I can't help the insistent buzz inside of me to protect Posie and Bentley.

Posie is a strong woman, but the past often has the power to creep back up on us.

I've slain all of my demons, but it terrifies me that there might be something out there trying to get her.

And I'm hellbent on making sure those shadows never touch Posie or Bentley again.

Even if I have to bloody my own hands for them.

After having Dutton here for half the day yesterday, Bentley and I eased into our afternoon, cleaning around the house. While we were tidying up, men arrived to install security cameras. I called Dutton and chewed his ear off for doing it without my permission, but I'm grateful for the added sense of security. I slept somewhat peacefully last night, even with Bentley in the bed with me. He'd wanted to try out the new bed, so I told him he could sleep with me just for one night.

Dutton didn't ask again about my association with the Boston Delinquents, but he's showing his concern by installing the cameras and promising to swing by every day. I told him it's not necessary, but I'm not opposed to it.

My kid hanging around dangerous men wasn't on

my bingo card. But he took a real liking to Dawson. I don't think it's just because of the ice cream, either. Dutton brought him ice cream, and while he likes Dutton, he isn't begging to see him like he is Dawson.

However, last night, when I put Bentley to bed, all he could do was talk about Dutton and how cool it was that they built the bed together. He's excited that Dutton is coming by later to take us to see Dawson.

AFTER PICKING up Bentley from school and giving him a quick bath, I get him settled in his room with his toys so I can do a bit of social media work. Ten minutes in, I get distracted.

I haven't bothered to search Bentley's father in all the years since I left Boston.

But now I do.

Bobbi Harley.

Yes, his last name is ironic, considering he's part of a motorcycle club.

His picture comes up straight away. I cringe at the sight of him, trying to calm my heart and remind myself that he won't know if I look him up. I can't believe I loved this man and put my life on hold for him.

Sighing, I open his page and then start scrolling through it. I find pictures of him with another woman. Zooming in on one image, I realize I recognize her. She's one of the women he told me not to worry about when we first got together.

Jokes on me, though, right? Because he was fucking her behind my back the whole time.

Scrolling down farther, I see a picture of them together, his hand on her round belly as she holds up an ultrasound picture.

I want to vomit.

Looking at the date, I pause. That can't be right. Can it?

It's from four years ago. So after he gave me money and told me to fix the problem, he knocked up someone else.

Asshole.

Clicking on her profile, I see a picture of her with her son, and he's wearing a little leather biker jacket.

What was so wrong with me that he chose to discard me like a piece of shit and have a baby with someone else?

Maybe I should have taken Dutton up on his offer to kill him.

I want to kill him. Make it so he can't ever breathe again.

When I left Boston, I'd decided that when Bentley was old enough, if he wanted to know who his father was, I would help him find him. I just didn't expect to find him now and so easily.

He always made me feel less than, and when I wouldn't comply, he got physical.

I find it ironic that the man I'm currently fucking is entirely dominant. But I know without a doubt Dutton would never hurt me. He might disagree with my opinions, but he respects them because he respects *me*.

I was too naïve back then to understand that the kind of love Bobbi offered me wasn't enough. I was just so desperate for any love or affection after my parents died that I was stupidly easy to mold.

Will he try to find me now?

A weight drops in my stomach.

If Waylon tells him I'm in Manhattan, how long would it take him to find me?

And what would he do if he did find me?

Thoughts of moving pop into my mind. I definitely don't want to do that. Not now that Bentley is in school and making friends. And I have a stable job that can get us on the right path.

Bobbi told me to fix the problem and come back; I chose to leave and never return. I changed my phone number and didn't have any family he could contact to find out where I was. So it worked. I got a clean slate. But, right now, it doesn't feel so clean of a break.

I hear a car pull up out front, and I slam my laptop shut as if being caught doing something I shouldn't be.

Bentley runs out of his room, squealing in excitement.

"Hey, put some pants on!" I yell after him.

"Dutton is here!" he shouts. I laugh as I quickly usher him to get dressed.

I open the door and lean against the jamb expectantly.

"Did your boss say you could finish for the day?" Dutton asks smugly as he walks up the stairs and onto the porch.

"It's okay; my boss is more focused on his receding hairline than what I'm up to. As long as I make him money, he doesn't seem to care."

He comes to a stop in front of me with a smirk. "Those are fighting words, *Mostriciattola*."

There's that name again. I need to remember to google it later so I can find out what it means.

"Dutton!" Bentley screams as he runs down the hall. "Are we seeing Mr. Dawson today? Because you promised yesterday."

"Hey, Bentley. We sure are. Are you ready?"

I laugh when I notice Bentley's shirt is backward.

"One second," I say as I take off his shirt and put it on the right way. "He had mud all over him from school, so he had to have a bath. Let me get my handbag. Are you sure your father doesn't mind if we visit him?"

"He's looking forward to it. And he even rented a jump house for Bentley," Dutton calls out.

I freeze as I grab my handbag, not sure I heard him correctly.

"Rented?" I ask, walking back into the entryway

Dutton shrugs as he says, "Well, they offered it to him for free."

"Whoa, he gets things like that for free?" Bentley asks with wide eyes.

I roll my eyes as I usher them both out the door to lock it up. Bentley skips toward the car, and Dutton leans in close to me, making sure not to touch me. I appreciate that he respects my boundaries around Bentley, especially considering we haven't yet had a proper discussion about whatever the fuck is happening between us.

"I appreciate the photo you sent me today," he purrs in my ear, and warmth floods my pussy. "I was in the middle of a meeting and couldn't stand up to offer the rest of my presentation because of how fucking hard I was."

I throw my head back and laugh. "You asked for it."

"When did you become so obedient?"

"When did you become so charming?" I shoot back with an arched eyebrow.

"It's always been one of my redeeming qualities."

I scoff and stop short as I notice the car seat in the back of Dutton's car. "Did you buy him a seat for your car?"

He shrugs. "It seemed inefficient moving yours between cars. Don't worry, I got the top of the line." He opens the back door for Bentley. "At least that's what the lady said."

I stare at him, not sure what to think. This man is becoming more and more considerate, and I reflect on how alien he is now compared to the brutal, commanding man I first met. Now he's buying car seats and installing them in his car when we're not even... what? Dating? A thing?

He turns and looks at me. "What? Do I have blood on my shirt again?" he asks, deadly serious.

I gape at him. Nope, still a psycho. "Do you do that stuff in broad daylight?" I whisper as I get into the car.

He leans in and whispers so only I can hear, "The best activities aren't exclusive to the night, Posie."

I'm out of my fucking mind with this man.

When we're all in the car, I'm not sure I want to ask him what he did for the day.

But Bentley says in a sing-song voice, "What did you get up to today, Dutton?"

Dutton glances in the rearview mirror, smirking as I give him a warning glare.

"Just did some boring work. I had to let someone go because he wasn't doing the things I asked him to do."

"Oh," Bentley replies thoughtfully. "Did you ask him nicely?"

"Very nicely," Dutton says, and I clear my throat.

WE PULL UP TO A BUILDING, and the first thing I notice is the van that delivered the bouncy house. Only one other car is parked in the lot. Dutton gets out and unbuckles Bentley from his car seat before I can even open my door. As soon as Bentley is set free, he jumps out of the car and runs straight to Dawson, where he waits at the door with a huge grin.

"Good to see you again, Bentley." Dawson laughs as Bentley's little hands wrap around his legs in a big hug. My heart twists at Bentley's immediate attachment to him, and I wonder if Bentley might've been like this with my father. I try to bury those sad thoughts.

"I was asking when we can hang out," Bentley says as Dutton and I follow them side by side.

Dawson looks over his shoulder at me and says, "It's good to see you again, Posie."

"You too," I reply with an awkward smile because the situation feels far too intimate and not like the sex-only arrangement Dutton and I were supposed to stick to. But him putting together my bed yesterday wasn't about sex either. Which reminds me...

I bite my bottom lip, wondering if I should show Dawson the photo I took of Dutton sitting amongst the pieces of my bedframe because I'm positive he'd laugh at it as much as I did.

"Can we go and jump?" Bentley is already hurriedly taking his shoes off.

"Of course. That's why we got it," Dawson says as he removes his shiny shoes and then holds his hand out for Bentley.

My eyebrows shoot into my hairline. "Your dad likes to jump?" I ask Dutton, confused, as he pulls out two chairs. The building is empty, and I wonder what type of business Dawson intends to put in here.

"Yes. He actually hated kids, and they're just drawn to him. But the moment he had his own kids, he was a goner. He was hands-on, especially when we were little. He would do all types of things with us. I wonder if it's because he never got to enjoy them as a kid that he wanted to provide us with as much as possible."

I side-eye him. Dutton had mentioned his father having secrets from his past, and it's not my place to ask, so instead, I say with a sad smile, "My parents were the same. They loved taking me places, and my father was probably the worst. He'd always use me as an excuse to go onto all the rides he wanted to go on whenever we went to the fair." I laugh, thinking about when I was ten years old and didn't want to go on a particular ride. I told him that if he wanted to go on it, he'd have to go alone. He didn't.

Dawson jumps, and Bentley bounces higher, squealing with excitement.

"Sometimes, I think my dad wanted a son. He tried to show me how to fish and things like that, but I didn't have much interest in them. I didn't like the dolls my mother bought me either. I just liked artsy stuff," I say, remembering how I'd entertain myself in my room for hours.

Quietly, Dutton says, "You don't talk about them much."

"They died, and then I had no one. I suppose I

don't like digging into the past." Look where it got me in Boston when I tried to pay my respects. Even though I don't say it out loud, I think Dutton understands as he studies me.

"Now you have Bentley."

I turn to face him with a smile. "Yes, now I have Bentley."

Dutton clears his throat.

"Who is his father, Posie?" I'm surprised he's asking again.

"Why do you care so much?"

I'm confident giving him the name wouldn't be a good thing like it'll manifest Bobbi onto my doorstep the very next day. There's a reason why I left him off Bentley's birth certificate.

"Because I saw how frightened you were when you spoke to Striker. I can protect you both." He sounds so earnest.

I swallow, a tendril of emotion sapping the fight out of me how I want to lean into this man. How I want to believe what he's saying. And the terrifying thing is that I do believe him. But when will the novelty of all of this end for him? I've fought hard to get Bentley and me here, and I want it to be enough. I want to have done enough to get us far away from that life. Even if I am scared of his father, I don't want to admit that to anyone. I want to push past that version of me.

"We don't need protection," I say, feeling that sense of fear closing in because if Dutton thinks Bobbi might come looking for us, then he most likely will.

"I would kill him for you." He says it without flinching. And this isn't the first time he's offered.

I sigh, looking at the killer beside me again. How do I feel so safe beside this man who can so easily dispose of anyone?

With a sense of defeat, I admit, "I don't want to take away Bentley's choice to know his father someday if that's what he wants." His eyebrows furrow in confusion because how could he understand? He doesn't have a child to protect, and he doesn't know what it's like to lose a parent.

"I always promised myself that when Bentley was old enough, if he wanted to know about his father, I'd tell him. If he wanted to find him, I'd let him. I don't want to be the reason why he can't see him. And I know the moment I give you his name, you'll take both Bentley's and my choice away."

"He doesn't seem like much of a father to me if he has nothing to do with his son," Dutton states. I look over to Dawson and Bentley as they continue to bounce and laugh.

"I don't entirely disagree with you. But, please. Going after Bobbi will only cause more bloodshed."

"Bobbi Harley?" Dutton asks, and I realize my mistake.

"Please don't do anything, Dutton. Promise me."

"What if Bentley isn't safe with him around?" he presses.

"Then I'll kill him myself. It's my fight, not yours," I say, trying to fill myself with all the bravado I can. Because deep down, I know I'm still that scared little girl. I wasn't raised as a fighter, and although I have a fiery temper, I'm half the size of most men. But if I had to fight for my son's safety, I'd take down a whole army before I let them touch him.

"Let me know when you need me, *Mostriciattola*. It's okay to ask for help."

It goes without saying that Dutton has already helped us more than he knows.

"What does that word mean?" I ask.

"*Mostriciattola?*" he repeats as he begins to remove his shoes. I follow his lead and do the same. He takes off his suit jacket, and when he stands and offers me his hand, he says, "It means 'little monster.'"

My eyes widen. "That's what you've been calling me this whole time? Why can't it be something sweet?!" I demand.

He chuckles, and when his father looks in our direction, I still place my hand in Dutton's as he helps me up from the chair.

"You've destroyed my office more than once. Do you think a *sweet* woman would do that?"

I *hmph* at him, walking ahead of him to the inflatable castle. "You're not interested in sweet, Mr. Taylor."

"No. The only sweet thing I like is between your legs."

Heat rises up my neck as we stop outside the bouncy house. I stare at Dutton for a moment before turning away and crawling inside.

Bentley screams with joy when we join them, and Dawson declares he is taking a water break, laughing as he leaves. Bentley starts bouncing around Dutton, who pretends to chase after him. For a moment, I see the man he truly is—the cold-hearted man who says he admires his father and is good with children. He gives himself too little credit.

I notice Dawson watching us again with a smile.

I know why he's smiling, and it feels as comforting as it is terrifying because this thing between me and Dutton is morphing into something more than just sex. And I don't know how to get myself out of the situation without getting hurt.

Dutton isn't ready for something like this—a family of his own.

And how arrogant of me to think that he could ever be.

THIRTY-EIGHT
DUTTON

I decide to give Posie and Bentley some time to bounce together, and I can't help but admire how she glows around him. He really is her entire world.

My father offers me a bottle of water, and I take it scanning the interior of the building.

"It'll be a warehouse. Figured we could expand our reach with a subscription-based service running out of here." I raise my eyebrows. "It was Posie who gave me the idea with her subscription of the photos from Pearl."

I can't help but feel smug and proud that she's inspired even my father. Although I run most of the companies and am now the face of Taylor Enterprises, my father still dabbles and expands as he pleases.

"What happened at Billie's party between Striker

and Posie?" he asks, and I'm surprised he waited this long to question me about it.

We both turn to look where she's joyfully chasing Bentley around as he squeals excitedly. She reminds me a little of my mother and Billie. My mother is one of the most nurturing women I know, yet she's a total badass in her own right. I watched her choke a man out when he attempted to pluck Billie out of her stroller. He was some dickhead trying for a ransom or some shit. That's the day I realized my mother was just as dangerous as my father, and she's made a point to put both me and Billie in self-defense classes at a young age. I'm certain that Posie has the same tenacity as my mother. That she would do anything for her son. I hope she never has to be put in that situation.

"Bentley's father is from that motorcycle club in Boston. When she found out she was pregnant, he told her to get rid of the kid, so she fled. She's terrified that if Striker tells him she's here, he'll come looking for her."

"Do you think that's likely?" he asks, and I can tell by the change in his stance that he's ready to fight the unseen threat.

"I don't know, but with how frightened she is, it's likely."

He hums to himself. "Eli just struck up a deal with them. If you kill one of his men, it'll fuck up the deal."

"I know, but I'm not letting that dickhead anywhere near them," I growl.

"Of course not," he snaps viciously. He strokes his jaw. "It might be time you take this seriously, son. I know you feel pressured by your mother and me regarding marriage and such things, but it was never marriage itself we were pressuring you into. We just wanted you to have something to focus on other than us and work. We wanted you to have something, or some*one*, to come back home to. Whether you're willing to admit it or not, I think you've found that."

I watch Posie jumping, her hair billowing around her in blonde waves. The way I care about her makes me uncomfortable. It'll make me weak. Destroy every belief I've had about myself. And I think it's unfair knowing I'll be a terrible husband.

I look at my father then, and my jaw tightens as if physically resisting admitting to the thing I've known for years. "I'll make a terrible husband."

His eyebrows shoot up in surprise, but then he smiles. "But will you? I thought the same about myself. But, Dutton, you're already doing all of the things a husband would do. You're providing for them. You're protecting them. And you most certainly love her. You just have to understand that she comes as a package deal. If you go ahead with this, Bentley will be your son. So you must decide whether you can be actively involved in his life. Not as a distant figure but someone who embraces him entirely."

He takes a seat, and I take the one beside him. I clasp my hands in front of me thoughtfully. "What if I'm not good at it?" I focus my gaze on my discolored fingernail. I struggled to build a bed, for fuck's sake. My reality of home life is very different than hers. "I'm a dangerous man; won't that give them more issues in the future?"

He considers this. "A *dangerous* man isn't always a *bad* man, Dutton. We've raised you to be a good person. At your core, you know how to provide them with what they need. And you'll protect them when it's required. And if you're not ready for that level of commitment, then you need to let her go now. Keep an eye on the house, make sure no one disturbs their peace, and kill that fucker if he comes anywhere close to them. But it's not up to you whether you're good enough for her. You need to let her make that decision and respect what she decides. You need to be willing to walk away."

The mere thought of walking away from her has me grinding my jaw. I don't know when she became the air I breathe or the yearning for her to look at me or be within my vicinity started, but it's obnoxiously insufferable right now.

"If she's yours and this guy does come for her, you have every right to protect your family. Striker will understand if one of his men is working independently. The same goes for Eli. Business deals aside, you know that we protect our own no matter what. You just have to decide whether you do it at her side or from the shadows."

A throbbing starts in my jaw from how tightly I'm grinding my teeth, and I'm startled as Bentley squeals and runs toward my father. He hugs his leg enthusiastically, gushing about all the fun he's having.

I can't help but compare myself to my father. Kids love him. What if I can't be like that? My gaze slides to Posie as she slowly approaches us, putting her hair into a loose bun. What if I can't be a good man for her? Or worse, what if she doesn't want me that way?

It's another matter entirely if I have the right to stand by her side.

Maybe she's only ever wanted me for sex.

And wouldn't that be ironic? The one woman I've fallen for might, in fact, be using me for the thing I've used countless women for.

Either way, I know I'll protect them both until I die.

"Hey, boss. Posie is in your office if you're looking for her," Mike mentions as he walks past me.

What the fuck is she doing here? I told her she didn't need to come in anymore and she could do everything from home. She's mostly been doing that for the last month anyway.

"Dutton?" I stop as Paula steps in my way.

"Is she dancing tonight?" I ask curtly.

Paula looks at me, confused. "No, I think she's just picking up a few things. But I do need to talk to you about hiring someone to replace her. The girls are a little strained."

"I trust your judgment, Paula. I have also emailed the payroll company about your pay raise."

"Pay raise?" she asks, surprised.

"Yes. You work hard and, in return, deserve more." That, and I know she holds a soft spot for Posie, not that I'd admit it.

She nods like she can't believe it as I step past her.

I couldn't sleep last night, not after the discussion I had with Posie about her ex. I know she thinks I don't understand because I'm not a family man, but it doesn't mean I don't have the urgency to protect what's mine. And for better or for worse, perhaps both of us have been hiding behind promiscuous lies. We've been hiding behind the act of sex instead of confronting an obvious truth. At least, I hope she feels the same way about me that I do her.

I don't want her with anyone else. And I pray to God she feels the same way because there's no way I'm willing to hand her over. And if she tries to leave me, I'll punish her. But I can sense the wall she's put up between us, and I know it's because of her son. They come as a package. And if I want Posie, I have to show her I'm willing to accept all of her.

Opening my office door, I find her putting things into her bag. She looks up at me as I enter. I shut the door behind me.

"Hey. I'm just finishing up so you can have your desk back."

"I don't want my desk back," I reply. "Where is Bentley?"

"He's with the sitter. I had to come in to do a few things."

I lick my lips. I wasn't expecting to have this conversation so soon, but I've never been a man to pull any punches.

"Do you have time for dinner?" I ask.

When I think she's about to immediately shut me down, she glances at the wall clock and then nods.

"I can do dinner, *or* we can go back to your place for a little fun. But I have to be back home in a few hours."

"Then we'll get dinner," I say, reaching for her. I tug her to me by the hip, and she raises an inquisitive brow at my choice of dinner over dessert.

"You always grab me. Are you afraid I'll run?" she says, sliding her arms around my neck.

"Well, you seem to have the tendency to run away from me before I wake up."

She smirks. "I don't run. I have a son to return to. There's a difference."

"Who you didn't tell me about, might I add," I purr as I dip my head and kiss her soft lips.

"There are many things you don't know about me,

Mr. Taylor. Now, are you taking me for dinner or trying to seduce me?"

I clench my jaw, my cock already semi-hard. I just can't keep my hands off this woman. But tonight, I have to at least until after dinner.

"Let's go. I want to discuss something with you," I say as I grab her hand and pull her toward the exit.

WE GO TO A LOCAL RESTAURANT, so we're not too far from the club and her car, and it won't take her long to drive home.

"Is it true you used to mainly ride your motorcycle, but now always drive your car?" she asks curiously.

"Who told you that?"

"Paula."

"Maybe I should rethink her raise," I grumble under my breath. She laughs as the hostess leads us to a table in a secluded corner.

I'd fallen into the habit of driving my car when stopping by my establishments. I didn't, however, expect to spend so much time at Pearl. But my curiosity was piqued by this little blonde monster. And I continued driving the car because it had more room.

Now, I have a booster seat permanently in the back for her son.

We order meals and a bottle of red wine. She talks about the ideas she has for the social media accounts, and I listen, agreeing with her on most things. How could I not? I've never seen this side of Posie before. She enjoys her work, I realize. She's so passionate about it.

When they place our meals down, I take a sip of the wine, watching her silently as she looks at her plate with anticipation. I've come to learn she really enjoys food. I figured this out because the meals I send her are the only gifts she's never thrown away. And I now know to ensure that nothing I send has nuts.

The conversation I had with my father a few days ago has been swirling in my mind, and I've come to a decision.

"Posie." She looks up at me as she takes her first bite.

I pause for a moment to admire her. She's dressed in all black, and her hair is tied back in a low braid. God, she's beautiful. "I think we should get married."

She chokes on her food, and I worriedly push her glass of wine toward her. She finally swallows, then sputters, "S-sorry, what?"

"You and me. Married."

"Yeah, that's a no." She shakes her head in bafflement.

"Why not?"

She stares at me like I've grown a second head. She puts her cutlery down, saying, "Because unlike you, Dutton, I want marriage and take it seriously. I want to marry a man who will put me and my son above all else. A man who will love me for all my flaws, and believe me, I have a lot. And I want a big gesture, not just some random thought that we should get married." She pauses. "Why do you want to marry me?"

"My father suggested it," I begin.

She laughs, and I'm startled that the thought of marrying someone like me is so hilarious to her. I'm not surprised, but I still don't like hearing her favorite word —no.

"That's the shittiest reason for marriage I've ever heard," she says, shaking her head. "So, no. We aren't even dating. And, to be honest, I don't know what we are, but I think you shouldn't strain yourself with the idea of marriage because your father suggested it."

"We can be whatever you want us to be," I remind her.

"Okay, well, you can be my boy toy."

"Boy toy?" I raise a brow at her.

"Yes. When I want someone to fuck me to help clear my head, I'll call you." She smiles.

I frown. "I do that already."

"Yes, and you do it very well. It's why you've been promoted from boss to boy toy. Now, let's eat so we can fuck in your car before I have to get back to my son." I go to speak, and she holds up her hand. "If you ask me to marry you again, I won't fuck you." I close my mouth, realizing I've been shot down.

I hate the idea of marriage, so why the fuck did I just ask her to marry me? It goes without saying that I want to protect her and her son, but she might throw her drink in my face if I mention Bentley.

She continues talking about work, and I'm reeling at the sinking feeling in my stomach that I'm of no more value to her than a vibrator. And I don't know how to communicate what I feel to her because I'm unsure if she feels the same. And if I do tell her, will she push me away?

I remember my father's words, suggesting I might have to be ready to walk away. But that option is unfathomable to me.

FORTY
POSIE

The food was amazing—so much so that when we walked out, I was tired. My food coma was fully activated.

Dutton rests his hand on my lower back as he leads us to his car. But instead of opening the passenger door, he opens the back door. I smirk *like old times*.

Climbing in, he sits and then taps the seat next to him. I don't know when things between us started becoming more than sex, but his proposing marriage was so out of the blue that I immediately shut him down. Especially when he said he did it because his father suggested it. It's nice to know I'm liked by his family, but I refuse to let myself and Bentley be some side prize. Dutton might not take marriage seriously, but I do. Sex, however, we can both agree on.

I smile as I climb in after him. When I shut the door, the lights go out, and it's dark. I know no one in the restaurant will see us through the tinted windows. He grabs me and pulls me onto his lap so I'm straddling him.

"So no talk about..." he says.

"Marriage," I finish for him as he slides his hand between us and straight up my dress. His fingers dance over the lace of my underwear. I untuck his shirt and slide my hands up his toned stomach and chest. Dutton has the best body I have ever felt or seen, and every time I touch him, I feel like a feral animal in heat.

"Then tell me what you want," he says and slips a finger under my panties. "What about talk of us seeing each other more?"

I gasp as he brushes against my clit, and I start moving my hips at the slight friction. I hate when he uses sex against me because if I'm not honest in these moments, he'll punish me and refrain from giving me an orgasm. Truthfully, these times are when we have the most honest conversations. But all of this talk of marriage has given me whiplash. I don't even know if Dutton understands what he's asking.

I claw at his chest, and he moves in and touches my lips with his. I love the way he kisses me, so soft and tender as if I might break, but then fucks me with his fingers and treats me like I'm a bad girl. It's the perfect combination.

"You already see me a lot. More than I see anyone else, apart from Bentley," I tell him as he pulls back. His hands slip from under my dress and move to undo the buttons at my chest, exposing my breasts. He leans in and kisses between them, glancing up at me through his lashes.

"I want to see you more."

"You sound needy." I smile at him. How does this man think to propose marriage before seeing one another more regularly? Then again, from what I've heard, he hasn't dated anyone, let alone had a serious relationship, and that terrifies me. What if I'm just a phase for him? I have so much going on in my life already; I don't know if it's worth taking a risk on a man who has only ever had to think about himself.

"I am," he purrs as I reach for his trousers and undo them. Freeing his cock, I lift up onto my knees and position myself over him. He looks down as I grab his cock and guide it to my entrance, pushing my underwear to the side. "For you," he adds just as I lower onto him.

When he's fully seated, filling me up, I start to rock back and forth, craving the friction. He grabs my ponytail and tugs my head back, exposing my throat. I'm forced to lean back, my hands bracing on his knees, as I ride him. "That's it, baby. Fuck me. Show me how much you want this cock to fill you up."

I can't reply, barely able to breathe, as his other hand starts rubbing my clit, providing even more friction. His mouth finds my breast, and he sucks.

Fuck me.

"Look at me," he growls. And I do as he says, awkwardly staring down at him as I ride him. "See how I worship you. *Only you.*"

My heart flutters, and I increase my speed, trying to distract myself from the confusion that is Dutton Taylor. He releases my hair and lets me take the lead, as if aware by the way my body speaks that I'm trying to gain control of this situation. Because I don't know how to read Dutton. I don't know why, all of a sudden, he's talking about dating and marriage when we've only discussed obedience and fucking.

It's the first time Dutton has ever let me take control instead of forcing me into submission, and I ride his cock like it's my lifeline. I fuck him so hard that I see stars. After I explode and start to come down, he grabs my hips and continues rocking me, not stopping until both of us are done.

Struggling to breathe, I lay my head on his chest, finding comfort in the man who is just as confusing to me as he is lethal. And I know I should've run away from Dutton the moment I realized he wanted me. But he makes me feel *safe*. And that wreaks havoc on my independence. Won't he just leave me like everyone else has?

I can't risk that for Bentley or me. We can't become attached to someone who will eventually throw us to the side.

"Move in with me," he says and kisses the top of my head.

I can't rely on something that might be temporary, nothing but promiscuous lies.

Eventually, this man might be my downfall, and I don't have the strength to pick up the pieces again.

"No," I reply, not moving. I can feel him watching me as I stare at his chest, avoiding his gaze. Because I know that's when Dutton always sees me. The *real* me. The truth and the hurt. And I'm not willing to let him see the uncertainty, scared he'll use it to his advantage in some way.

"I have to go relieve the babysitter. Thanks for dinner and dessert," I say, finally raising my head and kissing his lips. I attempt to crawl off him, but he pulls me back and kisses me again. Forcing his tongue into my mouth and forcing his dominance upon me. I moan, so used to melting into him that I have no choice but to depend on his breath to keep me sane. Gosh, how I love his kisses.

Managing to pull away, I smile at him and place a hand on his cheek. "You've become needy."

"Stay at my place tonight," he says.

"Take me to my car, Mr. Taylor. That was our deal." This time, I don't allow him to pull me back. I climb off him and readjust my clothing before I climb into the passenger seat.

I'm so confused as to what he wants from me.

We're good at sex. But moving in together, dating, marriage? It has no rhyme or reason. I look at him as he gets behind the wheel. Part of me wonders if this actually has anything to do with Bentley and me or everything to do with his family's opinions. Or even worse, the mention of Bentley's father.

FORTY-ONE
POSIE

"What type of mother comes home this late?"

I jump at the familiar voice as I get out of the car. When I turn around, my heart falters. Bobbi is standing at the curb, smoking a cigarette. He flicks it away as he starts toward me. I freeze. Everything within me that I shoved down all those years ago resurfaces: the fear I felt around this man, the uncertainty of what he was going to do next, as he told me he loved me in one breath and hit me with the next.

But it's not just me anymore, and I square up to my demon, even though I break on the inside, realizing he might've been watching the house the entire time I was with Dutton.

What if he...?

My jaw grinds, and then I'm startled as Amy opens

the door and steps out with her bag over her shoulder. "He's asleep. Good as always." She offers me a wave, then stops when she sees Bobbi.

"I suggest you let her leave," Bobbi whispers so only I can hear.

Fear grips me like a vise, but I find myself saying, "It's fine, Amy, you can go." She nods and glances at him one more time before she heads to her car.

As unpredictable as Bobbi is, my only saving grace is that it's early in the evening, and people are still out walking their dogs or tending to their lawns. I absolutely fucking refuse to let him inside my home, even if he puts a gun to my head.

Bobbi steps closer, and I can smell the scent of cigarette smoke on him. I fucking hate that smell.

"It's been a long time, Posie," he says, looking like he's aged fifteen years instead of six. How had I ever loved this man? I'm not sure what I found so attractive about him back then. Yes, he has that bad-boy vibe about him, but that's it. He looks like he needs to shower, and his clothes look like they could do with a wash. I used to do his laundry, and I wonder who's been doing it since I left.

I do have one thing for which I am grateful to him, though. He gave me the one thing I genuinely fucking love in this world.

"Has it?" I reply, making sure to harden my resolve and speak to him like I would any other man in the same way that I wouldn't let Dutton walk all over me when we first met. I'm not the same woman I was six years ago.

He smirks. "Always with that sass."

"You hated my sass," I throw back at him. He rubs a hand over his chin and nods his head.

"Yes, but you learned," he says. "You were a fast learner." He glances at the house then. "Is my kid in there?"

My heart rate picks up. *His kid.* How could Bentley be his kid if he never worried about him? How can a child so pure and sweet have the same DNA as this violent, controlling man in front of me? "Cat got your tongue?"

I point my nose in the air. "He is *my* kid," I tell him, hoping he doesn't hear the shakiness in my voice.

"Yeah, a kid I told you to get rid of."

"I did. I got rid of both of us. So you can leave now."

"That's not going to happen." He smiles evilly. "I might have to be careful with how I handle you because of the Monti family, but let me assure you it won't keep me away from my son. You know, paternal rights and all. I thought I'd pay a visit so we can establish some rules going forward."

My nails dig into my palm as I bite out, "You have a kid back in Boston. Why are you really here? You don't give a shit about him or me, so go back to your own fucking family!"

His smirk is full of venom. "So you stalked me? It looks like I'm not the only one who has struggled to move forward. And don't worry about that bitch and kid; they're just a temporary thing. You were always my main girl, you know."

I scoff. "We never had a future, Bobbi. Not while you were fucking another woman and telling me not to worry about it. There is no us, and he is not your son. You think you were the only one fooling around?" I lie.

He steps into my space. I make sure not to flinch, but I'm preparing myself for the worst. A dog barks in a nearby yard, which seems enough for him to reassess his decisions. This neighborhood, although not the nicest, is far safer than the one we lived in together, and people here will call the police.

He goes to pinch a lock of my hair, but I slap his hand away. He just smiles.

"You know, she fell pregnant once before you did, and like a good girl, she listened when I told her to get rid of that kid. Turns out, it was too late to abort the second time, though. Even when I pushed her down the stairs, the kid survived. So I realized he was a tough little guy, just like me."

My stomach twists with nausea. I hate this man so much that tears want to spring from my eyes.

I fucking hate you so much.

He smirks at my penetrating glare.

"Leave, Bobbi. No one wants you here. Least of all me," I growl.

"Oh, yeah. I heard you were with a Taylor. You know who that family is, right?" I don't bite at his antics. "They're more dangerous than me, Posie. You want our son around that? Striker might've told me I can't stir shit with them, but he has no place in the discussion between me and the mother of my child."

"At least he knows their names," I spit. Which I know I shouldn't have done because his nostrils flare, and he bites the inside of his cheek, trying to keep his temper in check. We used to have a habit of fighting. We would both throw fists and then make up, swearing it wouldn't happen again until it happened again.

I thought that was the type of love I deserved.

I thought that was all I was allowed to have.

Until Bentley.

Until Dutton, a small voice whispers.

"He doesn't know my name because you ran," he seethes, his foul breath covering my face.

"No, he doesn't know your name because you are a shit human who told me to get rid of him! Go back to Boston!"

"I'm the shit human? And what is it you do for work, Posie?" he says, smirking. "What if I took you to court to fight for full custody? Surely, you couldn't afford it. No one's going to believe a whore who dances for money."

I bite my tongue, doing my best not to react to his provocation.

"You don't want him," I grit. "You just want to get back at me."

Then, a sly glint enters his eyes. "See, I knew you knew me. And you know I'll do it to spite you."

"They will choose me over you," I insist.

"Oh no, sweetheart. My parents will be the ones fighting for him. I don't have time for a full-time kid." He winks and then turns, heading back to his bike.

His parents enabled his bad behavior. His father was a banker who made many good investments, enough that he can now live off them for the rest of his life. His mother is a housewife who idolizes her son, even if he is the devil himself.

"Bobbi," I call after him. He turns around to face

me. And there are so many things I want to say to him, but I bite my tongue. Lifting my hand, I flip him off. "Fuck you, you fucking loser. Take me to court. I dare you. With the amount of shit I have on you, no judge in their right mind would leave you out on the streets, let alone give you custody of a child." That's all it takes for him to stalk back up and slap me across my face. It stings, but I internally smile. "And now I have you on video," I add smugly. He looks around, trying to spot the cameras. I'm even more grateful now for the cameras Dutton installed.

His hand shoots out to wrap around my throat, gripping it tight. "You think you're so smart."

I struggle to speak from how tightly he's constricting my airway. "At least smarter than you," I manage to wheeze, tasting my own blood.

He releases me and storms off. I stand there, making sure he gets on his bike, and then I run to my house, unlock the door, grab my bat, and relock the door. Peeking through the blinds, I hear his bike rumble to life before I see him drive off. And know I won't be getting any sleep tonight at all. I run to Bentley's room, where I find him already asleep, and quickly start throwing essentials into a bag.

But then I pause, my face throbbing.

Every part of me is screaming at me to run.

But he'll only keep chasing.

I'll never get rid of him unless I deal with him now. But the thought of him threatening to sue for custody or even being anywhere near Bentley...

I know I wanted to give Bentley the option to know his father, but do I really want him to be associated with a man who, without thought, would throw a woman down the stairs and hit his mother?

I sag as I sit against the wall and stare at my sleeping son, trying to ignore the tears streaming down my face. Because I'm fucking furious, I've given him this power over me.

I don't want to run anymore.

FORTY-TWO
DUTTON

"She said she didn't want to marry me," I grumble to Eli through the phone.

Eli whistles, and I can tell he's trying not to laugh. "Well, you're an idiot for saying the reason you wanted to marry her was because your father suggested it."

I'm exasperated as I walk into my office at Pearl and close the door behind me. "Yeah, well, it sure as hell worked for you somehow."

He sounds smug as he says, "Yes, but I had something to blackmail Jewel with until she fell irrevocably in love with me."

I roll my eyes. "You're the last person I should be asking advice from."

"It's a big step for you, though. Are you sure this is

what you want?" I can imagine him sitting in his office at Lucy's, raising a drink to his lips.

I sigh. I've thought about this a lot over the last few days. I don't go into detail about thinking I'll be a bad husband or father. I mean, shit, if Eli is husband material, then surely, I am too. So I settle for, "I want Posie. And her son doesn't seem to hate me, so I'd like to try to be..." I can't finish the sentence.

Eli does it for me. "His father?"

What if Posie doesn't even want me? What if I properly convey all of this to her, and she still doesn't want anything more than sex? Fuck. When did I turn into this insecure creature?

"Something like that. Look, I've been staking out her place every night. If this deadbeat asshole of an ex comes back and threatens her in any way, I can't promise I won't kill him."

I turn on my laptop and then pull up the feed from her home security system. I see her car is in the driveway. I stare at the screen as Eli continues speaking, noticing a motorcycle parked at the curb in front of her house. My eyebrows furrow. I don't hear what Eli says as I spot another bike parked farther up the street.

"Hello, are you listening to me?" Eli says.

"There are two bikes in front of her house."

"What?" I hear a noise, so I assume it's him forcefully pushing back his chair and standing.

"I'm going now," I tell him. "Where are Ford and Hawke?"

"I don't know, but I'll call them and have them go there now."

"Good," I say and pocket my phone.

I push through the back door and stop when I see some asshole leaning against my car.

He has a cigarette hanging out of his mouth as he taps the side of the car. "This looks nice and shiny," he says as he keys the side of it.

I take three steps, but he raises his hand. "I wouldn't if I were you."

"Give me one good fucking reason not to," I growl.

He looks up at me with a sly smile. "You didn't think I'd come here alone, did you? I heard you beat up one of my boys. That shit might fly with Striker, but it won't with me. Two of my men are parked outside her house right now. If I don't call them back in ten minutes... Well, let's say things will get messy."

I don't have to guess whether he's bluffing because I saw it on the security cameras myself.

I should've been there with her tonight.

I underestimated how quickly he'd find her.

Fuck.

"I'm assuming you know who I am," Bobbi says.

"Not because you're significant," I sneer, curling my hands into fists, calling on all the self-discipline that I can not to launch myself at this motherfucker. One of my security guards opens the back door of the club, and before he can pull out his gun, I put my hand up and wave him back inside. "What do you want?" I grit.

He shrugs. "You're to stay the fuck away from Posie. That's all. I want you to stop thinking you ever had any interest in her. You'll fire her and let it go unnoticed when I take her back."

I grind my teeth. It's all about Posie, not one mention of Bentley. He doesn't even care about his son. This little fucker has no idea who he's dealing with. He's nothing but a cockroach trying to play in a league he doesn't understand. The only reason I don't kill him now is because I'm not sure how close the others are to getting to Posie and Bentley at the house.

"Do we have an understanding?" he asks as he keys the side of the car again with an antagonizing smirk.

"I want you to understand at least this much—I will kill you eventually," I tell him.

"Ah, but that'll create a war. You can't kill me while I wear these patches, or it'll bring hell onto your family. You can't tell me you think her pussy's that sweet. I'd know. I was there." He laughs at his reminder to me that he's had Posie before.

A determination to kill this fucker blazes beneath my skin. "You're playing at a game you were never invited to. You're nothing in the grand scheme of things. To them or us. You're just a little thug, and you'll quickly learn how much you've overstepped."

He grins, but I can tell he's becoming agitated. He saunters over to his bike and puts his helmet on as he says, "Dump her," before bringing down the visor. He revs his engine and drives off.

I immediately call Eli. He answers on the first ring. "Hawke and Ford just got there. I'm five minutes away."

"He was just here," I tell him as I go back inside.

"The fucking audacity," Eli says. "Did he threaten you?"

"He threatened Posie and Bentley."

"I can have Jewel kill him and make it look like an accident," Eli says matter-of-factly. "But I have a feeling that won't be enough for you."

"No. I want to kill him myself," I say, and a wave of relief passes through me at my cousin's approval. I would've done it anyway.

"They're family now, right? We protect our own," he says.

"Look after them until I get there," I say, then hang up.

"Close everything down!" I yell out. The girls seem surprised, and the security guard approaches me. I quickly brief him on the situation, to ensure everyone gets out safely. "We'll be closing for the next few days while I take care of business."

"What's happening?" Paula asks worriedly. "We're mid-show."

"Close it all down. Now," I order. Chaos erupts as the music is cut off, and everyone is ushered out. I walk out the back door, trusting my security guards. At least I know Bobbi is currently working with only two other guys.

I jump into my car, and as I pull away from the curb at lightning speed, I call Striker. He answers on the third ring.

"Which of your men are in my town?" I rhetorically ask him.

"Hi, Dutton. Yes, I'm good. How are you?" he replies sarcastically.

"I'm not fucking around. Unless you want me to send his head back to you. Your boy has overstepped."

"Fucking hell. Try not to kill him." I can hear a commotion around him. "I was only advised today that he'd left."

"Yeah, well, he's been pretty busy ever since paying Posie and then me a visit."

He curses. "Dutton, it's his kid."

"He threatened *them*, and then he threatened *me*. I don't give a flying fuck about what agreements you have in place with my cousin."

"You can't kill one of my men."

"What type of man is he, Waylon? And be honest." My veins are flowing with ice, and I'll fucking kill Striker as well if he tries to get between us.

"He's one of mine," he says.

"That's not the answer I am after, and you know it."

I hear some rustling and a door close before he starts talking again.

"He thought she would never leave him, and he went crazy when she did. Now that he's found her again..."

"Because you fucking told him!" I accuse angrily.

"He had a right to know!"

"She's *my* woman, Striker. So you better make him disappear and never return. Or you take his patch, and I end the fucker now."

"I don't answer to you," Striker snarls.

"And I don't let anyone touch what's mine," I bite back, then hang up on him.

I lower the bat and open the door. Dutton looks like a flustered mess. "He's here," I squeak, hating the vulnerability in my voice. Dutton's gaze lands on my face, and a raging storm swirls in his gaze.

"Did he hit you?" He drops to his knees. "I'm so sorry I wasn't here, *Mostriciattola*."

Tears well in my eyes as I drop to my knees in front of him, confused as to why he's the one apologizing.

"You didn't do anything wrong," I say, raising my hand to cup his cheek.

He shrinks into himself. "If I hadn't brought you to that party, none of this would've happened. I knew Striker would be there, and I knew you had some connection to that gang, yet I didn't understand the consequences."

My eyebrows furrow. "What? You did this?" I snap, shoving him.

"I'm so sorry."

I stand, towering over him. "Do you have any idea what you've done? He's threatening to take me to court, Dutton!"

"He doesn't care about Bentley," he says quickly, getting to his feet. "Let me help you."

I scoff. "Help me? Dutton, you've made it one hundred times worse. And for what? Because you wanted to flaunt me in front of your parents? You risked my son's safety."

He looks ashamed as he says, "Please, *Mostriciattola*, let me make this right." He reaches out for me, but all my rage springs to the surface. It's flooding over me, and I can't stop it.

I throw the bat at him, and he blocks it. I grab an umbrella leaning by my door and throw that, too. Every backward step I take, I find something new and throw it at him as the fury grips me like a vise.

"I know. I know. I know," he says miserably.

"You don't know shit!" I scream, my hair snarling into a wild mess as I throw things and cry and curse, my heart breaking. I don't want to run anymore, but I feel no less trapped. And I know it's not Dutton's fault, and I hate that he lets me take my anger out on him. That he's willing to let me take this out on him because he feels like he deserves it.

I did that once.

I crumple to the floor and sob. Then he's in front of me again, sitting with me in the middle of the living room as I cry because I can't do this anymore. I want to look after my son. But I'm struggling not to let this man in. I want to depend on him, but I don't know if I can trust him. Or myself.

"Posie, tell me what I need to do to fix this," he begs.

"You can't fix this, Dutton," I say with a sob. "He was always going to come."

Why? Why did he have to come when I finally thought I was getting ahead?

"Mommy?" Bentley's voice comes from the hallway. And it snaps me out of my thoughts immediately.

"Hey, baby," I say, turning my face to wipe away my tears. The living room is a disaster, and I'd completely snapped, forgetting to be quiet. Damn, I'm a shitty mother.

Dutton is moving, and when I look up, he's blocking Bentley's view of me. "Let me put him back to bed, and then we'll talk," he says, and it floods me with both pain and relief. It was painful to know that I must look so fragile right now to him. And I was relieved that he understood I didn't want my son seeing me like this and that he was here to pick up the pieces.

"Hey, Bentley. Sorry we woke you up. I tripped and accidentally broke some things," Dutton says as he picks up Bentley.

"Oh. Did you hurt yourself?" Bentley asks, still half asleep and rubbing his eyes. They round the corner and walk down the hallway, and my shoulders sink. Fuck, I really screwed up this time. I glance around the living room and at the open front door.

I sigh, walking over to close and lock it. When I do, I'm startled to find Eli standing there with his arms crossed over his chest.

"What are you doing here?" I ask.

He side-eyes me and then pointedly looks back at the street. I notice the twins waiting in a car parked at the curb. "I wasn't going to stand here for long. I didn't want to interrupt, but I wanted to be close while the door was open." And I realize then that, like Bentley and I are a package deal, this family of Dutton's, although dangerous, comes packaged with him. His silvery gaze flicks back to me as he says, "He loves you, you know. Even when he struggles to say it, he'll risk everything for you. And although I don't know where your mind is at with everything, I hope you can accept him for who he is. Because I'm terrified he'd go as far as to try to fit into a mold you shape for him if it meant he could be by your side."

The gravity of his words hits me. How can this powerful, violent man speak so emotionally about his cousin? When Dutton suggested marriage tonight, I thought it was because of his father. But I realize now that he might've been serious and asked because he truly wants to be with me.

I want to cry all over again. Can I let myself be vulnerable enough to accept another man into my life, into Bentley's life? But haven't I already welcomed him into my home? Into my heart? I can't use Bentley as an excuse anymore.

"Thank you for watching over us," I say to Eli, who simply nods before pushing off the doorjamb and heading back to his car. I pick up the bat, mortified that they most likely saw all of that. I place the bat beside the door and inhale a shaky breath. Now that my violent, wild temper has calmed down, I prepare myself for an entirely different conversation.

It's not Dutton's fault Bobbi is in town. Whether it was now or in the future, he was always going to find us. It's unfair to blame Dutton when I've always told him this was my battle to fight alone. But he wants to help me.

This is when the realization hits me that there's more than just Bentley and me in our little bubble now. Maybe I don't have to do this on my own after all.

I'm making coffee because there's no way either of us are going to sleep tonight.

"He's asleep again," Dutton says from behind me.

"Thank you."

He's cautious as he walks up behind me, wrapping his arms around me and just holding me. I sigh against him. I can't even fight him anymore.

I don't *want* to fight him anymore.

We remain there for a while, and I simply absorb his strength as he stands behind me like a pillar.

"Do you want me to stay?" he asks. And I know he's asking whether I'll let him stay in my home or if he'll simply sleep in his car outside.

A part of me wants to tell him no, that I can do this myself. But when I turn to face him, I nod my head.

I don't have anyone else, and Bobbi knows that. So he'll use that against me now just as he did our whole relationship. Fucking asshole.

"I'm sorry for throwing a bat at your head," I whisper as I wrap my arms around his neck. "Thank you for coming. I know this isn't a situation you would have picked."

"Picked?" he asks. "What does that even mean?"

"Well, you're a man of power; you can literally have any woman or anything in the world, and instead, you're caught up in the mess that I've been lugging around for years."

"I don't want to be anywhere else but here, Posie. I would never hurt you. You know that, right?" I nod, and his gaze narrows on the mark across my cheek. He cups it, a wild storm brewing in his eyes, but he handles me gently. "I'm so sorry I wasn't here."

"This was never your fight, Dutton," I remind him because he's taking it on like the world's on his shoulders, and he's failed.

"Your fight is my fight." He licks his lips. "I didn't explain myself well enough tonight at dinner."

"You don't have to, Dutton."

"Stop trying to push me away." He inhales deeply, then continues, "If you don't want me after what I have to say, then..." His throat bobs. "Then we'll work on it again tomorrow."

"You don't handle rejection well, do you?" I jest, trying to lighten the mood.

"You're the one woman I can't have reject me, Posie," he says. "This isn't just sex, and you and I both know that."

The coffee machine stops brewing, but we ignore it, not breaking eye contact. The truth sits between us.

"I want to be here to protect you and Bentley," he tells me.

"And what past that, Dutton? I should be focusing on whatever is happening with Bobbi right now instead of this." I point between us.

"Stop deflecting. Because you know the two go hand in hand. I can make Bobbi disappear."

I push away from him, not because I don't want to be touching him but because I need space. My mind is a clusterfuck of emotions right now. "I don't want to take away Bentley's choice."

"I might not be a parent, Posie, but I know your son wouldn't want a relationship with a man who would hurt his mother. Sometimes, we have to make hard decisions."

I look at him. "That's not fair." But I know he's speaking the truth. I've been thinking about it for some time now. But Dutton makes me accountable for my actions. It makes the option of running away impossible. He deals with everything head-on. And although I usually do the same thing, when it comes to matters of the heart, I always flee instead.

"And then after this? What happens in six months? A year? When you get sick of us? When the novelty of our happy little family is too much?" I question, throwing my hands in the air.

"I can't promise I'll be a good husband or father, but I'm willing to do everything I can to be that for the both of you."

"How does your mind jump to marriage and parenting?"

His eyebrows dip. "Because shouldn't it? It's not just you I'm saying yes to. I've thought about what our future will look like. I travel a lot. I focus on my work and know I have undesirable methods of getting things done, but I can't apologize for who I am or how deeply I feel for you."

"I won't marry a man who isn't open-minded to change. In seven years, we might have to. Nothing is set in stone, Dutton. You can't just say we're this way and will never change. I won't be a perfect little housewife, submitting to your every whim. In the bedroom, yes. In our relationship, no."

"I know," he insists. "Fuck, Posie, I know that more than anything over these last few months trying to get my way with you." He encroaches on my space. "You've fought me at every point, and I don't want to fight you anymore. I just want to be here, as best as I can, and in any capacity you'll accept me."

Tears spring in my eyes as I let myself follow his thought process, envisioning a future with him, because for so long, I told myself it couldn't even be a possibility. "And where would we live, Dutton?"

"Wherever you want. We can live in one of my homes, buy a new one, or even live here in this rental." Knowing he's used to a particular lifestyle, I scoff at that last option. "The where doesn't matter. Where you want to make memories is where we'll be. Granted, most of my work is based here in Manhattan, but we can figure it out. If Bentley wants to go to the best school in Paris, we can do that. Although, personally, I'd rather go to Italy," he says, and I realize he's rambling. For the first time, the cool, collected man is at a loss, and it's the rawest version I've seen of him. He looks younger at this moment, inexperienced even.

"It sounds like you're trying to plan out our lives already," I say, bringing him back to the moment.

"It's not that. I want you to know that it's not just you I'm saying yes to, *Mostriciattola*. I want to make sure I'm the best choice for Bentley, too." My heart breaks a little more because I didn't know Dutton had thought about that at all. I didn't realize he'd taken us so seriously this whole time. "I know I come across as cold and, at times, strike up adult conversations with a child and seem awkward, but I promise you, I will give him just as much of my heart as I will you.

"I want to be his father, Posie, if he will accept me. And I want you to be my wife. Because I know without a doubt there is no one else for me. I didn't even know someone so perfect could exist for me until you first said 'no' to me. I may not be able to teach him fishing, and I'm assuming you definitely don't want me to teach him how to use knives—"

"Out of the question," I snap, interrupting him, and it brings him back to the room, back to me. He's breathing heavily.

"I just want us to be a family, and I'll do whatever I have to so I can keep you both. I just need you to be willing to take the first step with me, *Mostriciattola*. Please." He gently clasps my hand.

My bottom lip trembles because I know that taking the first step with this man will be irrevocable. Men come and go, but someone like Dutton? I'm terrified because I now understand how much he wants to stay.

"I don't want you to change, Dutton. I'm just... I'm

scared," I admit, and his gaze softens as he cups my cheek. And it's so surreal to see this side of him. No one else sees this version of Dutton—only me.

"Let me protect you, Posie. I can make him go away."

"Won't it make it worse for you and your family?"

"You and Bentley are my family, Posie, and I'm trying my hardest to ask for permission before I kill the fucker who dared to hit my woman. But I need you to say yes. I don't want you to hate me for taking away Bentley's choice."

I have a feeling that Dutton will do it anyway, but there's no doubt in my mind the situation with Bobbi will only worsen. His fixation and demand to have control over me won't stop. And he clearly has no intention of getting to know his son. He only wants to use him to get to me.

I nod quietly, and his expression relaxes as he presses his lips to mine. I never thought I'd feel such a wave of relief asking someone to kill for me. Maybe I really am, as Dutton calls me—a little monster. But I'm willing to do whatever I must to protect my son. To protect my family.

FORTY-FIVE
POSIE

Bentley isn't used to another person staying in the house besides Amy. So when he finds out that Dutton is staying over for another night, he asks him to stay in his room. Dutton politely declines his request, which makes Bentley sad. But we put on a movie and eat popcorn, and by the evening, he falls asleep on the couch. When I stand to get him, Dutton beats me to it, picking him up gently and cradling him in his arms. I watch as he carries Bentley to his room, and then I follow behind them. After Dutton lays him down, Bentley spreads out, remaining fast asleep. Turning and walking out, I shut the door behind us.

Last night was a whirl of deep discussion, and although neither of us slept, we lay comfortably in my bed. It was nice to have him here. And I feel like we'll be safe no matter what, even if Bobbi does show up.

No one is more capable of protecting us than Dutton.

He reaches for me, lifting me in one swift movement, and walks me across the hall to my bedroom. He opens the door and steps inside, then closes it behind us and locks it.

"What if I said I don't want to have sex tonight?" I ask as he sets me down on the bed and then steps back. He stares at me as he starts unbuttoning his shirt.

"Okay," he replies, discarding his shirt on the floor and kicking off his shoes. He undoes his pants and then pulls them down. He has on boxers, and I can see his hard cock tenting the material.

"That's all you're going to say?" I ask as he walks around to the other side of the bed, pulls the covers back, and climbs in. He looks funny, this big scary man, lying in my bed covered in a pink comforter. Though, he doesn't seem to mind.

"Yes. Now, lie down before I change my mind."

I shake my head at him, then get undressed, leaving myself in nothing but a pair of panties. Lifting the covers, I climb underneath and scoot close to him. Lying on his chest, I lift my head and look down at him.

"That's really unfair," he grumbles. "You, naked and lying on top of me." I can feel him growing harder. I smile as I wrap my arms around him and put my head on his chest, listening to his heartbeat.

This is so different from any love I've known, and how right and peaceful it feels terrifies me. But even I know this little fantasy bubble we've lived in over the weekend will eventually pop.

"Are you going to turn out to be a regret, Dutton?" I ask.

"No," he says adamantly. "I hate that he hurt you." And I feel guilty for him being aware that I was comparing him to my ex.

"You hurt people," I remind him.

"Never you." I believe him.

My hips start moving, and before I can help myself, I lean up and touch my lips to his. He kisses me back, his hands finding my ass and gripping it, but he doesn't take control. My hands roam his sides until they reach his face. I cup his cheeks as I whisper, "Fuck me."

That's all the invitation he needs before he flips me on my back, throws the blanket off of us, and tears at my panties. He crawls backward, and his head goes straight between my legs. He kisses his way to where I want him and starts sucking and licking. I moan, trying to keep it down so Bentley doesn't wake up, but it's hard when Dutton is eating me out like I'm his favorite meal that he can't get enough of.

Just before I come, my core vibrates with need, but he stops and pulls away. He's now on his knees, pulling his cock out of his boxers and looking down at my spread legs, and he starts stroking himself.

"Dutton."

"Yes?" he says with a slight smirk. I sit up and grab him, and he laughs as he falls back to the bed with me. "Needy, aren't we?"

I lift my hips, and he slides straight into me. I groan when he's fully seated and try not to scream when he starts moving quickly. I can feel him everywhere.

And then he slows down, his steady thrusts making me claw at his back. He leans down, never breaking the rhythm, and kisses me.

My tongue slides against his at the same time he thrusts his cock all the way in, making me gasp.

"I think I'm falling in love with you," he admits quietly, just as my legs start to shake and my head goes fuzzy. "Posie. Fuck," he pants, and I know he can feel it too. Not just the way we are but so much more.

And now he loves me.

I'm afraid of what falling for this man will do to me. I barely survived the last man who told me he loved me, and he didn't have a hold of me as much as this man does.

I think I'm fucked.

And now I'm falling for a killer.

At least he's hot, I guess.

Knowing that resistance is futile, I cup his jaw as I whisper, "I think I'm falling in love with you, too."

FORTY-SIX
DUTTON

I dress and quietly sneak out of her room early. As I brew a cup of coffee, I check my messages. I see Will sent Bobbi's location, and I immediately shared it with the others. Will can find anyone, so thank fuck he's on our side. His services don't come cheap, though, but I would pay him whatever it took to find where that asshole is staying.

"You're here again," Bentley says sleepily as he enters the kitchen, rubbing his eyes.

"I am."

"Can you make me breakfast?" he asks. I look around, not sure what he eats.

"Cereal?" I say, and he scrunches up his nose at me.

"Mom makes me avocado on toast. She says cereal

is full of preeeservatiiiives." He draws out the last word but says it as if he's heard it a million times.

"How about McDonald's?" I ask. His eyes go wide, and then he runs to the door. "Let me tell your mother first. Don't open that door." He nods and hops from foot to foot as he waits.

I enter Posie's room to find her cuddled up in the blankets. Leaning down and kissing her cheek, I whisper, "I'm taking your son to get breakfast. Do you want coffee?" She nods and turns over to her other side. Bentley hasn't moved from where I left him when I walk back out to the entryway. I ruffle his hair as I tell him what a good job he did at listening before we head out to get some food.

The only reason I'm okay with leaving Posie alone in the house is because Ford is sitting outside in his car. He and Hawke have been taking shifts watching over the place, and I'm grateful to Eli for extending the protection.

Today's the day we're going to lure Bobbi out of hiding.

Bentley tells me all about his school on the ride, and I never once thought I would enjoy listening to a kid tell me about his day.

Yet, here I am.

When we return, I see Posie standing on the front

porch in a nightgown, wiping her eyes. After I unbuckle Bentley, he jumps out of the car and runs over to her to tell her what we got. She scoops him up and hugs him hard. When she looks at me, she smiles softly.

"I was asleep. I thought..."

"I'm sorry."

"No, it's okay. You told me, and it didn't click. But it's okay." She turns and heads inside, and I can tell how worried she was by the death grip she has on her son. Following her into the kitchen, I place the food on the counter. "Wow, you got a lot."

"I didn't know what you wanted, and Bentley wanted almost everything on the menu." I chuckle.

"You can put me down now," Bentley tells her. When he's back on his feet, he climbs onto a chair and opens the bags, pulling out the pancakes followed by hash browns.

My phone buzzes, and I look at it. Posie offers me a small smile. "We can't stay here forever," she says.

Last night, we discussed tracking Bobbi down. Now that we know his whereabouts, the plan is in full swing. Eli is currently waiting outside the pub where Bobbi and his two goons are staying.

"I have to go," I tell them. Her gaze meets mine, and she looks at me with sad eyes. Which is so unlike her; this woman is strong. "I'll be back," I promise as she wraps her arms around my midsection.

"Thank you," she says before she pulls away. "I'll see you later." She turns back to Bentley. I give him a little wave as I leave. I hope this time, when I come back, she hasn't run.

I hate that Dutton is so thoughtful. That this man, who is a known killer, and possibly even worse, is kind to me. That he shows me how I should be treated. And he and his family have been kind to Bentley. I never thought of bringing a man into Bentley's life. Yet Dutton has slid straight in without an invitation, and he did it so effortlessly.

He started as my boss, and now he sleeps in my bed.

"School today?" Bentley asks, his voice hopeful. I've kept him out for a few days while we sorted out a plan of action. That, and I don't want him out of my sight until Bobbi is taken care of. But now that he is, I don't see why Bentley can't go. I don't want to hit pause on our life because of Bobbi anymore.

"Go and get changed, and let's go to school."

He jumps up and rushes to his room to get ready. I follow him, go into my room to get dressed, and pack his backpack. When I drop him off at school, he runs off excitedly to play with his friends.

When I arrive back at home, the car Hawke and Ford have been sitting in is gone, most likely because they've already caught the assholes involved in this.

I sit in the car and stare at the house for a moment. I'm exhausted, and it's going to be hard to focus today, knowing what's happening. I check my phone, noticing I have a missed call from Dutton. When I go to return it, a motorcycle parks behind my car.

I grip my steering wheel. In true Bobbi fashion, he's somehow managed to avoid Dutton and the others, most likely at the sacrifice of his men.

I quickly call Dutton.

"Bobbi is here," I rush to tell him. And while I want to handle this situation myself, it's nice to know someone has my back. Because I know things with Bobbi are about to get ugly. But without my son being here and knowing nothing can happen to him, my fighting instincts are coming out in full force.

"Fuck," Dutton curses from the other end of the line. "We only got his men; Bobbi slipped out somehow. Where are you?" he asks, and I can hear tires squeal, telling me he's on his way to me.

"In my driveway."

"Good. I'm almost there. Back the car out now and leave."

"He's parked behind the car," I tell him.

"Run him over," he barks as if that was the obvious answer. Shaking my head, I know I can't do that because of the big-ass motorcycle that my sad tires won't get over. So I put the car in park and open the door. I'm sick of running.

And I feel the fire spark to life in the pit of my stomach.

Dutton says something else, but I hang up on him. Knowing he's on his way is enough for me as I come face-to-face with Bobbi.

"Avoiding me?" he asks. I shut the car door and turn to face him.

"Like any human with a brain would do," I snap back.

His hands curl into fists at his sides. "I see you're fucking the Taylor kid," he sneers. "They broke into the place I was staying and took two of my men. You wouldn't know anything about that, would you?"

"The Taylor kid?" I laugh at him. "You're literally only a few years older than him, and your brain is smaller." Then my gaze drops to his crotch. "Come to think of it, you're smaller than him in more ways than one."

I knew it was coming before the words even left my mouth. But I couldn't help myself. He swings his arm, and his fist connects with my jaw. I feel it crack and hope to God nothing is broken as I cup the side of my face.

"Get up, you stupid bitch. See, if you would have stayed with me to begin with, I wouldn't have to teach you how to talk to me."

Just then, a car screeches into the driveway. Dutton jumps from the car and strides straight over to us. He doesn't even pause, stepping right up to Bobbi, and a fight breaks out. Only a few punches are thrown because Bobbi keels over when Dutton punches him in the stomach. I only hear a loud grunt as Dutton blocks my view of him.

"Did you think it was smart to come back here? I warned you that this was a bigger game than you were ready for," Dutton says coolly.

"You stabbed me," Bobbi says breathlessly, the handle of a knife sticking out from his gut.

I grab Dutton's hand and pull him back. He turns and looks at me. His eyes go wide when he sees the discoloration blooming on my jaw. He touches it, and I flinch, even though he's gentle as he does.

"Go inside and ice your face," he tells me just as Eli and Hawke pull up in another car. Ford is most likely with Bobbi's men.

I inhale a sharp breath because although I agreed to this, signing someone's death warrant is serious business. I harden my resolve, reminding myself Bentley might've been here.

"The stab wound is not lethal; it's why he's still standing," Dutton informs me, and he's back to being the cold, calculating version of himself. Then he turns to address Bobbi. "I want you to know the only reason you're still breathing is so I can show you how to treat a woman later."

Bobbi shoots me a pleading look. And it's unbelievable that he still thinks I'm stupid enough for him to manipulate. "You wouldn't let them do anything to me, Posie. I'm your son's father."

"What is my son's name?" I ask. When he doesn't answer, I smile even though it hurts to do so. "You have no idea and will continue to have no idea. You put yourself in this situation."

"Striker will come after you for this; it's best you let me walk now," he threatens, gripping the knife as if afraid it will go in deeper.

"Waylon could try, but we both know he would rather not start a war over a piece of shit who thinks it's fun to hit women. You kept that secret quiet, didn't you? I understand that he doesn't want your kind back," Eli answers as he stops next to Dutton. "I suggest you walk over to that car and get in nicely."

"I'm not going anywhere with you people. I know who you are," Bobbie spits, attempting to step back. But Hawke is behind him and, with a smile, throws his arm around Bobbi's neck as if hugging him but terrifyingly tight. I watch as, after a few moments, Bobbi sags to the ground like a sack of shit.

"Ice. You need ice." Dutton grabs my hand and leads me to the house.

"What are they going to do with him?" I inquire.

"You don't have to worry about him again," is the only answer he gives me. Like that's enough, I glance back as we reach the front door and see Eli and Hawke dragging Bobbi to the car.

"How sore is it?" Dutton asks as I lift my hand to my face, flinching when I make contact.

"It's okay," I lie. And we both know it's a lie. "I don't know if I'm doing the right thing," I whisper, the reality of having faced Bobbi one more time finally sinking in.

"It's okay, Posie. This is my decision. The blood

will be on my hands, not yours. Now, get in that house and ice your jaw before you have to get your son later."

I walk to the kitchen on autopilot, and Dutton follows closely behind me. He goes straight to the freezer, grabs the ice cube tray, and finds a plastic bag to put the cubes in. He then gently removes my hand from my swelling jaw and places the ice bag on it. I flinch in pain, glaring at him accusingly.

"You need to ice it," he says and tries again to put the bag against my face.

"It's cold."

"That's the point." He chuckles. And when he tries a third time, I let him and try not to pull away. He drops down in front of me and holds the ice against my jaw while he stares at me.

"Marry me."

"Stop asking," I reply, my jaw throbbing.

"I won't." He smirks.

"Can you kiss me? Just here." I tap my other cheek. And without moving the ice pack, he leans forward and goes to my ear first.

"I will make you my wife one day and be your husband. I want to be very clear on that. No other man will ever hurt you or touch you again because if they so much as look at you, I will kill them." And then his lips brush my cheek, and he ever so gently kisses me.

Closing my eyes, I dream of what a life with him might be like.

And I hate that I'm already in so deep that there's no looking back for me.

For the first time in a long time, there's a new future for Bentley and me.

But first, the past has to be buried... permanently.

FORTY-EIGHT
DUTTON

I left her, even though it killed me. I told her I would take her to pick up Bentley when I returned. And she told me a non-negotiable time to be back, or she would get him herself.

I glance at the watch on my wrist, then smile as I turn my focus back to Bobbi, who is currently trying to wiggle on the bed he's strapped to.

"You can remove the gag," I tell Ford, ignoring the other two men who are tied against the wall.

Ford is holding two crowbars. I always thought they were crude weapons, like Hawke's spiked gloves. *But I suppose we all have our things*, I think as I eye the knife my cousin is holding for me.

Ford does as instructed, and Eli watches from his seat on top of a crate. I understand I've cost him a lot of money in this deal. But, somehow, I'll make it up to him. I'm not one to usually create trouble for others, especially my family. But for her and Bentley, I was willing to set the world on fire, fuck the consequence.

I never understood love until now.

Provider.

Protector.

I was all of these things. I just hadn't found the right family to whom to extend my unwavering loyalty.

"Picked the wrong woman to hit," Ford says as he steps to the side. Hawke sneers as he sits beside the two club members. They're a distant blur in my mind as I remove my suit jacket, roll up my sleeves, and wash my hands. Then I turn to face him. His eyes scan the room, and he grunts, trying to break free of his restraints. Oh yes, that knife is still in his belly, too.

When his gaze lands on me, his eyes widen in fear. I take the knife from Eli and approach the bed. I want this arrogant asshole to see the monster he picked a fight with clearly.

"Do you feel powerful picking on women and children?" I ask, looming over him in the same way I know he's done to countless women.

"Please. You can have the bitch. I'll leave and never come back," he snivels.

I crack my neck from side to side. "You have a

brain, correct?" He nods in answer. "Do you honestly believe calling her a bitch is helping your situation at all?"

"All fucking women are bitches and disposable," he says, a little bite coming back into his tone, then grunts as he tries to move again.

I smirk, not needing any more ammunition why this fucker needs to die.

Women are the best, literally the fucking best. And this piece of shit has no idea how to treat a woman. I reach for the knife in his stomach. I like that knife, so I want it back. He cries from the pain when I yank it out none-to-gently, then I discard it on the floor and lift the other one in my hand.

This is when he realizes his words about women aren't going to help him. When he starts pleading for his life. And, to be honest, I've already begun to block him out.

I always believed that no one could love this part of my life, but I was mistaken.

"You can have her!" he screams.

"You say it like she was yours to give," I reply calmly.

I place the tip of the blade at the bottom of his shirt and slide it up, cutting through it and his vest and exposing his stomach and chest. His hands are tied above his head, and he tries relentlessly to pull them free. But he doesn't have any luck, and I don't plan on untying him anytime soon. I study his chest, which is covered in hair, and wonder what work of art I'm going to create on this canvas today. I do plan to kill him, but first, I want to play.

"If you kill me, they'll come for you. You'll start a war!" he shouts.

Eli then speaks up. "That's our decision to make. You fucked up thinking my deal with Striker would make us look the other way while you terrorized my cousin's woman and her child."

Eli spoke with Striker the moment it was revealed that Bobbi was an abusive motherfucker. Striker decided to turn a blind eye to what we had planned for him. Apparently, much has changed in the last year since Striker took over the club, and those who held old values were still being flushed out. The two goons who decided to follow Bobbi were simply caught in the crossfire, and by default, we'd clean up the mess.

Though Striker did confess that if word got out we finished them, there might be backlash in the form of other club members coming for us. I can't disagree with it, considering I'd do the same.

Once I've decided what I want to carve, I take a deep breath and begin. Bobbi whimpers at the first light touch of the cool blade to his skin. And when I apply pressure, piercing his skin and making the initial slice, he screams in earnest.

He wails in agony and tries to see what I'm doing as I carve her name into his skin. When I'm done, I shoot him a satisfied smirk.

"H-how c-could you," he stammers, tears running down his face.

"How could you hit her, not once but twice?" I growl. I step back and head to the sink, tossing my knife into it. "Don't worry, it won't be there for long. I'll peel it off shortly. I just wanted you to remember what put you in this situation to begin with."

It is time to have fun with my prey.

I'll take my time ruining him because there is no amount of torture I could inflict on him to ever make amends for the hell he put my woman through all these years.

FORTY-NINE
POSIE

Before I pick up Bentley, I make sure I have layers of makeup on, and I wear dark sunglasses so there is no speculation about what's happening with me at home. I'm not sure how I would answer any questions regarding the bruising on my face. How do you explain that your ex-boyfriend threatened you and hit you, and the person you're currently... sleeping with plans to kill him?

Bentley draws and paints most of the afternoon as I wander around the house, cleaning things just to keep myself busy because I don't know what else to do. A part of me wants to know what Dutton is doing to Bobbi, while the other part is scared to find out the answer.

Just as the sun sets, there's a knock on my door. I

take a deep breath before I answer it. I'm not going to lie; I assumed it would be Dutton. But when I pull open the door, it's an older version of him staring back at me.

Dawson smiles at me, then his gaze flicks from my eyes to my jaw and then back again.

He doesn't look thrilled at what he sees. He has that same hard line on his forehead that Dutton sometimes gets when he's angry or contemplating something.

"Dutton asked us to stop by," he says.

"You didn't have to come," I tell him, just as Honey, who I didn't see, comes up beside him with a bag of food.

"Hello, Posie. I hope it's okay if we join you for dinner. We brought food." She holds up the bag, and Bentley runs out, spotting Dawson. Dawson scoops him into his arms as Bentley starts telling him about his day. I hold the door open for them, welcoming the distraction. I know they're here to ensure we're safe, which fills me with so much love and gratitude that I don't even know how to process it.

I feel like I'm not so alone. Going forward, I already know I don't have to fight my battles alone.

Once again, I feel like part of a family.

Honey says something, but I don't hear her at first.

Then, it registers that she is asking where the kitchen is. I wave my hand in that general direction, and as she passes me, she grabs my hand and gives it a small squeeze.

Dawson's already sitting on the living room floor, where Bentley shows him how to paint something. And I notice that my anxiety eases now that they're here. I guess this is what it's like to have support from people who love you.

I don't even have to question whether they accept Bentley and me because they have from the moment they meet us. My sense of self-preservation and fear prevented me from seeing that.

I follow Honey into the kitchen, where I find her searching through cabinets for plates. I point to where they are.

"So, I bake. It's what I enjoy and what I do when I'm stressed," she says as she pulls out a tray of cupcakes. "How are you holding up? And please don't tell me everything's okay. I know what it's like to be a mother and worry about my child."

That's exactly what I was going to tell her, but a lump forms in my throat, and instead, I choke out, "I'm sorry." Her eyes widen, and she puts the tray down. I'm startled when she wraps me in her arms. I awkwardly hug her back, whispering, "I've caused a lot of trouble for you all."

"You haven't caused any trouble for us," she says, leaning back so I'm forced to look at her. I laugh at myself as I wipe my eyes. "Have you forgotten that our family's middle name is trouble?"

"But you didn't have to do any of this for me. I know what it might cost your family."

"It costs us nothing. We look after our own, no matter what," she says adamantly. "Posie, you have my gratitude."

"What?" What did I do to deserve that from her?

Honey bites her bottom lip as if she's unsure as to whether she should continue. She squeezes my arm as she focuses on the food in front of her. "I was worried for my son. I thought he was closing himself off to the possibility of having a life like this."

"Like this?" I ask curiously, leaning against the counter and wiping beneath my eyes.

"With someone he loves," she clarifies.

My stomach drops because a small part of me is still so scared that this could be ripped away from me. What if I make the wrong choice? It'll impact Bentley as well.

"Dutton was an easy child growing up. Too easy. He was inquisitive and intelligent but mischievous and calculated. And he was very protective of his sister. That ease, we realized, was him acting in the ways he thought was expected of him. As a teenager, he became a little less easy to control. Not that we wanted to control him, but we guided him to stop picking fights with everyone, so he did stop... publicly, that was," she says, eyeing me, and I can't help but smile.

"He became more distant in adulthood and only focused on following in his father's footsteps. I don't think Dutton realizes it himself, but he adopted all the good qualities from Dawson, readying himself to be a provider and protector. But whenever we asked if he met anyone, I felt the moment he shut down as if that wasn't a viable option for him. It felt like he hated something about himself, and that terrified me. Looking back, we probably didn't have the right conversations around it," she admits. "But even when they're adults, your children are still your children. You want to guide them as best as possible and see them happy. It's been a while since I've seen my son genuinely happy. Not until you came along, Posie." She plates up two cupcakes. "He'd never brought a woman around to meet us before you." She smirks. "And Billie told me he asked you to marry him."

"How did she know that?" It slips out of my mouth before I can pull it back.

"One thing I'll give you a heads-up on is that this family is nosy. We're always in each other's business, but we mean well. In short, Dutton asked Eli for advice, which was overheard by Hawke, who told Billie, who asked me about it."

I stare at her, trying to follow the chain of events. And then I recall someone saying Hawke has a big mouth.

"He didn't propose." My eyebrows furrow. "Well, he sort of did. He kind of said it in the moment. I wouldn't really call that asking. Getting down on one knee and making a heartfelt speech is how you are meant to ask someone to marry you."

"I couldn't agree more." She smiles.

"It's not just me I have to think about. I have to consider Bentley as well," I say, peeking into the living room at Dawson and Bentley painting. I hug myself.

She places a hand on my arm. "I understand that. And so does my son. But you make sure he asks you properly. No loopholes or half-assery. And I certainly expect a wedding. But not until you're ready. No matter what happens, Posie, we're your family if you'll have us. We're not going anywhere."

I take a sharp breath, trying my hardest not to break into a million pieces. As if knowing, Honey collects the two plates and takes them out to Dawson and Bentley. "What are you painting?" I hear her ask.

Tears well in my eyes as I realize that it might've once been my parents doting on Bentley and me. Something I think about more than I care to admit because it's something I can't change. For so long, it had only been Bentley and me, and now the expansion of our family feels like it's flooding my lungs with a breath of relief and grief.

When I initially moved away after I found out I was pregnant, I only looked forward. I left Bobbi in the past, and never did I think that being confronted by him again would make me feel like that scared and angry teen again. I hated that my parents were so easily and quickly taken from me.

I was in survival mode, cultivating every moment preciously, like time was about to run out.

In all those years, the only good thing that happened was Bentley.

And then I met Dutton.

When I first met him, I just assumed he was a stuck-up asshole who had more money than he knew what to do with, and so he decided to open a strip club. Granted, he's still an asshole, but he has so many good qualities that lie hidden under the surface.

Today, I made a decision I never thought I'd make

—taking away Bentley's right to ever meet his father. And I'm scared he'll hate me one day for it. But deep in my heart, I know it was the right decision. I just needed a bigger monster who had my back to help me make that difficult choice.

To pick up the blade when I was too weak to slay the demon while I created a sanctuary for him to return to.

When Bentley finishes his cupcake, Honey starts to tidy up the mess. Dawson stands and smooths the front of his pants down before he looks at me.

"Dutton is here," he says.

"Come on, Bentley, let me see where your room is," Honey says, taking his hand and leading him to the hallway. Bentley practically drags her to his room.

"Can I show you the bed me and Dutton made? It's in Mommy's room. And then I can show you my new LEGO set." He barely takes a breath while chattering to her.

"That sounds exciting," Honey replies excitedly. And I'm grateful for her because I don't know what to expect with Dutton's arrival. But I've decided to love the monster for all his glory. Not just the bits I don't want to confront. But in the near future, there definitely will be a conversation about no blood or funny business in front of Bentley.

I open the front door as Dutton gets out of the car. His eyes find mine, and I walk toward him, relief sweeping through me that he looks perfectly fine— maybe a little tired but in one piece. He holds his arms out for me, and I pick up my pace, wrapping my arms around him as I step into his embrace. He cups the back of my hair and holds me tightly.

For a moment, we just stand here, holding one another, until I finally whisper, "Is he dead?"

"He's gone, *Mostriciattola*," he says, petting my hair. I hold him tighter, the wave of relief immediately slipping off me. Am I selfish for being happy that I have an out like this? Not every woman has someone who would literally kill for her. But I'm grateful that my cold-hearted man found me and never gave up.

"How is Bentley?" he asks, changing the subject.

"He's good. He's showing your mother his room."

He nods, and I notice he's changed his clothes.

"Did you get blood on your other clothes?" I ask, nodding to his shirt. He smirks and glances at me as he hooks an arm over my shoulders and leads me back to the house. Dawson is standing by the door, waiting. He and Dutton exchange a brief glance and nod as if silently communicating something.

"Did you save me some food? I'm starving," he says to his father. I go to slip into the kitchen to grab him a plate, but he grabs me around the waist and pulls me into him. "Stop worrying. I got you." And for the first time, I believe that.

"Come in and eat," Dawson says.

I step back just as Dutton kisses my forehead and whispers, "I'd rather have my dessert." And I know exactly what he's talking about. Shaking my head, I turn and walk to the kitchen. His arm stays around my waist.

I decide to leave Dutton and Dawson alone in the kitchen to speak for a few minutes, and I go check up on Bentley. It's late in the evening, close to Bentley's bedtime. Honey is sitting on the bed with him, reading a book. She glances up when I walk in.

"Dutton loved me reading to him every night," she explains. Bentley is rubbing his eyes tiredly.

"Can Mrs. Honey finish the story before the bath?" he asks.

"Sure, sweetie." I smile at him and then step back into the hallway. When I do, Dutton is there, grabbing me from behind and turning me before his soft lips, which are known to be ruthless when speaking to others, land on mine in a gentle kiss. When he kisses me, he takes my breath away, and I can't help but press into him. He cups my cheek tenderly, being careful of my jaw. When he ends the kiss, he looks down at me.

"Marry me," he whispers. This time, I smile at him and shake my head.

"Stop asking me like that."

He raises a brow in question.

"She wants you to get on one knee and make it romantic," Honey calls out from the bedroom. I cover my mouth with my hand to stop the laughter as Dutton frowns.

"Romantic?" he asks. "I suck at romance."

I lay my hand on his chest.

"You actually don't. So try harder, and the answer might be different." I grin up at him before I step out of his grasp.

"That's just teasing," he grumbles, following me back to where his father is seated in the kitchen. Having these two powerful men in my small home feels strange, but I'm realizing it's something I'll have to get used to.

Six months later...

"HOORAY!" Everyone claps and cheers as Bentley blows out the candles on his birthday cake. He's lost his front tooth, and I was scolded when I tried to put a hundred-dollar bill under his pillow. Apparently, the Tooth Fairy isn't so flush with cash. So fuck the Tooth Fairy. I bought him the newest Transformers LEGO set instead so that I could get credit for it.

Bentley claps his hands excitedly as I hold Posie from behind while she takes photos. My mother helps Bentley cut the cake.

We're in the backyard of my brownstone. Ulti-mately, we gave Bentley the choice as to where he'd like to live, and he wanted this one because he thought it was cool that it had a fireplace. I felt rather smug at having them installed.

It also felt like a fresh start for me and Posie.

After everything that happened with her ex, we needed it. Eli tells me that everything with the Boston Delinquents has been going swimmingly.

"We need more plates," my mother says, and I release Posie, kissing her on the cheek.

"I'll go grab some." I excuse myself, nodding to Will and Alina, who have been traveling so much lately that we haven't seen much of them, so it was nice that they could make it today. Especially for my mother since she and Alina have been good friends for so long.

I walk through the back door into the kitchen and hear it before I see it.

"What are you doing?" Hawke shouts.

My sister has her shirt halfway over her head, Ford's hands at the bottom hem, and Hawke is standing in front of them, looking over at me, stunned.

I see red as I storm toward them, pushing Ford off her. "What the fuck?!" I snap.

"Dutton! It's not what it looks like!" Billie yells. "I had a bug on me!"

My heart is pounding in my ears as my gaze

bounces between the twins. They're looking at each other, and I can never tell what they're thinking.

"Is that true?!" I demand.

Hawke bites his bottom lip. "It was pretty fucking big, but don't tell Eli I'm scared of them or anything."

My eye twitches as I glance around, searching for said bug. Ford is quiet, but that's not unusual.

"And why were all three of you in here anyway?" I question, trying my hardest to calm my raging, murderous thoughts.

Billie now has her shirt back in place, and she rolls her eyes. "You can't seriously be pissed right now? And we came in to get the cake."

"The cake's out there," I say suspiciously, staring her down. Whatever she sees makes her pause, but only momentarily before she starts arguing.

"Hello? Did you forget I enjoy baking? Did you really think we'd only bring one variety of cake?" She flicks her honey-colored hair over her shoulder. "Gosh, you're so insufferable. I need to find Hope and Ivy to get away from all this testosterone." She huffs, shoving past me. "Besides, shouldn't you be getting your shit together?" she asks with an arched eyebrow.

I swallow. She's right. Today isn't only Bentley's sixth birthday party.

Ford hands me a stack of plates, and I nod in thanks

before leaving, giving them one more assessing look. As I leave, I can hear Hawke furiously speaking with Ford in a low voice. I don't know what the fuck is happening with those two, but something doesn't feel right.

When I get back outside, half the cake is cut up and being served. "Everything all right?" Posie asks, and I smile at her, this beautiful fucking woman I've been blessed to call mine.

"It couldn't be better," I reply, then call Bentley over for a family photo. I pick him up, and Posie takes a selfie for us. I notice Paula and Mike taking a photo from a distance. They've become another addition to our family.

"Mommy, Dutton has a question for you," Bentley says suddenly, and I'm put on the spot as I set him on his feet. The little fucker threw me right into it. I don't like everyone watching, but I swallow my pride because this isn't about me. It's about Posie. My *Mostriciattola* flipped my world upside down but became the home I didn't think I deserved.

"What's up?" she asks sweetly, and her eyes go wide when I grab her hand and slowly drop to one knee.

Her other hand goes to her mouth as she squeaks, "You can't be serious. Now?"

I run my thumb over her knuckles as everyone watches us. "It was Bentley's idea to propose on his birthday."

"I helped pick out the ring!" Bentley announces with a huge grin. I can't help but smile at him before turning back to Posie, who is tearing up.

"Use my son against me, why don't you," she says through a laugh.

"Well, we come as a package deal now, *Mostriciattola*. You know why I'm here on one knee. You know I love you more than anything and want to give you everything. So, please, do me the honor of becoming my wife so you can keep me in line until the day I die. Although, I'd much prefer if you threw fewer things at my head."

She chokes on a laugh as she drops to her knees and hugs me, crying. "You deserve it half the time, asshole," she whispers.

"She said yes!" I announce to everyone, and she laughs, kissing me. As relief floods me, I claim her mouth, covering Bentley's eyes with one hand. I certainly didn't want to be rejected in front of my entire family. But I'd have done it again and again until she said yes.

When we pull apart, she looks down at the ring,

and I let Bentley pull it out of the box so I can slide it on her finger.

"We liked the blue one," he explains. "But Daddy said we had to get the biggest one."

"What did you just say?" Posie chokes out, and I look at Bentley, shocked.

Bentley seems unsure of himself as he awkwardly looks at the ground. "Is it okay if I call you that?" he asks uncertainly. Posie looks at me, tears welling in her eyes, and I pull him in for a hug, clearing my throat. I didn't know how much I needed to hear that until I had.

"Of course it is, son," I say, and tears stream down Posie's face as I bring Bentley close to me, hugging him, grateful for his acceptance.

Grateful for this family I have for myself.

The family I'd kill for all over again.

ALSO BY T.L. SMITH

Connect with T.L Smith by tlsmithauthor.com

ALSO BY KIA CARRINGTON RUSSELL

T.L. SMITH

USA Today Best Selling Author T.L. Smith loves to write her characters with flaws so beautiful and dark you can't turn away. Her books have been translated into several languages. If you don't catch up with her in her home state of Queensland, Australia you can usually find her travelling the world, either sitting on a beach in Bali or exploring Alcatraz in San Francisco or walking the streets of New York.

Connect with me tlsmithauthor.com

KIA CARRINGTON-RUSSELL

Australian Author, Kia Carrington-Russell is known for her recognizable style of kick a$$ heroines, fast-paced action, enemies to lovers and romance that dances from light to dark in multiple genres including Fantasy, Dark and Contemporary Romance.

Obsessed with all things coffee, food and travel, Kia is always seeking out her next adventure internationally. Now back in her home country of Australia, she takes her Cavoodle, Sia along morning walks on beautiful coastline beaches, building worlds in the sea breezes and contemplating which deliciously haunting story to write next.